To Steal
an Irish Heart

by

Darcy Carson

To Steal an Irish Heart

Cover Art by *The Wild Rose Press, Inc.*

The Wild Rose Press, Inc.
PO Box 708
Adams Basin, NY 14410-0708
Visit us at www.thewildrosepress.com

Publishing History
First Tea Rose Edition, 2020
Print ISBN 978-1-5092-2987-1
Digital ISBN 978-1-5092-2988-8

Published in the United States of America

Dedication

To my son Kevin, daughter-in-law Kelly,
and oldest granddaughter, Keyla.
My very own special cheering section.

She'd never been kissed before. Not like that. Oh sure, lads had stolen a few pecks, but nothing compared to Kirkland's tantalizing kiss. Still, it would be a cold day in hell afore she'd admit that and stoke his inflated vanity.

"Sure, and if you be asking me to rank them, I've had better and worse." She took a deep breath to calm her rapidly beating heart. "I warn you now. There'll be no next time. 'Tis wrong. You don't understand."

A smile lifted the corners of Kirkland's lush mouth. "It is you who doesn't understand. After all, we are wed. All I want is for you to soften toward me. I never meant to kiss you. It took me by surprise as well. Unless you wish me to…"

"A lie. You'd say whatever you thought I wanted to hear in order to gain your freedom." In spite of her accusation, confusion swamped her mind. She glanced at the giant wolfhound peacefully sleeping on the floor, then out the diamond shaped windows of Padraig's bedchamber as if answers lay in the far beyond.

Kirkland stepped closer. "I would be happy to kiss you again."

"You put yourself in mortal danger by kissing me," she told him. Mayhap she wasn't insane. He was! His behavior courted danger.

Chapter One
Dundalk Bay, Ireland, 1661

Simon William Lancaster considered Ireland hell on earth. Not for himself, but for the poor inhabitants of this land.

He hadn't reached this conclusion hastily. His carriage had passed bands of hollow-eyed devils tramping across the rain-soaked countryside in search of what meager food and shelter they could find. Cromwell's Ironsides had done their best to annihilate the inhabitants. The people had nothing left to lose and everything to fight for. No wonder the Irish were a rebellious, troublesome lot.

Surrounded by the misery, he'd grown up in a different hell—ostracized, lonely, mistreated—and had survived. Not only survived but thrived. Being ignored by his father and bullied by his brother had taught him survival skills that gave him the will to succeed. Now he controlled his own fate.

That said, he'd needed an excuse to leave London for a while. He rather preferred his neck attached to his head and needed to protect it from an angry king. Out of sight, out of mind worked well with Charles II while he cemented his throne. People wanted a return to normalcy, which the new king promised to provide.

In Simon's last mission as a privateer, His Majesty ordered him to capture a Spanish treasure ship, but after learning civilians traveled aboard, he had let the vessel pass unmolested. The action had outraged Charles, who coveted the cache for his treasury.

It had only been a couple months since he'd given up the life aboard ship and added the *Black Sheep* to his merchant fleet. He'd consented to take his brother's grandiose vehicle—snow white with gilded lanterns and handles—for convenience sake, only to realize it was ill-suited for the rigors of muddy and rutted roads. His good deed to check on the family estate had gone from bad to worse when the carriage broke an axle on the journey home.

While he waited in an inn for a blacksmith to arrive from Dundalk to make the needed repairs, Simon took a swallow from the earthenware mug one of the numerous patrons had pressed into his hand.

One of the locals, he couldn't remember which, saluted him. Most were named O'Casey, a clan of dark brown-haired fellows with a few blonds and redheads thrown in for good measure. When the O'Caseys saw him eyeing them, several lifted their mugs. He'd never been offered so many free drinks in his life.

A maid with a soiled apron around her thick waist brushed her ample bosom against him each time she passed. A group of strangers surrounded him as he stood before the wooden bar. Perhaps too friendly. Their good humor could not be real, not for the likes of him, an Englishman.

Still...all the ale he'd consumed cast a rosy glow on his jaundiced view. He hadn't had a good fall-down drunk in years, and didn't see the harm now. Besides, common sense warned him not to insult these people. They might construe it as rudeness for an Englishman to turn down a drink from an Irishman.

Voices and the scuffle of feet behind him caused him to turn and glance at the revelers.

"Sur-r-re, I'm going to offer a toast to the groom," said a tall, well-built man with bright red hair and blue-green eyes. He had to shout over thunderous drumming that produced a sound that seeped into a person's bones and made them sway with the music. A trio of men with their arms draped over each other's shoulders started to sing a melodious tune.

Simon liked the man's friendly face instantly, and the sensation grew when the man signaled him to join him at a table along the wall.

The fellow's companion was a younger O'Casey with the strange name of Sean the Third. Simon's memory spun, but he did recall being introduced earlier in the day. The young man looked to be in his early twenties with thick, shaggy brown hair matching that of nearly everyone pressing into the inn. Only the fellow's expression hinted at sadness.

"Wait 'til Roanne arrives afore you begin to celebrate," Sean the Third cautioned the first man. "You know what happens when you drink too much."

"Aye, I'm notorious as a lover." The taller man grinned. "An amorous, loving drunk. Women adore me. They cannot resist me charms." He winked at Simon. "What about you? Will you lift your tankard in a toast to the lucky groom?"

The room swirled before Simon. "Pray tell, who might be the lucky fellow?"

"Trust me, my lord. He'll be quite near and dear to you."

"Ah, someone here then. It's a game. I'm to guess

the man's identity."

Sean the Third nodded at Simon's mug. "Best enjoy your drink. The bride's a-coming soon enough."

"The wedding's to be held here? A bit unprecedented."

The redhead's grin widened at his inquiry. "Sur-r-re, and everything will work out. God's presence is in all houses."

"And who might you be, friend?" Simon asked.

"Rory O'Casey of the clan O'Casey." His brogue slurred the tiniest bit. "I'm the sixth brother to the bride. There's twelve of us, you know, counting Roanne."

Simon scrunched his face, doing his best to envision such a sizable family. "Twelve! Your father breeds his own brigade."

In a flash, both men's expressions hardened.

"Our Da went to his heavenly reward three days past." Sorrow laced the tall man's voice. "His wake was held yesterday."

A break in the music made the announcement all the more solemn. Before Simon could murmur a befuddled condolence, a dark brute stumbled up to the table. He scowled like a man ready for a fight. "Damn Sassenach, thanks to you and your kind, we've little to be grateful for except our women."

"Murdock!" The man called Rory looked about to spring at the newcomer. "Keep a civil tongue in your head."

"Not fair. She's me sister," the broad-shouldered brute moaned. "I want to do right by her."

A foot away from him, the two leaner men patted the giant on his back. "Find yourself a pretty *caitin* to dance with, Murdock," Sean the Third suggested.

4

"No one here I want to dance with," the big man answered, slopping down his drink.

Simon chuckled into his mug. Sassenach meant foreigner in Gaelic. Maybe he wasn't as drunk as he believed. He laughed at his own thought.

Murdock swung around at the sound. "Enough of this. What about him?"

"Me? What did I do?"

Murdock curled his hands into huge mallets. "You exist."

Simon accepted being lumped into all things English. He couldn't blame the Irishman. Rumors of their unfair treatment under Cromwell's reign had reached far out into the sea. The series of penal laws had brutal consequences, and the impact was severe.

Before Simon could respond, the inn's door opened. The music stopped and a hush fell over the crowd as everyone turned in that direction. Then they chanted, "Roanne! Roanne! Roanne!"

Simon's attention went to the door, and he thought he'd died and gone to heaven. Framed in the open portal was a vision silhouetted against a jeweled backdrop of verdant rain-drenched hills beyond the door. Her willowy height caught his attention right away. Being tall himself, he always preferred women who did not make him bend in half to steal a kiss.

She hesitated to enter the dingy establishment. The privateer in him applauded her good sense. It never hurt to be cautious.

The hint of a green gown peeked beneath the opening wedge of her drenched cloak. When she slipped off her hood, a cloud of fiery curls was set free to frame her lovely face like a halo.

"Who's the angel?" he asked no one in particular.

****

Roanne stood on the threshold of Finnigan's, despair filling her mind. The daub and wattle public house might be a poor excuse for an alehouse, but it was all they had. The story went that Finnigan's Norman ancestors built it over five hundred years ago. Since many families in the county claimed lineage from the Normans, no one disputed the boast.

She refused to step into the cramped depths. Her nose twitched from the sharp assault of turves smoke, unwashed bodies, and stale spirits. Somewhere inside stood her soon-to-be lord husband. A man she'd never met.

Someone played a *bodhran*, a hand-held drum as they approached. She listened to the fast rhythm, and the grief smoldering within her increased tenfold. Her brothers would never fathom the hollowness this forced marriage caused her. To leave the only home she knew. To lose the precious freedom she cherished so highly. It wasn't fair. She cast a dark glare at each one who dared to meet her gaze.

Now she understood Finn and Padraig's urgency in fetching her here. She whirled to face them, her chin lifting in defiance. "All right, which drunkard is he?"

The redness in Padraig's face deepened to match the color of her hair. "Faith, such coldness from the bride."

"You condemn me to the slow torture of marriage to a stranger."

Finn stepped closer and put a consoling hand on her arm. "Blessed Mary, Roanne, we all know how difficult this is for you. Do you not think we'd change

6

the prophecy if we could?"

The prophecy! She cursed whoever originated the hated prediction. It gave no daughter of the O'Casey control over who they would marry. Oh, she knew her family loved her, but her brothers weren't obligated to follow the blasted prophecy or fear dying.

She exhaled a deep sigh, letting her resistance melt ever so little. "Aye, you would. Forgive me." She turned to survey the crowd again. "So, tell me…where's my future husband? What's his name?"

"He be Simon Lancaster, the Earl of Kirkland," Padraig said.

"Kirkland, you say." She frowned, shooting a glance at Finn for clarification. He shrugged. "I'm unfamiliar with the title. Where is this lord from? The East Country?"

"You could say that," Padraig said. "Best meet him first. He be handsome for a—"

A fiddle and pipes joined the *bodhran* to cut off his words.

Roanne's trepidation doubled. "For a what?"

Padraig straightened to face her. "An Englishman."

Roanne stumbled back into the rain, thunderstruck. She slipped her fingers into her pocket to find her rosary. She clutched the amber beads, drawing comfort from them as they warmed at her touch. This couldn't be happening. After twelve years under the thumb of English conquest, her family had survived warfare, famine, and plague. Thousands of her countrymen were not as fortunate. Many had died, fled or been deported to the colonies.

And now she was to be sacrificed to one of the fiends!

"Holy Mother," she cried. "What depravity is this? An Englishman. I'll not wed him."

Padraig scowled. "Aye, you will. According to the prophecy our instructions were to find the first marriageable lord we could. We did our best. He isn't our choice either, but he's what we found hereabouts."

"Curse your black souls! Curse the whole O'Casey clan!"

"Too late, we are already cursed," Finn said with the same bitterness filling her.

Roanne stomped her foot, splattering the trio with mud. "What's wrong with him? Is he touched? No sane English lord would want to marry me—an Irishwoman. What have you promised him?"

"I need to find my wife and a drink," Finn said.

He slipped away and left her and Padraig to argue alone. He joined the revelry next to a pregnant woman standing with a short man Roanne recognized as Father Thomas. The Jesuit traveled from town to town administering to his scattered flock right under the noses of the authorities.

"Mind your tongue." Padraig hissed, his anger showing. "You'll feel better once you see the fellow. They say he's handsome for a Sassenach. Finnigan's daughter is beside herself fussing over him."

"Then let her wed him. And more joy to her."

"Trust me and the lads, Roanne." He held out his hand and wiggled his fingers. "We will not abandon you when you depart for the man's house. Those whose responsibilities can be set aside will travel with you to make sure you're treated kindly."

Despite the assurance, Roanne remained unconvinced. She backed farther out of reach. "Spare me, I beg you."

"Spare you, sister?" Remorse laced Padraig's tone. "Haven't we always done right by you? Luck be with us. What else would an English lord be doing on Irish soil unless he has Irish blood hidden somewhere in his past? Being in his cups, he's already admitted to being Catholic."

Rain dripped onto her face and she found herself trembling. "He's still the enemy. For the sake of an accursed prophecy you're putting me in his arms."

"Come, now," Padraig tried to soothe the situation with an explanation. "A sizeable Peter's pence has been paid to the church to have the banns waived. All is in readiness. We are your family and we love you. You will be his wife…and you will save yourself."

"I don't want—"

Padraig grabbed her arm. "You'll wed tonight. We promised Da to keep ye safe, and we'll not break our word."

Guilt stabbed at her that her brothers took on the burden of her welfare. They were barely surviving themselves during these hard times. The realization became another reason to hate the prophecy.

Roanne squared her shoulders. Resigned to her fate and against her better judgment, she said. "Aye, it seems I have no choice. Where is this Englishman?"

****

Teetering off balance, Simon shouldered his way across the compact dirt floor of the alehouse. He hadn't glimpsed a fine-looking woman in ages and wanted a better look at the bride. Along the way someone handed him another tankard. He arrived just as a man in brownish gray leggings and tunic and an extremely pointed nose and small, rounded ears stopped before the soon-to-be wed young woman. He barely reached her shoulders.

"Ashamed you should be, Roanne O'Casey!" he accused her. "You're marrying the enemy."

Her face reddened. "How dare you say that, Lubdan! Everyone in Ireland knows our prophecy. I have no choice."

"If the truth fits," the man countered in a high-pitched whine. "You might as well hear what everyone be thinking. They call you a traitor to all who suffered and died."

Simon guzzled his drink. With the insult ringing in his ears, he took matters into his own hands even though he saw several men step toward them. Worried relatives? More than likely. Something he did not have in common with these O'Caseys. Even though he acted as his brother's agent in Ireland, there was no love lost between them. His brother couldn't care less if he lived or died.

"Are you daft, man? That's no way to speak to a lady on her special day." He smiled at the slender woman standing in the doorway. She stared up at him over a button nose and eyes sparkling with amber and beryl flecks. Tiny raindrops shimmered in her lustrous red hair, catching the brilliance of candlelight. He imagined dazzling jewels gracing her neck.

"Thank you, my lord, but I can stand up for myself. Especially against the likes of Lubdan." She gave her accoster a dismissive shrug.

The little man's nose twitched like a rat sniffing the air. "A pox on you, Roanne. You forget your place. Already you defend the enemy against a loyal

Irishman."

Her gaze blazed with fire. Without warning, she slapped him.

An expression of pure hatred covered the short man's face. He flexed his fingers until they clenched into a fist. When his hand rose, Simon burst into action. No man struck a woman in his presence. He swung at the fellow. His fist landed with a jaw-breaking punch that slammed him to the floor.

Simon stepped over the body and puffed out his chest. He had defended the angel's virtue to the best of his ability. "Fear naught, my lady, he'll not besmirch your good name again."

A dark look materialized on the angel's face. "Too much ale gave Lubdan courage he doesn't possess while sober. I could have handled him without your assistance."

"I rather enjoyed putting the scum in his place," Simon replied as O'Caseys dragged the unconscious man off. They dumped him like a sack of potatoes in a corner. "First things first. Let's get you out of this rain."

The wide-eyed stare she gave him made him want to laugh. He knew perfectly well that he had no right to issue an edict when her relatives filled the alehouse.

"By your accent, you must be Simon Lancaster," she said, stepping inside.

The fresh scent of rain came with the lovely miss. He cocked a brow, more intrigued than before. The accent he understood. But how'd she know his name? And even though she did, he tried to wrap his head around why she hardly seemed pleased to see him. "At your disposal."

"Shouldn't we proceed with the ceremony?"

Strange-she sought his permission. He wished he wasn't so deep into his cups. It made intelligent conversation difficult, and he so wanted to impress this woman, for she heated his blood in a way he'd never felt. Though his vision blurred, he still noticed her gown had been worn shiny and felt a pang of sadness. Such a creature deserved better. She would do great justice to lush satins and silks.

Except they stood in a shabby tavern, not exactly the place for the finery.

He shrugged and nearly toppled. It must be a local custom for the bride to mingle with the guests before the ceremony. If Irishmen chose not to keep an eye on their womenfolk, especially the attractive ones, who was he to argue? "You must be excited on this momentous day. Will you spare a traveler a dance?"

She tilted her head and gaped at him as though he didn't know who he was or what he was doing. "This is absurd," she protested.

A fiddle started a jig that made him tap his foot to the lively music. He set his tankard down and extended his hand. "Come, dance with me. I'll do my best not to step on your toes."

"One dance is all."

A tingle of pleasure wove through him at her quick acquiescence. And apparently her relatives approved as well. Revelers cheered when they mingled with the other dancers. He bowed over her hand and hoped he could stay on his feet without embarrassing himself.

The bride narrowed her gaze at him as he stumbled around the room. "I cannot go through with this farce. You don't understand the dire importance of the situation."

He had no idea what she meant and concentrated on remaining upright, once again wishing he hadn't consumed so much ale. "What is the name of this tune? It sounds familiar."

"Really? You want to talk about a silly song?"

He swung her around, drawing her back. "It's as lovely as you."

She rolled those amazing eyes of hers. "The song is called, 'I'll never love thee more'."

"Ahh, a truer statement has never been uttered."

"You're drunk," she said.

At that moment, even while on the dance floor, someone handed him a tankard. He had the good sense to decline the drink. "Apparently so."

She glared at him, stopping completely. "The prophecy… It must be fulfilled. It is my destiny. I…"

A glitter of something reflected in her eyes—alarm, courage, and fear. She should never be afraid, not around him. "I know nothing of any prophecy, only your beauty intoxicates me far more than mere ale."

She scowled at the people sweeping by them, dancing, singing, happy as could be. "And I think swill spills from your tongue as easily as from any Irishman, my lord."

Swill, indeed! He laughed, enjoying her company.

She blinked several times, glaring at him the whole time with a fire that made him catch his breath. "What brought you to Dundalk?" she asked.

"Fate, I could say…though I wish it was you."

She huffed. "Mockery doesn't suit. The prophecy dictates I wed after my da dies. I have no choice, even if the groom is a stranger. 'Tis that so hard to understand?"

Her response caught him unprepared. Arranged marriages were common enough. His own parents' marriage had been one. The thought stopped him cold in his tracks. His brother, Hugh, took great enjoyment taunting him about why their mother left—because of him. The departure had broken his heart. Still, after all these years, the memory of her abandonment cut deeply with a pain for which he had no defense against.

At the moment, however, his befuddled brain decided encouragement would best serve to ease this bride's concerns. "You need not be afraid. Marriage is a noble endeavor. One that has stood the test of time."

She tsked at his attempt at humor. "A poor answer if ever I heard."

Simon tried to process her reaction, and found it problematic to do just that. "So lovely, and such a sharp tongue. But, oh, so much courage. I extend my gratitude to your betrothed for being tardy. His loss is my gain." Simon's gaze darted from her to check for newcomers in the dim interior. "Though I am curious who you intend to marry."

She huffed at him. "A fool, it would seem. I am to wed you."

Chapter Two

Blue eyes wide, the groom reeled backward to slump into a chair. "I've never been wed afore. What a novel idea. I'll beat my brother to the altar and that'll piss him off."

Roanne swore animosity colored his tone. She sank into the seat across from her soon-to-be husband. "You mean you didn't know?"

One of her brothers slid a tankard across the table. She glared daggers at the culprit. It was shameful to trick the earl into marrying her. There could be ramifications. Her brothers should be ashamed of themselves for keeping the fellow tipsy and in the dark.

The earl stared at her with a frown turning his mouth down. He gave her a weak smile, emptied the tankard, wiped his mouth, and passed out. His head hit the table with a loud thud.

She closed her eyes. This foreigner, the Earl of Kirkland, an overdressed Englishman in his fancy coat and tight breeches, the quality of which the O'Caseys hadn't seen in over a decade was the man she must wed.

Suddenly, Padraig loomed beside her and stood silent until she raised her gaze. "'Tis time, sister. I've come to bring you and your groom before Father Thomas."

"How? He's out cold."

Padraig signaled Rory. "Take one side and I'll take the other."

"Aye, I'm more than happy to lend a hand." Her brother rushed forward with a silly expression brightening his face, and hoisted her husband-to-be off the chair.

The none-too-gentle handling roused Kirkland. "W—what is it?"

"Father Thomas is awaiting, my lord," Padraig said, lifting him to his feet.

His eyelids fluttered and he grinned. "Oh, aye, the nuptials. I'm to be wed, you know. Mustn't delay the celebration or be late to one's own wedding."

Padraig and Rory flanked the Englishman until they reached the forefront of the bar. Finnigan's daughter handed her a posy of yellow and purple wild pansies. She nodded her thanks, for the sad-faced flowers fit her mood.

Padraig leaned in. "All will be well. You'll see."

"For all the O'Casey men, you mean," she whispered.

He placed a kiss on her brow, and gave her hands a squeeze before stepping back to the crowd's edge where his wife, Meagan, stood.

The alehouse stilled.

Outside, a storm boiled with wind gusts and pelting rain. Roanne's heart beat with the same fierce pace of the weather. For better or worse, marriage was a journey meant to last a lifetime.

Father Thomas performed the ceremony and had both her and Kirkland sign the contract with a hastiness she swore was designed to prevent them from calling off the proceedings.

Before the ink dried, her brothers and other family members surrounded her. They flashed huge grins and she allowed herself to be hugged and congratulated, fighting the sensation of being smothered in good wishes. All the while, she wondered if the fool who was now her husband had passed out again. She should probably seek him out to see how he faired.

Then the music started up again with the fiddle, pipes and *bodhran* blasting away. Someone tapped their feet, and she was swept out onto the dance floor to the cheers of the onlookers. Pretty soon couples joined her.

When the sun set, O'Casey womenfolk nudged her upstairs to a prepared room. Her knees buckled at the sight of where she would spend the night. The room contained little furniture—a rickety chair, a corner table holding the stub of a candle…and the bed. It appeared to be a timber frame with rope supports and a mattress bag stuffed with straw.

An hour later, they left her standing in her best nightdress. Roanne listened to rain and wind beat against the window. An omen of things to come? The turves had smoldered in the grate to small flickering coals, and the room's faint chill came as a welcome relief after the stifling crowd below.

Before long, male braying signaled the approach of the groom. The door slammed opened with a bang. Her husband stumbled inside. To her horror, the crowd accompanying him tried to follow.

It took her drunken husband several minutes to convince the crowd of relatives otherwise. Grateful not to have an audience for the bedding, Roanne stood and stared. The fool had the nerve to wink at her as he struggled to remove his fancy long coat. In his inebriated state, the simple task proved nearly impossible, and she had no intention of aiding him. She ignored the imploring glances he shot in her direction.

He succeeded in stripping off the garment and beamed at her. "Ahh, that feels much better."

She glared back. He was a stranger. What kind of man was he? Kind? Cruel? Insensible? She had no clue and that made her hate the prophecy all the more. "This is madness. Utter madness."

"What madness? What are you talking about? You have nothing to worry about." He shrugged his broad shoulders. The motion caused him to sway and bring the hint of bay toward her. "Fear and trembling are common among brides."

"Lord Simon, I—"

"Don't call me that," he interrupted. "M-my name is S-Simon."

"Simon," she repeated softly.

He grinned at her. "That's much better."

She retreated until the backs of her knees bumped into the bedside. Her rapidly beating heart revealed she didn't know what to expect. He was kinder than she anticipated.

He stumbled toward her, arms outstretched as though to wrap her in a hug. The scent of bay grew stronger. "Tonight, we will be friends as well as husband and wife."

She dodged him. "A drunkard is a sorry friend and an even sorrier husband."

He threw her a silly grin. "As I recall, you vowed to obey me in all things."

"You were not listening, my lord husband. I vowed to take thee to my hand, my heart and my spirit. I promised to remain by your side in sickness and in health, in plenty and in poverty. There was no mention of obedience."

"Well, there should be." He frowned as though puzzled. "Your vows claim you'll take me to your heart. That implies affection or love, although I confess the possibility hard to swallow since we've just met."

She shuddered as he tossed one of her own concerns back at her. The blue-eyed devil reminded her that they were strangers. Her conscience wondered how she could live with the enemy. Even a handsome one.

Smiling, he leaned forward, only to lose his balance. His body hit hers, his weight pressing her into the mattress. Overpowered. And surprised in a titillating way, she had the impression Kirkland was not a man to take advantage of a woman.

"Now this is more how I envisioned our night together," he murmured, brushing hair away from her face.

"Is that before or after you crush me to death?"

He raised up on his elbows, sniffing the air. "My apologies. I smell spices."

"I suspect my sister-in-law Meagan sprinkled them on the bed linens."

His smile widened. "Ah, then you must thank the lady for me."

In the next instant, Kirkland kissed her eyelids, tickling the sensitive skin with the tip of his tongue. A tingle ran down to Roanne's toes. She recalled how he had swept to the entrance with a scowl aimed at Lubdan. His actions had surprised her, coming from a Sassenach. None of her brothers had come to her rescue. *Only him.*

The kindness allowed her to close her eyes. Only her senses would not let her shut off the salacious emotions the man's attention caused.

This was her wedding night. She shoved riotous nerves aside to raise her arms and encircle his neck. The events of tonight would bring about a child—a part of the prophecy that also needed to be fulfilled. Once she bore a wee one, a safe and secure future awaited.

Her fingertips explored the bristles of his unshaven face.

"Ah, my lovely, you have a gentle touch," her husband said.

His praise gave her incentive. She pressed her mouth against his, tasting malty hops. He returned the kiss with such tenderness that a lusty sensation kindled within her belly, far more pleasant than she imagined possible. She tugged on the ribbon ties of his clothing.

Her newly-wed husband captured her fingers, and drew back a few inches. "You are truly lovely, gentle bride." He hiccupped. "Alas, the ale I've consumed has rendered me incapable of performing my husbandly duties."

Did he say what she thought? Blessed Mary! This couldn't be happening. Not now. "'Tis my one and only wedding night, my lord husband."

He rolled onto his back, tucked his hands behind his head, and yawned. "I beg your understanding. While you hold much appeal, I fear I have consumed too much of your Irish ale and now grow drowsy."

At his words, panic climbed in Roanne's chest. Damn her brothers. They should have realized an Englishman couldn't hold his liquor like them. "No, no. You mustn't fall asleep. The prophecy... It will not work if you do."

"I promise to attend you later. Just a few winks now."

"No!" Roanne shook his arm and felt the hard muscles beneath the linen fabric, but it was already too late. A sound, soft and rhythmic, emanated from the man.

"My lord husband," she whispered. "Simon, are you awake?"

No answer. She leaned closer. No mistaking that particular sound—a low snore.

****

Dawn had long passed when Simon stirred awake with a grimace and creation's worst headache behind his eyes. His mouth felt as though a wounded animal had crawled inside and died. He tried to lie still in the bed, fully aware any movement would double his pain.

Yesterday…his head had spun from all the liquor.

Last night…he'd been intoxicated by an angel.

Today…what had he done?

The O'Caseys had plied him with more tankards of ale than he could count. Like it or not, he'd been a dolt to accept everyone. The fault lay squarely on his shoulders for going along with the wedding. Perhaps the comely bride with the fiery hair, the nuptials, and the celebration had all been figments of his intoxicated mind. Even drunk, he admired her beauty, her woman's body that fit against him in a tempting manner.

Moving slightly led to an odd discovery—he still wore most of his clothes…including his boots. Most confusing. He must have passed out for his usual preference while sleeping was being naked. No wonder slumber had seemed uncomfortable. He stretched slowly and realized some of his shirt bindings were loose.

Running his hands down his front, the glint of gold on his finger caught his eye. A simple wedding band. *His*? The thought took him aback. He wore none upon his arrival in Ireland.

He rubbed his eyes to assuage the pounding in his head while doggedly mulling over the events of last night. Logic dictated that it had been an elaborate hoax. Or a traveler's scam. Though, in all fairness, the bride didn't have the jaded look of one of those professionals. New to the trade?

And he would have sworn she didn't want to participate in the ceremony.

He was pretty sure the bride's name began with an 'R'. Riona. No, that wasn't right. Frowning, he tried to dredge the girl's name out of his befuddled noggin. Radha. Ryanne. Roxanne. None of those sounded right. What was it? After several moments of digging into his memory, her name came to him.

Roanne.

Success brought a smile to his mouth.

Had the fellow who performed the ceremony even been a priest? It took a brave soul to wander Ireland, even in disguise, under the peril of death for no mercy was shown to those caught when Cromwell ruled. This time Simon really considered himself a fool for not questioning him beforehand.

The ring on his finger certainly added to the reality. Of course, it could be a prop to enhance the impression. He wouldn't put anything past these O'Caseys. They might be experienced flimflam artists.

Heat radiated at his side. Simon glanced down to

discover a slender body with a cloud of red hair spread over the pillow next to him. So lovely. He felt every inch of her lush body through his clothing. He was positive they hadn't lain together. Such a shame. Being drunk, performance had been impossible.

The woman made a wistful sound. Or did she sob in her sleep?

Then wincing, white hot sparks of rage flared up inside him—at himself, at the O'Caseys. While he considered himself a rational man, the anger hit him so fast his gut tightened. His childhood had been plagued with cruelty and jests to leave deep scars and bitter memories. Too many times his brother boasted their mother left because of him. Hugh never explained why, which only added to Simon's misery.

He had to get out of this room. Out of Finnigan's. Out of Ireland.

He set his jaw and climbed out of bed. The room spun as he collected his bearings and eyed the thin, well-worn gold ring again. It had to be someone's family heirloom. Pilfering was out of the question. So, thinking, he pulled the ring off and set it on the stand next to the candle.

A second glance at the slender figure beneath the thin covers made him back away. His chest tightened. The beauty deserved a long, happy life—without him.

In the middle of shrugging into his long coat, the door burst open and pounding feet rushed inside the room. He grabbed the only weapon he could find-the chair. He raised it in the air, ready to smash the intruder.

Six O'Caseys stumbled to a halt.

Sean the Third grinned. "We come to escort the

happy couple to the manor, my lord."

Simon set the chair down and leaned against it to steady himself. "That won't be necessary. I continue my journey back to England." He scooped the ring off the table and tossed it on to the bed where it bounced once before coming to a rest.

The loud entrance had woken Roanne. She sat up and peered blearily at her brothers. She rubbed her eyes, then frowned when she spotted him with the chair still in his hand.

Shock washed over the young man's face. "W-what? Without your bride? I think not. We stayed the night in case Roanne needed us. 'Twould seem our instincts were right."

The tall redhead called Rory shoved his way to the forefront. "Easy now. Roanne can be a handful at times, but she has many fine qualities, too. Give her time to adjust. You'll not find a more caring or loyal person."

Simon wasn't in the mood to hear the virtues of a woman he had no intentions of becoming better acquainted with. His head pounded with the raised voices, and he'd give anything for a large tankard of water to quench his thirst.

Then, the image of his mother flashed in his head. He felt five years old. Betrayed. Abandoned. The exact thing he planned to do to the lovely creature in the bed-sneak away without bidding a word of good-bye. The notion made him push aside the sliver of appeal curling within him. "So you say."

Roanne snatched up the ring before jumping from the bed. "I can speak for myself."

"Let me warn you, Lord Kirkland, being a nobleman won't stop us from thrashing you if you mistreat our sister," boomed a voice from the back of angry Irishmen.

Simon straightened. "I am not the Earl of Kirkland. That responsibility belongs to my brother, Hugh. He is the earl, not I. I'm Simon Lancaster. Hugh is the heir. I'm the spare."

A platter crashed at the bottom of the stairs in the alehouse.

Sean the Third pushed his face into Simon's. "You're a fraud?"

The announcement amused, more than insulted, Simon. Truth be told, a grain of reality existed in the accusation. "I'm not the one who made the assumption."

"It cannot be." Sean the Third's complexion paled until freckles showed across the bridge of his nose. "You have no notion what you've done."

"What *I've* done?"

"Aye, you."

Perplexed, Simon waited for an explanation. When none was forthcoming, he sighed and watched Roanne grab her well-worn gown off the chair where it had been placed the previous night. She jumped back under the covers and squirmed into it. Simon would have laughed at the sight if the situation were not serious.

From the back of the group came another O'Casey roar. "He tricked us. I knew it. Let me kill him."

Simon recognized the dark-haired brute who pushed forward from the previous night.

Red-faced, the giant man scanned the room as though seeking permission to fulfill his threat. His huge chest puffed out. "I warned you we couldn't trust the damn Sassenach."

"For the love of God." Rory launched his long body at the other man. "Shut up, Murdock. Let the fellow explain himself."

Before he spoke, Roanne flung off the covers and stood. "Ye can't totally blame him for being a cursed wretch. None of you bothered to fully explain the prophecy to him. We cannot blame him for not knowing what's at stake."

A good guess about his character, and on the mark, Simon deduced.

Six pairs of red-rimmed eyes stared at her, then turned to him with varying glares of distrust. While he applauded the Irishwoman's spirit, the accusation put him in danger.

"Best you not be up to any shenanigans," one of her brothers warned Roanne.

A middle-aged giant scowled at her. "Faith, that's it, isn't it? She isn't one who likes being told what to do. Da spoiled her. She's torturing us for marrying her off to someone not of her own choosing."

Simon didn't believe the criticism for a solitary minute. He wondered if the bigger the O'Casey, the worse their temperament.

"Brian's right," answered one of the younger O'Caseys whose name Simon couldn't remember.

A throbbing head didn't improve his memory or disposition. While condemning the situation he found himself trapped in, even worse, he abhorred the woman being subjected to criticism because of him. He opened his mouth to champion her when she threw the brass candleholder at her brothers.

Two O'Caseys leaped apart as though they expected additional objects to careen in their direction.

She scowled at them. "My temperament isn't in question. The blasted Englishman is the one we need to concentrate on. He's ruined everything."

"Aye, a sorry pain in the arse she can be when she wants," the last fellow continued as he edged inside without a care.

Simon harbored no illusions about these O'Caseys. They were single-minded in their pursuit of separating him from his coin. Watching his supposed wife, the shattered expression on her face made his sense of self-preservation take a distant second. His heart beat faster. He never abided someone being picked upon, and a sense of injustice rose.

"Roanne wouldn't lie about something this serious," Sean defended her. "It's that piss-ugly Englishman trying to weasel out of his vows."

"I agree with Sean the Third," Rory added.

The heavily muscled Murdock joined Roanne's side. He wrapped her in a bear hug and gave her a squeeze. "Roanne wouldn't seek vengeance at another's expense."

For some odd reason, the kindness made the brutish giant tolerable. That is, until the fellow posed a new development.

"'Sides, who's to say the marriage was consummated?"

The statement caused everyone to stare at her for confirmation.

"A fair question, Roanne," Sean the Third finally said. "Did the fellow bed you?"

She pursed her lips, her gaze flitting around the room. "Nay," she whispered. "Nothing happened."

Rory moved over to her. "Best explain. Even

drunk, from what I saw last night, Kirkland seemed besotted with you."

Simon noticed, though none of the O'Caseys focused on him, somehow, they had strategically placed themselves between him and the door. They had no intention of letting him depart until explanations were given and the situation clarified.

Roanne clamped her hands on her hips. "'Twas you who got him so drunk he fell asleep and snored the night away."

Simon smiled to himself. The girl wasn't a liar. She had her facts straight. He'd give her that.

Murdock laughed. "Leave it to a Sassenach not to finish his own wedding night like a real man. Though 'tis the first time I be grateful to one."

"What can we do?" Sean asked, wide-eyed looking at his brothers.

Murdock gave Roanne a sad smile. "I say we give him a good clobbering and send him back to England a little worse for wear."

Rory's blue-green eyes twinkled with amusement. "Sure, and if you had half a brain, you bugger, you'd know using your fists won't solve our problem. I say we take him to Padraig."

After a few heartbeats of listening, Simon announced, "I don't see the problem. Just let me go and I'll continue merrily on my way."

"Sure, and you played us false," Rory responded.

"Me?" Simon didn't have to feign surprise. "What is amiss? I concealed nothing from you."

Murdock took a threatening step forward. "You misled us. What about your carriage?"

That explained the confusion. "My—my carriage?

It belongs to my brother. You see the crest and think I'm the earl. Who's the fool now? I would have gladly told you whatever you wanted to know. I have no secrets."

"That a fact. It's never too late." Rory's voice went soft, deadly. "How about now?"

Simon's gaze roamed the chamber until it rested on Roanne. She stood quiet and defiant, lips pinched tight, although movement beneath her gown revealed shaking knees. The poor thing was probably frightened to death. He had admired her at first sight in the doorway. Looking at her through clearer eyes, he loathed being the one responsible for bringing woe and consternation into her life. Instinct told him she deserved to be cherished and treated with kindness.

Being cautious came naturally. He wondered how much information to supply. "My life is boring. Nothing unusual. I was born in Stafford in west-central England," he began, because it amused him to do so. "The locals call it Staffs. My brother and I call the locals Stuffy Staffs because we always thought they had sticks up their…"

Roanne's head snapped up. "You keep saying brother. Only one? No others? No sisters?"

He held up a single finger. Best to be vague. These people were strangers, potentially charlatans. "One brother is all. And one uncle who lives in London with his wife of forty-odd years. My older brother, Hugh, resides at the ancestral estate, Hollyhock. We tolerate each other now, though throughout our childhood, we battled for all sorts of imagined slights. Hugh never reached my height or size, and I suspect jealousy played a part in his behavior. What else do you want to know?"

Simon stopped talking. No sense giving away all the Lancaster secrets.

"Are you in line for any title? A viscount? Baron?" asked a skinny O'Casey with tawny brown hair and dark eyes.

He inhaled and hoped dredging up the past would prove to these people they had the wrong man. "Hugh retains the viscount title for his heir, once he is born. All my name can lay claim to is Honorable, and even that is questionable at times. Since I've been forthcoming with you, how about answering a few of my questions."

"Like what?" Sean the Third demanded.

"This prophecy everyone keeps referring to. What is it?"

Sean stepped closer, eyes narrowing. "It's everything. Our past. Roanne's future."

If a simple misunderstanding caused this disaster, Simon deserved to know, but he doubted that. The passion in their voices unveiled true belief. "A few details would be helpful."

A huge sigh preceded Sean's explanation. "The prophecy came into being when our Norman ancestor arrived in Dundalk. It claims when the O'Casey clan leader dies, his daughter, if unwed, must wed the first lord her family can find."

"What if a daughter is never born?" He spared a glance at Roanne to see her reaction. She lifted her chin as she followed the conversation.

"That has never happened," the young Irishman answered with the ring of confidence in his tone.

"She must be wed and breeding within a year," Rory added, surveying the room.

The O'Caseys nodded in agreement.

A sour taste grew in Simon's mouth. He never approved of women or any person being considered chattel. From cabin boy to first mate, he treated every individual equally, on their own merit. Irritation rose at the callous treatment of someone who should be a beloved relative. "I hear an *or*."

"Or she dies." Sean the Third stepped closer. A sad expression flashed across his face as he glanced at his family members. "Remember the Talberts of Kerry?"

The O'Caseys exchanged glances with each other.

The young O'Casey looked at Simon. "They had a similar prophecy, but it included the whole family. About a hundred years ago, the oldest son refused to uphold the family tradition of wedding his closest neighbor's daughter. Instead he ran off with a girl from town who he fancied, and everyone perished in a great bogslide."

Simon's gaze flashed to Roanne where she sank on to the bed. She didn't flinch under his scrutiny. "A bit far-fetched, but extinction explains your rush."

"This is not something we make light of." Sean the Third's voice rose. "We love our sister. It be a grave burden that we gladly accept as our responsibility. We want to see her wed, to live a long life, and be well cared for."

"I think I'll kill him after all," Murdock snarled.

"Silence." Rory held up his hand. "Not another word until we talk to Padraig. He's the O'Casey. He'll decide what to do." The redhead slung a traveling cloak over his sister's shoulders. "We return home. With Roanne and with you."

"Move," threatened Murdock.

An O'Casey shoved Simon toward the stairs. He'd been in tighter spots. He just couldn't recall exactly when or where.

Dull light from a single window spilled inside the main room now empty of patrons. Stale ale and the scent of smoke permeated the room.

The creak of a door opening or closing in the back of the alehouse caused Simon to glance over his shoulder. More likely Finnigan or his daughter were up and about, eavesdropping. So be it. Let them. He had nothing to hide.

Outdoors, a layer of clouds masked the sun and brought the smell of rain closer. He wasn't surprised to find the elegant carriage with brass side lanterns mended and sparkling clean like a regal white swan swimming in the Thames.

"Where's my driver?" Simon asked, hoping the O'Caseys didn't harm an innocent.

"We gave him some coin and sent him on his way," Sean the Third said.

"Ian, you drive," Rory ordered. "Brian, Timothy, and Sean, you ride inside and keep our new brother-in-law company with Roanne. Murdock and I will take the ponies and ride ahead."

"Why can't I ride inside?" The giant brown-haired Irishman spat on the ground. "With me there, there will be no escape."

Rory acknowledged the truism with a nod. "Brian can handle one Sassenach and is slower to anger than you. I want the groom to arrive alive and in one piece."

During the course of the exchange all trace of amusement left Simon. These O'Caseys weren't charlatans. They were in earnest—nothing mattered to them except their belief in their ancient prophecy.

Could he truly be wed?

During his years as a privateer, Simon had suffered many discomforts and faced death a hundred times. Speed and cunning had served him well and saved him from untold enemies, yet today he faced an enemy he was unable to outfight. The most dangerous one of all—superstition.

Simon took survey of the situation. Odds of six against one weighed heavily in the O'Casey's favor, but that wouldn't stop him from escaping. He waited for Rory and Murdock to head for the stables to retrieve their mounts. Then, without warning, he lunged and knocked Brian to the ground, feigning right and going left. He barreled past a corner of Finnigan's, already spying his escape route—the deep woods beyond.

Suddenly, he was struck in the back of his legs and fell onto the muddy ground. The youngest O'Casey whose name he finally recalled as Timothy tackled him. Simon rolled, pummeling his fists on the young man in a futile attempt to make him release his hold. The O'Casey clung to his legs like sticky thistle.

Their brief scuffle allowed time for the others to catch him and pin his arms.

"You be going the wrong way, Sassenach," said Sean the Third with a grin.

Brian clamped an arm around his neck and dragged him back to the carriage.

His clothes were a muddy mess, but he was still a gentleman. He extended his arm to aid Roanne as she started to climb aboard. She tossed him a look of disgust and ascended by herself.

Timothy went next, with Simon clambering after

him. Despite his mud-covered clothes, he sat next to Roanne. Timothy squeezed beside Roanne, leaving the opposite side empty.

Roanne snorted and moved. "Stay away from me. I'll no be having either one of you sitting next to me in your filthy clothes."

Next the massive Brian ducked inside, his weight dipping the carriage.

"Comfortable?" Simon asked, wedged between the brothers tighter than caulked planks.

Finnigan stood in the alehouse's doorway, watching the whole episode with a grin.

Brian snorted. Timothy shifted his weight a scant margin. A heavy object, being secured to the top, jostled the carriage.

Lastly, Sean the Third settled next to his sister.

The sound of reins cracking over the horses' backs signaled for the carriage to jerk forward.

Simon rocked on the seat and willed himself to sit still. The cloudy memory of Roanne stroking his face brought a smile to his lips. He'd thought her soft mouth and the sweet kiss a dream. In the periphery of his brain, he recalled she had responded to his caresses.

Today, she hadn't bothered to pin her luscious hair up as was the practice of married women, and he didn't mind in the least. He rather enjoyed the flyaway curls surrounding her face in feathery red wisps.

He leaned across the carriage to pat Roanne's knee. His fingers came into contact with the threadbare green skirt. He knew he was in trouble, but wanted to make the best of a bad situation. "Take heart, madam wife, I will be perfectly safe."

She raised her chin to eye him with a gold-green

stare that he could only call a dare. "What makes you think I care?"

"Such coldness. And us newly wed."

A beefy hand clamped over Simon's wrist. "Don't be touching our sister."

"She's my wife," he reminded the middle-aged man named Brian.

Brian tweaked his hold ever so little. "Padraig will decide if you be her husband or her be a widow."

Simon withdrew his hand. The warning sounded genuine. Plus, he'd felt the bone-crushing power in the fellow's huge paw around his throat and now his wrist. No sense provoking a fight.

"Should I be worried?" he asked the younger, affable O'Casey across from him.

Sean the Third chuckled. "You're an Englishman in Ireland. What d'you think?"

The others laughed, including the stoic Brian and Roanne.

"The situation could be worse," he replied, though he couldn't imagine one.

Each revolution of the wheels caused the carriage to heave and bounce over the rutted roadway and brought him closer to his mysterious destination. He kept an eye open for landmarks—a twisted tree here, a tumble of boulders there. He memorized what he saw.

As the captain of the *Black Sheep* he wasn't worried about getting lost. Once he escaped, the stars would guide him to Dundalk where he could catch a ship home.

Dusk fell over the land when the vehicle lurched to a stop before an impressive five-storied square tower manor rising out of the ground with *fleur-de-lys* carved on the tie beams and oriel windows of various sizes spread across the front. Simon guessed the ancient structure dated back to the Normans with each generation adding to it. Similar ones dotted the English countryside.

On the south side of the manor, tall oaks stood guard and provided shade against summer heat.

A half-dozen dogs-wolfhounds-bounded around the carriage as it stopped. Their deep barks were loud enough to frighten away the bravest soul, and make the carriage horses skittish. Whip-like tails banged the exterior, turning the vehicle into a drum. He immediately recognized the rare breed of sighthounds that Cromwell had forbidden exported.

"Our family has raised the dogs for centuries," Sean said, noticing Simon's interest.

"I thought only the nobility could own them."

Sean snorted with derision as he left the carriage. "Who said we own them? They have minds of their own."

He watched Sean the Third exit and stagger against the onslaught. The man laughed as several in the pack rose on their hind legs to lick his smiling face.

Roanne departed next and ran straight for the manor to disappear inside.

When he exited, sure enough, the huge dogs broke away to circle him, sniffing at his boots and legs. He'd always been good with animals and harbored a soft spot for large dogs. Surprisingly, these yellow-eyed beasts behaved with more gentleness and affection than the smaller spaniels belonging to the ladies of Charles II's court.

The largest male, a red brindle, ducked his giant

head beneath his hand. Simon understood the silent request for a scratch and complied until a shove between his shoulder blades sent him stumbling forward through the manor's door left open by Roanne.

Inside, empty spaces revealed where furniture once stood, and ghostly outlines suggested tapestries stripped from stone walls not long ago. A pang of regret struck him at the further evidence of the war's legacy to Ireland.

Brian continued to push Simon up two flights of stairs and along a hallway to an unknown destination.

Chapter Three

Roanne hurried into the solar to catch Rory and Murdock relaying the devastating tale to Padraig and Meagan that her husband was not a lord. A moment later, Brian pushed Kirkland inside, and everyone quieted. Kirkland whipped around and slammed his fist into her brother's face. Is this what having only one brother produced? The O'Caseys tussled with each other and never took offense or meant harm to one another. Couldn't her husband take a little shoving? Or was it fear? He had no choice but to accept her brother's decision on the status of their marriage.

At least that's how it appeared.

Still, she questioned his motives. Did he have no sense of his own safety? Was he trying to provoke a donnybrook?

Murdock and Rory rushed to pin Kirkland's arms before he threw punches again without reason. Padraig stepped in front of Brian to defuse the tense situation.

Roanne slipped her hand into her pocket in search of her rosary beads. Instead she palmed the ring Kirkland had tossed on the bed at Finnigan's. The ring represented so much happiness, trust, and now betrayal. Sadness sliced through her at that last thought.

Once the commotion settled down, Meagan burst into tears. She dashed out of the room and down the passageway.

"Mercy, Meagan, don't run off," the O'Casey hollered after her, raking his hand through silver-streaked hair.

"Let your wife go, Padraig," Murdock said. "Weeping be good for a woman's soul. Give her time to adjust and she'll come around."

Padraig's shoulders slumped, giving the impression that he'd reached his limit and all of his age. He turned sharply to face Kirkland and didn't mince his words. "They tell me you're not the Earl of Kirkland. Be that so?"

Whispered voices rustled like brittle fall leaves over the floor. Kirkland didn't answer. Instead he sank onto a chair before Roanne's desk where she had left the cubbyholes stuffed full of writing paraphernalia and sheets of vellum strewn across the top.

"If I had been informed of the importance," Kirkland began at last, "I would have mentioned it sooner. It would seem hasty actions have their drawbacks."

"We can't take his word that he isn't a lord," Finn said. "He could be lying. What if we fetch Sir Percy? He's always had an eye for Roanne."

She shuddered at the man's name. She'd been taught to treat all people equally, to give kindness to noble and peasant alike. Of course, there were exceptions. "The man's a debaucher," she snapped with more venom than she intended. "'Sides, I hear he only beds virgins."

"Which, it seems you are," Padraig shot back in an instant.

Blessed Mary! She frowned. She hadn't been the only one to react at Sir Percy's name. Murdock had growled like one of the wolfhounds. No love-loss between the two Irishmen, yet none knew the reason, and because it was Murdock, the family knew better than to make inquiries.

"We have three months before Roanne needs to be with child," Rory said. "Percy is full of airs. Always thinking he's better than us."

Roanne's stomach rolled when one of the family's wolfhound's tail struck the chords of her harp. The mournful twang echoed through her soul to bewail her predicament. "And I'll have Sir Percy's gizzards on a platter if he's the next man I'm forced to wed."

"We have no idea if what's being said is true or false." Padraig faced Kirkland. "As head of this clan, my responsibility is to make the correct decision. If you've spoken true, you'll have our sincere apologies for getting you drunk and forcing you into this marriage. Until then…let me think."

Roanne's cheeks burned with sudden heat. She wanted to scream in frustration. "Padraig, can't we undo the damage afore more occurs? Can we not petition for an annulment through canon law?"

With saddened dark brown eyes, the O'Casey shook his head. "I hate to think we're ill-starred after all these generations, sister. The ceremony was performed in accordance with the laws of the church. Tis no easy thing to undo. The prophecy has held the O'Caseys in good stead through the eons. Don't lose faith. Blessed we are that the marriage wasn't consummated." He paused to peer at Kirkland again. "No offense, but we do not know you well enough to trust your word."

"You knew me well enough to wed your sister."

"A decision deeply regretted," Roanne felt

compelled to add. She stared at her husband, hating the niggle of attraction in her belly.

He coughed a half-laugh, half-snort. "And here I wondered if this is a traveler's dodge. Was I right or wrong?"

Roanne couldn't take insults heaped upon injury, especially when aimed at her family. "The O'Caseys are many things, but thieves or liars, we are not."

"Mistakes have been made on both sides. I take full responsibility. I shouldn't have gotten drunk." Her husband crossed his long legs at the ankle, looking pleased with himself. "Is there no resolution we can mutually reach? I would be willing to go to London and find a diocese willing to grant a quick annulment."

She sucked in a breath. A lie. Now she knew for sure the man didn't possess a grain of common sense. "Are you serious? Do you really think that utterance works with us?"

"Silence," Padraig ordered. His brows knit together over a worried expression. "What happened is unfortunate but will be resolved. My immediate concern is how to confirm your claim, sir. Bad blood betwixt our countries runs high. Right now, peace is as fragile as a newborn. The English aren't welcome in Ireland. Nor is it safe for the Irish in England."

"You mean to send someone to England, don't you?" Sean the Third asked, a twinkle shining in his eyes. "Let me be the one."

The O'Casey smothered a smile. "Who else would I let take on such a perilous journey?"

"Tie a string to his left hand," Rory said in a teasing tone, "in case he forgets the reason you send him."

"Sure, and make it red," Murdock added. "'Twill be a more potent reminder."

"Ian shall go, too." Padraig appeared unaffected by the jesting. "He'll keep the ponies in good health. And Finn, as well. His wife is near her time to birth their second child, so he'll be eager to return with Godspeed. A ship's raising anchor on the morning tide. All three can leave for England aboard it."

Roanne kept a close eye on Kirkland during the exchange. His feeble attempt at escape at Finnigan's seemed below the man. Now, the way his steady blue gaze eyed the leaded windows made her think he contemplated smashing through them to make his escape. He'd be a fool if he tried. The thirty-foot drop from the solar would be deadly. His body would break on the grounds below. Her stomach flipped at the thought and she swallowed hard.

"May the saints accompany you on your journey. I wish you all safe travel and your troubles be few," she offered. "Though I would feel easier if I knew the answer now."

"Wouldn't we all," Padraig said. Suddenly he turned to glare at the man who was her husband. "While the situation is inconvenient for you, it is serious for us. Roanne is our only sister and doing right by her is foremost in our minds. We will not be the first O'Caseys to lose a sister to the prophecy. Meanwhile, we'll keep an eye out for another lord."

Roanne freed a pent-up breath. "Can you, at least, promise me a say in the next man you select for me?"

The Englishman held his hand over his heart. "You crush me, dear wife."

She didn't find his jest humorous. The man had no

sense. Didn't he possess a smidgeon of good judgement or a sense of self-preservation?

Murdock aimed a malevolent grin at the man. "You won't be amused if a sad accident befalls you. They happen so often."

Kirkland leaped to his feet, his expression fierce. "Threats? Am I a prisoner or a guest?"

A fair question as far as Roanne was concerned. Where did this Englishman stand in their household? Instinct warned her he required watching. After all, what Englishman could be trusted? Then she remembered the press of his hard body against hers the night before. A flash of heat rushed to her core. She held her breath, and turned to her oldest brother for his answer, and hoped she agreed with him.

"'Twould appear you are my brother-in-law," the clan leader began with a none-too-pleased scowl. "For now, we will honor your status and let you wander free wherever you wish within the manor and on the grounds, however, you'll not go unguarded. An O'Casey will remain with you a 'tall times."

"We can't trust him. He should be thrown in chains and locked up," Roanne spoke up.

"Is that any way to treat your husband?" the man quickly added. "Why so argumentative? I am as much a victim in this situation as you are. Can't we make the best of it?" He rose and stepped in her direction.

A solid wall of O'Caseys saved her by appearing in front of her husband before he took another step.

That's what he deserved for goading them, Roanne decided. From the other side, she bit back rage.

"Another room will be readied for you," Padraig spoke next. "You'll not be laying your head upon our sister's pillow until we uncover the truth."

When her brothers edged aside, Roanne hazarded a glare at her tall husband. He beamed a triumphant grin back as if he'd won a battle. She shook her head. The man must be addled. Didn't he grasp the direness of the situation? His lack of a title ruined everything. It took every speck of control she possessed not to bolt from the room.

She'd show him. So, she bunched her skirts in her hands and walked out of the solar with her head high like a lady. Satisfaction soared within her. The small victory felt so good, because she doubted many won against the man.

****

So spirited, so challenging, Simon thought. He hated seeing his wife depart, then she stormed back into the room, her freckled face flushed pink. He envisioned holding the red-headed vixen close to his solid frame, before leveling a penetrating stare at her. "Have you returned to play me a song on yonder harp?"

She scrunched up her button nose, her green-gold eyes blazing at him. "I be pleased to play and sing at your wake. The sooner, the better."

"So angry, m'dear," he said, not offended, but curious. "Something else drew you back, then?"

Her chin tilted up. "Aye, it has."

Simon saw her brothers inch closer, being protective. "Well, by all means, enlighten me. I'm most eager to hear what you have to say."

"You be wrong about us. The O'Caseys' word is our bond."

Several brothers nodded in agreement. It reminded Simon of the closeness within this family. No such sentiment existed in his. He paused to reflect…only a few individuals at Hollyhock offered him friendship. His mind traveled back to one in particular-Old John-the tenant farmer hadn't feared repercussions from the lord or his heir. The thought caused a warm tendril to spiral through him.

"No offense, dear wife, but I'm not in the mood to hear you extol the virtues of your illustrious family. They, after all, were willing to wed you to the first lord they could find. Is it my fault they erred? Now they keep me prisoner. And threaten to kill me." He flicked a glance at Murdock, then the clan leader. "I'll take my leave. Someone deliver me to those promised quarters."

Murdock's gaze drifted to the O'Casey, who nodded.

Murdock and Rory escorted him to a chamber one level up.

"Don't be thinking you can escape during the night," Murdock warned him, seemingly only too happy to boast. "One of us will keep vigil outside the door the whole time."

Simon didn't bother answering. He'd heard threats before. He entered the chamber and studied the near empty room. A track of narrow windows lined the far wall. He strode to them, and looked out in the fading light to spy a row of tall oak trees. Many years at sea gave him excellent vision at night. The sight informed him this chamber was on the south side of the manor. Freeing a sigh, he eyed the distance from windows to the trees as he considered leaping to the closest branches. Probably a bad idea. Too far, and the spindly branches would snap with any pressure.

Which left the four-inch ledge running along the

manor out as well. He valued his neck too much. Of course, staying with these O'Caseys' put him at risk of death. He let his mind drift. How long did he have before escape became mandatory? Once they learned he spoke the truth, they'd be furious, but there was nothing he could about their reaction. He valued his own hide.

The door closed with a solid thud and he turned around to survey the room. A simple timber frame bed held a mattress that appeared stuffed with straw. At least he wasn't expected to sleep on the floor. He fingered the linens neatly folded at the foot of the bed and shook his head. The thin fabric, even tied together, would never be strong enough to hold his weight if he fled through the window.

He continued his surveillance of the interior, and spotted his domed traveling trunk against the far wall. The O'Caseys weren't outright thieves. Roanne had spoken true. He gave them that much, assuming nothing inside was missing.

He lay on the thin mattress, which proved more comfortable than he expected. He mulled over his choices. Scaling down the manor wall was no different than when he escaped his bedchamber as a child. He might be better served to go along with the O'Caseys' crazy scheme for the time being. Escape meant returning to London, and if the king remained angry with him, a cell in the tower of London awaited him. Fortunately, this room held much more appeal.

The prophecy nonsense troubled him. Changing peoples' minds with logic was always a long shot. The Irish were no different. Although this clan seemed filled with more suspicious nonsense than most. It meant persuading them to reexamine age-old beliefs. Thus far, all he'd seen or heard convinced him that the ancient edict controlled these O'Caseys' every action, their every thought, and had regulated their actions for eons.

The temptation to play along-if only for the pleasure of exposing them-became powerful bait, although nothing compared to his attraction for Roanne. In truth, he doubted he could ask for a better wife. She appeared loyal to those she loved. She wasn't a liar. She'd already proven that. Her spirit caught him totally unaware. He didn't believe another woman could be more beautiful. All he had to do was look at her and he wanted to bed her. If they were truly wed, was that so bad?

And something he'd trusted all his life-his inner compass-told him that their lives together would never be dull. The intuition had never steered him wrong.

Eventually, sleep overtook him. He woke at dawn to the sound of branches scratching against the manor's sides. His gaze flicked toward the windows.

He rolled out of bed, donned fresh clothing, and opened his door a crack.

A napping Murdock jerked upright in his chair. The wolfhound at his side lifted his head, his tail thumping the floor.

"Hope you slept well," Simon greeted, moving past the giant O'Casey, only to hear a grunt and the sound of a chair scraping the floor. "I certainly did."

"The hours went by with nary a notice. Come, Braith," the Irishman called to the wolfhound.

Simon laughed at the snarl in the man's tone. "More likely nary a wink."

"You be a fool, then, to think an O'Casey can't sleep sitting up. I've slept in worse places than a chair."

"I had the sweetest dream." Simon decided the man used rudeness and anger to keep people at bay. "No superstition or worrying about a silly prophecy robbed me of a night's rest. Now, where do we break our fast? Or is starvation a condition of my detention?"

"Are you worth feeding, Sassenach, is more the question?"

Chapter Four

In the solar, Roanne wrapped a shawl around her shoulders to ward off the morning chill. Her world crumbled around her and no helpful fairy magically appeared to resolve her problem. She sat ramrod-straight on a stool near the brackish-smelling turves fire.

Nor was she alone. Her oldest brother paced the length of the room in long strides, his leather doublet flapping behind him. His face contorted with concern.

"That worried look troubles me, Padraig. What displeases you so?"

He stopped to glower at her, combing salt and pepper hair with his fingers. "Stop and think, sister. Use your head to abet me instead of asking the obvious." He went to stand at a window with his hands clasped behind his back.

Roanne narrowed her eyes. Padraig never snapped without cause. She decided to give him a few moments to calm rather than coerce him into giving her answers. He would tell her when ready.

She flashed a smile at Padraig's wife, Meagan, to show his sour mood didn't offend her. She noticed the older woman wore a rounded straw hat and heavy wool cape and carried a wooden *bascauda*, a long shallow container.

"Going picking, are you, Meagan?"

"Aye, I spotted some dandelion greens on the far hill, ripe for picking. Harvesting them will add tangy flavor to our supper."

"Best stay in and keep dry. I slipped out earlier and the clouds freed their rain to pelt the ground so hard it felt like I was being punished for a sin I have no memory of committing."

Meagan chuckled. "I appreciate your warning, Roanne, but I'll be fine." She rolled her brown gaze and made a silly face. "I put some bread loaves in the ovens an hour or so ago to bake. Be a lamb and remove them for me."

Roanne loved to help in the kitchen where the scent of spices filled the air. Unfortunately, her skills were sadly lacking when it came to cooking. Still, the request pleased her. "Should I ready a stew for the evening meal?"

This time outright laughter burst from Meagan. "Best wait for me. Everyone lost their appetites the last time you put your hand to cooking. I promise to return long before the need to begin our supper arrives."

"How will I ever learn to cook, if I do not practice?"

"There's no need for you to master the skill," her sister-in-law countered as she headed for the hallway. "As a noblewoman, you'll have servants aplenty to do your bidding. Methinks you'll no have to fix feasts, just know what to prepare."

"Meagan speaks true. You should listen," Padraig said after his wife left the room. "Meanwhile, we wait for Sean the Third, Ian, and Finn to return."

Disappointment swept over Roanne like an outgoing riptide. "They're gone? I'd hoped to give them these." She uncurled her fingers to reveal three four-leaf clovers. "'Tis why I went out. I wanted to find a wee bit of magic to keep evil away on their journey and wish them Godspeed."

"They should be three-quarters to Dundalk by now. The only ones remaining are those I've bade guard your husband."

It wasn't fair. "He's husband in name only," she snapped.

"And a fine good morn to you," the man himself said behind her.

She nearly jumped out of her skin at the sound of his voice. She had no words to counter Kirkland as he stood under the lintel, all fresh in a blue coat that made his eyes a piercing blue. The width of his shoulders left no room for her brother to pass. Nor did Kirkland show any sign of moving, which she decided was intentional. Murdock growled behind him. Her husband's gaze bored into her as if she were a tasty morsel for him to devour. Not a feeling that invoked pleasure in her.

"What d'you want?" She forced her gaze away from him. His handsome face had beamed at her. Oh, she was fully aware that she snapped at the wrong person. Her brothers were the ones who'd blundered. She didn't understand why the fellow appeared jovial about being confined against his will. He left her in a constant state of confusion. She vowed to live up to the definition of her family's namesake, Casey, which meant vigilant.

Her husband stepped into the solar and Murdock swept around him. "Have you eaten?" Kirkland asked her. "I, for one, enjoy company when I eat. I had thought you might join me. I brought bread fresh from the ovens."

The damn man was being kind again. In truth, she liked him more than she should. It was annoying. "My company will not be to your liking."

Her rejection seemed to mean nil to the fiend. He smiled. "Let me decide."

He held up two round loaves of sweet-smelling soda bread, then proceeded to rip one into equal parts. The scent of fresh baked bread tickled her nose and her belly grumbled. She hadn't broken her morning fast yet.

He tossed half to Murdock and the other to Braith trailing on their heels. Slightly piqued, she couldn't understand why the colossal red brindle favored the infernal Englishman. Usually, the hound remained wary around strangers, trusting only family.

Murdock tossed his bread to the floor, a stream of curses permeating the room as he stomped to a far window seat and flopped down.

Far more appreciative, the wolfhound swallowed his offering in a single gulp, then padded over to the portion Murdock discarded, sniffed, and ate it as well.

"Dense you must be to antagonize my family," Roanne said, disturbed at the waste of food when days of being hungry were still fresh in her mind.

"The hound seemed to enjoy my offerings." He tore the second loaf in half and held the larger piece out to her.

Being hungry, she accepted the proffered food. She bit into the hard crust with its soft center and moaned with delight.

In the next instant, wolfhounds outside started barking and howling like the devil himself approached the manor. Insistent banging at the main door heralded an anxious visitor.

Within moments, Sir Percy waddled into the solar in a cloud of cloying perfume that even the rain couldn't wash away. A wig with curls down to his shoulders slid over his head with every bob and weave, and his common features were put to shame by glittering red and gold finery. Roanne didn't know if she should hold her breath or cover her eyes.

Braith growled. Murdock, in the far window seat, shushed the dog, even as he scowled with hatred at the man.

Sir Percy hurried toward Roanne, leaving a trail of muddy footprints across the floor. An expression of sympathy skimmed over his face as he dipped low in an exaggerated bow. "My deepest condolences, sweet, sweet Roanne. A blessing on you for the loss of your father. I've just returned to my manor from an important trade matter to learn of your tragedy."

The smile he flashed left her cold and the condolences fell flat as far as she was concerned. It was common knowledge that he cared only for himself. She flicked a gaze at Padraig, willing to follow his lead.

Padraig stepped forward with a smile frozen on his face. "You have our gratitude, Sir Percy."

Percy puffed himself up in an effort to appear taller. "Say nothing. We are nearly neighbors. Kindness between us goes without saying. All of County Louth is aware of the O'Casey prophecy and I have come to offer my humble self as a means to fulfill it. Roanne will have a life of ease as my beloved wife."

Roanne stiffened her back and swallowed down bile. The man disgusted her. Her animosity had nothing to do with his appearance or how he flaunted his wealth. It had to do with the way he put himself above anyone else and the way he treated those less fortunate. Rumor had it that he ruled his household with his fists. And though his departed wife had denied it, Roanne had seen the bruises on her fair skin with her own eyes.

For a split second she didn't mind being wed to the hated Englishman. Stealing glances at him, she couldn't help wonder what it would feel like to be pulled into his embrace and kissed with passion by him. The image ignited feelings that she wasn't ready to deal with. She stared at her guest. "Your gracious offer won't be necessary, Sir Percy."

His lips thinned. "What game is this? There's not another lord within miles of Dundalk. I do not find your words humorous…"

"There's me." Kirkland stepped forward with a stony expression and put an arm around Roanne's waist.

Roanne bit her lip to keep from smiling.

Sir Percy's gaze locked on the much taller man. "Who are you?"

"Her husband."

A look of relief passed over Sir Percy's pudgy face and he waved away the announcement. "Word from the innkeeper at Finnigan's is that you're no lord, nor was the marriage consummated."

Roanne could not let the statement pass. "Surely, Sir Percy, a man of your esteemed standing does not succumb to alehouse gossip," she said, doing her best not to laugh as the man's ego deflated.

"Of…of course not."

Roanne almost felt sorry for the vile braggart. *Almost.* "As you can see, all is well here."

"Then I take my leave." Midway to the solar door he stopped, spinning around to face Padraig, nearly losing his wig. Percy slapped a hand on top of his head, saying, "If the tale proves accurate, my offer stands as long as Roanne remains untouched. But do not delay for long."

Kirkland snarled at the demand and stepped slightly in front of Roanne, squaring his shoulders and making himself a target. He seemed unmindful of the Irish lord's titled position. "Farewell, Sir Percy. As you can see, your proposal won't be needed here."

Percy flushed. A stunned silence fell over the gathering while they watched him spin on his heels and depart.

After long seconds, Padraig grinned. "Well, the fellow's boggers now."

"Good riddance to rubbish," Murdock grumbled.

"*Ack!*" Roanne tossed her hair back and glared at Kirkland. She had to admit that she appreciated his help. "Thank you."

Kirkland performed an elaborate shudder. "If he is your only choice for a husband, I understand your willingness to kidnap an Englishman and hold him against his will. He curdled my gut and I'm known to have a solid one. Though, surely, you are aware there are consequences to your actions."

"Best explain what you mean," she said, trying to subdue her curiosity.

The Englishman's smile disappeared. He waited until everyone stared at him. "You might end up with all of England rising up against you."

The O'Casey meandered near the window seat where Murdock sat. He faced the window with his hands clamped behind his back. "Peace has just returned to our land. Surely, the king won't risk his crown after newly securing it. Especially over a nobleman's second son."

"Unless, of course, the man in question is a favorite of the crown," Kirkland answered. "I do not mean to boast, but I have his ear."

Roanne couldn't interpret the man's neutral voice. Tension crackled in the air. Rain drummed beyond the room's windows like the tramp of soldiers on the march. The image made her shudder and let fear dance a jig inside her. If it was true, not only was she doomed but her family could be destroyed as well. "Why should we believe you?"

Kirkland waved away her question. "I daresay that would be a fine tangle now, wouldn't it? I have the ear of the king."

Their gazes locked on each other. This time a twinkle danced in the blue gaze. Did he think the situation amusing? Reluctantly, she conceded a certain admiration. A lesser man would have caved against the uneven odds of facing her family alone. Though not Kirkland.

"If you are trying to irritate me, you're succeeding." She hated herself for sounding like a harpy. "Now, d'you or don't you?"

He shrugged. "Charles' gratitude is well known to those who aided in his return. His Majesty's generosity is well-documented—land grants, fine estates." He gave all three O'Caseys a broad smile. "Why, I daresay he might consider this tower manor fair compensation for my detention."

The not-so-subtle threat against their ancestral

home caused Murdock to launch himself off the window seat and halfway across the room. His face bloomed red. "Bastard! Let me choke sense into the buffoon, Padraig. 'Tis what he deserves."

Kirkland didn't flinch. He stood his ground. "Try, if you dare. All you'll receive for your efforts is failure and I hear the taste is bitter."

Murdock growled low.

Without so much as blinking, the Englishman continued, "I was willing to credit you people with sense not to spurn the king's order, if it came."

"Hold." The O'Casey stepped between the two men. He signaled Murdock back and peered at Kirkland. "I'm thinking you said what we needed to know. Those I've sent will be in and out of England afore the king finds out."

"You can hope," Kirkland said, then added, "Mayhap, I can offer a proposition. A gentleman's agreement."

Roanne stomped to the far side of the solar, whirling back around so fast her head spun. How could they trust the man? She'd wager a fair bride price that plans for escape filled his head. "What can you offer? If I remember correctly, you admitted to being scarcely honorable."

Padraig raised his hand to stall further argument. "Let the fellow speak, Roanne." He turned to Kirkland. "Tell me what you propose."

"My word that I will not try to escape."

Roanne's gaze slid to his handsome face. He disturbed her at a level she didn't understand. Was it her? Or him? Why should they agree to anything? The O'Caseys held the upper hand. At least, she hoped they did. If he truly was a friend of the king, they could be in trouble. "What d'you want in exchange?"

"Why 'tis simple." Kirkland closed the distance between them. "A truce and the pleasure of your company to guide me about the manor. I want to spend more time with you, m'dear. You are much prettier on the eye than your brothers."

Roanne wasn't fooled by the flattery, though she did wonder why his proximity fired her temper. In all honesty, she didn't know the fellow well enough to blame him for her world ending. "If it's company you want, find another."

Kirkland went on as if she hadn't spoken. "Plus, when the rain ceases a tour of the grounds. I'm sure by that time fresh air and a change of scenery will be a pleasant break."

He reached out to catch her hand. Their fingers brushed. She jerked at the jolt rushing up her arm. The sensation surprised her. She didn't like him being so nice.

"First, my company…then what?"

"You should'na agree to his request, Padraig," Murdock said. "He shouldn't roam free."

The discussion ended when Rory entered the room with her youngest brother, Farrell, tagging along. Both were tall with Rory's well-defined muscles and Farrell lanky and still developing. The two promptly threw themselves into chairs, long legs sticking out before them.

"I missed the beginning but heard enough to think Murdock worries over much," Rory said, grinning.

A petty voice cried inside Roanne. She stamped her foot. "We'd do well to listen to Murdock."

"All the more reason for two pairs of eyes to keep watch," Padraig added, walking over to stand in front of Kirkland. "All you want is Roanne's company?"

"Is that so difficult to understand?"

"Your offer is a bargain worth taking, I'm thinking," Padraig answered, his tone final.

Roanne's shoulders slumped. Defeat slammed into her, but she wasn't surprised. In all fairness, she had expected it. While no longer in favor, one element of Brehon law still applied to the O'Casey clan—*family was more important than one individual.*

She was as much a prisoner of the O'Casey's as the Englishman.

For the good of the clan, she must defer to their will, but like it, she would not.

"I await your pleasure, dear wife." He beamed at her.

His smile, no matter how genuine it appeared, irked her more than she could say. He believed he'd won this round. Well, he'd be sorry. It took more than one loss to defeat her. Being bound by the agreement of men did not mean she would make it pleasant for the egotistical man. She paused her thoughts to glance at the fiend watching her…an Englishman.

The enemy.

Her husband.

Why wasn't he concerned about escaping? And why be amused at his imprisonment?

Didn't the fiend care about his personal safety? She didn't understand him.

****

Simon studied the five people surrounding him with interest, especially the spirited Roanne. He battled a surge of approval that burrowed into him. Her loyalty to her family was a characteristic he never knew. The way she interacted with all her brothers, treating each with equal fairness, showed him that she would be good with children and would make a good mother.

Her angry attitude reminded him of a deckhand aboard the *Black Sheep*. The fellow had argued at the slightest provocation. Simon took him aside and discovered the real reason—a dying son. He did the only humane thing he could think of—gave the seaman coin at the next port and bid him to return to his sick child.

Now, Simon was fast discovering watching the defiant woman's cheeks pinken immensely enjoyable. He shook his head. The time had come to focus his attention on the situation around him. Good advice for any man caught in his predicament.

"What man accepts confinement with a smile?" Roanne's voice filled the solar. "You're cracked, Padraig, if you cannot see this Englishman is up to no good."

Laughter rolled out of the O'Casey. "Is that woman's intuition I'm hearing? An undependable emotion. Truly, I am aware of the danger."

Simon blew a deep breath through his nostrils. "Blame me if it eases your conscience, dear wife, although we all know the truth. Your brothers are to blame."

So saying, Simon chose not take the manor tour just yet. He returned to his room. All in all, the last two days had been confusing to say the least. He found himself liking his jailors. They argued, debated, and agreed with each other without animosity or grudges.

He recognized it as being a similar bond that his crew possessed on the *Black Sheep*, and one he could appreciate.

He felt a kinship with Rory's sharp mind. Padraig appeared a calm leader, who took in all the information before making a decision. He liked Sean the Third. The young O'Casey had an adventurous streak in him that he'd possessed early in his seafaring days. Even the churlish Murdock's loyalty to family could not be denied.

He especially found Roanne appealing, though she wanted nothing to do with him. He always enjoyed a good challenge and wondered what it would take to change her opinion.

****

A sennight later as dawn broke the horizon, Simon stood before a small polished metal looking glass mounted to the wall, wishing for a shave. Looking at the reflection, he knew he preferred action, yet had barely lifted a finger to free himself because of the situation in London. An angry king equaled an uncertain future. He couldn't leave just yet.

He scratched his jaw, his beard itching. Too bad the O'Caseys had removed his razor. He found that the only item missing from his trunk.

Turning sharply, he paced the length of his prison. A quick glance out the window did nothing to ease his anxiety. Trees blocked his view, but what he saw showed rolling hills and gray sky.

His introspection came to a swift halt when someone knocked on his door.

"Enter," he called.

"I heard you moving about."

Simon managed a smile. "Make yourself comfortable, Padraig. Are you my jailer for the day?"

"Not me. Brian or another will be up after eating. I'm headed out to move the flock to a different meadow," the O'Casey replied.

Simon rubbed his jaw. "I'll be happy to lend a hand."

"What d'you know about sheep? Can't have you getting in the dogs' way," the clan leader said.

"I keep telling you I'm the spare. My family had no interest in how I spent my days as long it didn't involve them. I lent a hand to the tenants wherever needed. What must I do to prove myself?"

Padraig nodded. "A fool who trusts too easily is soon parted from his gold."

"We're not discussing gold."

Padraig rolled his shoulder in a dismissive shrug. "*Ack*, but we are."

Simon stared at the older man, puzzled.

"You left your wedding band at Finnigan's. It belonged to our Da. Roanne gave it to me for safekeeping, but you should have it, I'm thinking."

"You humble me." Simon accepted the proffered ring, slipping it onto his heart finger as he pushed back a twinge of guilt poking at his conscious. A deep ache inside him wished Padraig had been his older brother instead of Hugh.

"Call it faith." Padraig opened the knapsack he carried and took out bread and cheese. He handed several pieces to Simon. "Every hand is appreciated. We'll find you a pair of boots. There's enough around here. Some are bound to fit."

A hard day's work always filled Simon with a

sense of accomplishment. He loved working aboard ship alongside the crew, using his muscles until they ached. It reminded him of when he helped a tenant till his land or bring in a herd of cows. Those were always his favorite days at Hollyhock.

Plus, it wouldn't hurt to get a closer look at the lay of the land. If and when he eluded his jailors, having a familiarity with the area would be beneficial. "Best I change into different clothes."

"Aye, a good idea."

Afterwards he followed Padraig through the manor to a door where several thick-soled boots tall enough to cover his calves were scattered about. He found a pair that fit perfectly.

Outdoors, they skirted a rock wall too high for Simon to see over. On the other side several O'Caseys laughed and joked with each other, another reminder of the connection between the close-knit family.

At the end of the walkway, pastures were sectioned off with lower rock fences. Padraig ducked into a barn where several ponies nickered from their stalls. Simon followed him inside and inhaled the strong scent of hay and manure. It was an aroma one never forgot, like the briny scent of the ocean.

The clan leader gave one pony a rub on the nose as he passed before stopping to open a bin and tossed out several handfuls of feed for chickens to fight over.

Back outside, Simon spotted an older woman leading a milk cow with a full udder into a small outbuilding.

Puddles dotted the path. Simon's boots sloshed over muddy terrain as he studied the verdant grass, bare patches here and there. Though these people fared better than most, it required hard work to survive. His admiration grew for them not giving up.

Next to an empty hog pen, a dozen sheep, their white bodies caked with mud, huddled together. The color of their wool looked like dumplings covered in gravy.

Two dogs-black and brown-sat with wagging tails at their approach. Puppies leaped up but seemed to have no sense of order. Padraig called to the dogs in Gaelic, and while Simon understood not a single word, he grasped the meaning as the older dogs circled the flock and herded them toward a gate in what could only be called military precision. The sheep bunched together, stubbornly defying the dogs.

"Lambing season is beginning," Padraig said. "We'll move them to higher and drier pasture."

Simon stayed with the O'Caseys because he wanted to. Had to, really. Better safe than sorry. Like many monarchs, Charles II could be petty and needed time to forget about being upset with him for not following his orders. Besides, he wasn't in any hurry. A nobler cause awaited him—his wife, Roanne, deserved his full attention.

The morning flew by. He walked rolling hills that reminded him being aboard ship riding gentle waves. He liked the silence and the sense of solitude, even though never truly alone.

Each loose flat rock he found, he stacked on the fence line.

A gentle wind blew over the land, smelling of rain. Clouds raced over the sky, enormous cloudscapes with gray hearts. He expected a good drenching by the end of the day and yet found himself enjoying the outdoors.

Until he spotted potential disaster.

A ewe pawed the ground, a sign of nervousness, next to a scum-roofed pond. She arched her back and kept curling her lip. Definitely going into labor. And sure enough, when the animal moved, a black lamb lay at her feet, nearly invisible on the muddy ground.

Almost immediately, with the lamb in front of her, she pushed out another. The second newborn staggered right for the water on wobbly legs, too young to know the danger.

Simon hollered at Padraig, pointed, and took off on a run. Behind him, shouts erupted to roll over the land. He hadn't been wrong about being under observation. Let the O'Caseys think him escaping. There wasn't a moment to waste to stop and explain.

He vaulted over a low rock fence separating the pastures, and reached the pond just as the vulnerable newborn went under for the second time.

He plunged into the water, iciness cutting into his bones. A small dark head broke the water right in front of him and uttered a pathetic bleat. He scooped the lamb into his arms, only to lose his balance with the struggling animal. Together they slipped into deeper water and went under.

Simon rolled on his back, holding the lamb on his chest, and kicked with all his might. After a short distance, he tested his footing and found solid ground. He headed for shore with his precious cargo.

Pandemonium reigned around him. O'Caseys stared at him. Puppies barked on shore. The ewe bleated loudly. One of the adult dogs nipped at its heels to encourage it away from the water.

Simon gingerly set the newborn down. It flapped

his ears as his anxious mother licked her baby's nose. Both babies found a teat and began nursing.

A puppy ran straight for Simon and leaped onto his chest. He fell backward onto the rain softened ground.

Padraig stood at the edge of the water and grinned. "You smell like pond scum."

Simon couldn't help himself—he laughed outright. He hadn't had this much fun in a long time. He'd grown up working hard on various tenant farms on his family's estate. It brought back pleasant memories. "Today is a good day."

"Have to admit, you are not what I expected." The clan leader looked about and waved his relatives away. "We're done here. The others can finish up. Best we go inside and get you into dry clothing."

His sense of freedom vanished with those words. "A bit of water doesn't bother me."

****

Excited shouting drew Roanne to a solar window.

Kirkland raced across the open pasture, his long strides devouring the distance faster than any O'Casey. Was he escaping? Her heart thudded with fear...hope. She was slowly coming to the conclusion that keeping him prisoner was unfair.

Far behind, bedlam pursued him. Padraig raced after him. Two other brothers tossed down their rakes to give chase. Kirkland's speed proved impressive. No one appeared capable of gaining on him. Could they catch him before he escaped? Who did she root for to succeed?

She grimaced with irritation as she shoved the thought away. Siding with her family should be second nature.

Kirkland reached the green-coated pond and did the unthinkable. He leaped into the murky water. She couldn't believe what she witnessed. The man had lost his mind.

When a lamb's head popped out of the water in front of him, she cheered aloud.

"What is it?" Meagan said, coming up behind her and putting a hand on her shoulder.

She shifted her gaze to her sister-in-law. "Look at him. The fool jumped in to save a lamb"

Together they watched him swim to the shore and set the wee animal down.

A second later, an exuberant puppy leaped at Kirkland and knocked him on his backside. Oddly enough, instead of raging at the undisciplined dog, he laughed with such gusto that it reached all the way to the manor.

Roanne shook her head in bewilderment and turned to Megan. "He confuses me. I want to hate him, but his kindness keeps me off balance."

Meagan grinned. "The Englishman is not what he seems."

"No, he's not. And like it, I do not!"

A soft chuckle came from Meagan as she resumed her seat.

Roanne remained standing at the window and saw Padraig command her brothers to resume their chores. One slapped Kirkland's back in approval. Their bewildered expressions matched her own feelings.

As Padraig and Kirkland returned, she couldn't take her gaze off her husband. Attraction wasn't love. Oh, he was handsome enough, no question about it. If he turned out to be a lord, she idly visualized herself enjoying spending time in his company.

Shocked by her own thoughts, she snorted and whirled away from the window. "I can't stand being idle. I'm off to the kitchen to balance our accounts."

Chapter Five

The O'Casey led Simon to the side of the manor where Braith waited next to the door. They entered a spacious, high-ceilinged kitchen with shelving ringing the walls holding containers of all sizes and shapes. A stone fireplace dominated one side of the room. Crocks were parked on shelves and around the room in a haphazard order on the floor. A single window provided plenty of light. Simon counted six heavy worktables.

But what stopped him dead in his tracks was Roanne hunched over one of those tables. Every time he saw her, she impressed him. Dressed in a plain cotton shift with a faded pink bodice and skirt that had seen better days did nothing to detract from her loveliness. Her button nose was buried in a huge account book, her full attention absorbed by pages.

"What's she doing?" he whispered to Padraig as water pooled at his feet.

The O'Casey's eyebrows knitted together. "Our accounts, few as they are. It's warm in here and she likes to lend a hand, if needed. Best not disturb her."

He wanted to know his wife better. "There's no harm in bidding her a good day."

Padraig shrugged. "The Irish have a saying worth heeding. A woman is more obstinate than a mule—a mule more than the devil. And, at times, that's a blessing."

The brindle wolfhound circled in front of the hearth where an iron cauldron hung over a small fire. An aromatic stew bubbled inside.

Stubborn fit Roanne, and if Simon were honest with himself, he found the trait rather appealing. He found her different from other women he had known. And he'd met many in ports around the world. "Why offer me advice about your sister?"

"Because I have no wish to see her hurt. And instinct tells me you have the ability to do just that."

The retort set him back. He'd never considered his effect on women. Those he'd met and bedded were ladies of the night with no expectations from him. Now...now Roanne and her family anticipated something from him.

On silent footsteps, he approached Roanne from the side. Her profile, a work of art in his eyes, delighted him. A murmur rose from her soft-looking lips.

"Do you need assistance?" He inhaled the spicy scent of cloves and orange. At first, he'd thought the tangy aroma came from the kitchen until he realized it emanated from Roanne. He then tried to breathe in the fragrance as if to draw the woman closer.

The low muttering stopped when she became aware of his presence. Scowling, she turned to give him a sweeping glance. Her gaze paused on the golden ring on his finger, then shifted to his face. "If I did, seeking yours would be last on my mind. Timothy checks my figures when I ask him."

Her intelligence impressed him, and that independent streak intrigued him. The situation definitely called for finesse. Or flattery.

He chose finesse.

"I'm sure you are quite capable, m'dear. But I daresay I'm decent at numbers," he said.

Her nose wrinkled the tiniest bit. "So, you can add."

Warmth swirled through him. "Do my ears deceive me? Is that outright praise?"

Padraig leaned against the far wall. Moments before he'd snatched a carrot off the table and now nibbled on it.

Roanne wiggled in her chair and then turned her golden green glare on him. "Leave me be, Sassenach. I have accounts to balance."

The tilt of her chin warned him she meant business. "Of course, m'dear. Hard work should always be appreciated." His own deepening voice brought an acute realization. He'd meant his tribute. That, and the brief look of vulnerability on her face before she managed to squelch it. Hurting her was the last thing on his mind.

Finesse wasn't swaying her to his side in the least. Yet yielding to the fiery Irishwoman wasn't in him. "For now, I'll settle for your company and that promised tour."

Amber-green eyes went wide. The look of surprise became precious to him. "Sure, and you jest," she replied. "I've work to finish. And…and you are stinking wet."

He smiled at her. "Take pity on me. I could use a bath and a shave. Although your brothers saw fit to remove my razor from my traveling trunk."

"You think giving you access to a weapon makes good sense?"

"Point taken, but I still need to clean up."

"The man speaks true, Roanne." Padraig pushed away from the wall where he had waited. "Heat up some water and he can bathe in his chamber."

For several seconds Roanne glowered at her brother, lips pinched tight. "Fine, but I'll not tend him in his bath. 'Tis Meagan's responsibility as woman of the house."

"She's out picking herbs."

"What about one of the lads? They've had more practice than me."

Padraig shook his head. "They have their own chores, but I'll have some tote the water." He looked over at Simon, then back to her. "You'll not have to bathe him. He possesses two functioning hands and can do that himself. But a good shave with a tender touch he does deserve. That you can do."

"Alas, you crush me," Simon hollered over his shoulder, glad she couldn't see his expression. He was positive the disappointment welling up inside him would have shown on his face.

Braith followed them to his chamber and made himself at home at the foot of the bed.

A knock on the door signaled the appearance of his tub, a wooden barrel. A brigade of O'Caseys with buckets of steaming water poured into the room. Each dumped their load into the barrel until halfway full. One or two even gave him a nod of approval. He assumed saving the lamb had found favor with them.

Simon stripped off his filthy, wet clothes with gratitude.

Slipping into the water felt heaven-like. With a sigh of appreciation, he eased himself lower until water covered his shoulders.

He had no time to relax. Padraig handed him a sponge and a coarse bar of soap made of mutton fat, wood ash, and natural soda.

"I have been meaning to ask." Simon scrubbed his torso. "You are one of the few O'Caseys who maintains a civil courtesy toward me. Why is that?"

Padraig retreated to the bed and sat down. "I learned long ago to extend courtesies even to the English. In the Spanish court, I was well-taught to temper my actions and tongue."

"Spain?" Simon stopped washing. Of all the O'Caseys, this man was the hardest to read. Well that explained a lot. Being in court taught diplomacy. "Somehow, I cannot imagine an Irishman in that hot, burning land."

"Ireland is my home. It always will be." Padraig leaned on an elbow, clearly using the time to gain some valuable rest. "When Cromwell became Lord Protector, a blind man could see the deed signaled worse treatment for all Irish. Before the invasion, I whisked Meagan and our little heathens back to her family in Ulster for safety's sake, then hied myself off to serve King Philip IV as an advisor. One learns immense patience when dealing with royalty."

"Sad, but true." The conversation made Simon wonder if enough time had passed for Charles to forgive him for not attacking the Spanish treasure ship. Charles never stayed angry for long and never held a grudge. His reputation as the Merry Monarch was growing by the day.

The O'Casey offered a weak smile. "The funds I earned kept my family afloat during the worst of the crises. Sean the Third turned into an adventurous soul and convinced three others to travel to the colonies, where they were welcomed in Maryland, the only place to accept Catholics. Colin is still there. Ian joined the Irish army established in France. Others took their families and sought sanctuary in Russia and Poland."

Simon used the soap to wash his hair. "What befell your family, all the families in Ireland, will be hard to forget or forgive."

Padraig eyed him as if he'd lost his mind before Simon ducked his head to rinse out the suds. "Who said anything about forgiveness? The cruelty which took place in our country will never leave our memories. We don't want to forget. Never will. When Roanne wrote of our Da ailing, I returned posthaste. The others followed soon after. Now as clan leader, I can ill afford to let another blunder occur."

In the blink of an eye, sadness blanketed the chamber. "How did your family escape Cromwell's resettlement plan?"

"We didn't. Those who stayed were forced to move. 'Twas a hard time for everyone. We can thank Saint Brigit for watching over my Meagan, and those left behind with Da. We lost Sean the First to plague. Finn carries the scars in his hairline from his battle with the plague as a reminder. At least none were left in a ditch to have their eyes picked clean by ravens. Other families fared worse."

The tale horrified Simon. Even on the high seas, he'd heard rumors of the mistreatment, but never encountered cruelty on such a level and prayed he never would. He stood to climb out of the barrel. The water had cooled fast. "Still, you and your family survived," he spoke with honesty. "We-you and I-have a chance to rectify the damage of the past."

Padraig rolled his eyes. "If you are asking to be released, I cannot. Roanne is our only sister. Da spoiled her. Yet she is precious to us. Every O'Casey is compelled to see her wed. Happily would be best."

"Your prophecy has warped your perspective. It motivates you to commit a gross wrong. All I'm requesting is for you to consider how it infringes upon my life. Ask yourself if that's fair?"

Padraig didn't answer. He tossed Simon an over-sized cloth to dry off.

In silence, Simon dressed. He didn't have the slightest doubt once the trio of O'Caseys returned from England they would verify his account.

And Roanne would have to marry again.

His insides twisted.

He didn't like the idea, but what choice did he have? On the off chance that the prophecy was real, her marrying someone else was the only logical deed that could happen. To keep his concern hidden, he rubbed his scruffy face. "All I need now is that shave."

"Roanne will be here shortly."

Simon arched a brow. "You vouch that she won't cut my throat."

Padraig shrugged from his position on the bed. "No one controls her actions. Be on your best behavior when she arrives and try not to irritate her."

As if knowing they spoke of her, a knock sounded at the door. Roanne stepped into the chamber, toting a steaming bucket of water, a bowl tucked under her arm, a towel, and a paper-thin blade for a razor.

"Sit down," she ordered Simon.

Simon took his cue from Padraig, who nodded. He settled in a straight-back chair. Once again, the scent of oranges wrapped around him as Roanne walked toward him. He inhaled deeply in an attempt to draw her closer. "I hear you have a gentle hand in the art of shaving."

"I make no promises. Now, close your eyes."

When he obeyed, his world became one of sounds. The creak of floorboards told him Roanne moved about. A noise from the bed sounded like the clan leader had adjusted his position. He followed the scuff of Roanne's slippers, and the swish of skirts on the floor. The sound of soap being whipped into sudsy lather came from near the table. A blade clinked against the table and he sensed Roanne's slender presence next to him. For a moment his heart raced. In the silence he envisioned her enticing face studying him, his throat, and swallowed.

A rush of breath fanned over his skin as Roanne exhaled. He controlled the urge to wrap his arms around her waist. Best to let her continue without interrupting. After all, she held the knife. Then a warm hand lay on his shoulder and he knew she leaned over him. Somehow the light touch felt right.

He held himself still at the first bite of cold metal against soft flesh.

Without a word, Roanne drew the blade up from under his chin. The distinctive scrapping told him a honed and sharp blade performed the task. After each pass, the rinse of the blade in water sounded. He heard the soft drag of metal on cloth as she cleaned the razor. She repeated the process over and over.

He let himself enjoy the soft press of Roanne's body against his shoulder as she reached over his side to perform her task.

"All done," she announced.

He cracked open his eyes to find the sun setting beyond the windows and tentatively rubbed his face, discovering it as smooth as a baby's bottom. "You have my sincere thanks. A job well done."

She grunted.

Her response was short and sweet, the complete opposite of the woman before him. Yet, unexplainably, her appeal continued to grow in him. "Looking on the bright side, I'm alive. That is good. I'll have that manor tour now," he said, refusing to have their time together end.

A deep sigh fell from her mouth. "*Ack*, I give up. If the tower interests you, I'll start with that." She handed the razor to Padraig, and stomped out of his chamber. Her steps flagged at the door, and she whirled around. "Well?"

"After you," he said.

He raced alongside her as she dashed for the stairs, not slowing until reaching the uppermost landing. She seemed to enjoy the mad race and that he kept up.

Thudding steps and the clink of nails on the floor followed them. Simon wasn't surprised that Padraig and the wolfhound huffed after them.

At an arched door, Roanne lifted a latch and pushed the heavy door open. Pitch blackness hid the details from view. The sharp click of flint sounded, and a sputtering light bathed the trio in a yellow glow from a candle. Shadows fluttered on bare walls in a cavernous room.

Roanne pointed at a toppled heap of a half-dozen trunks. "Three times this number once were stored here.

Empty now, each one held precious finery."

Padraig confirmed her statement with a nod.

Afterwards, Roanne grabbed the candlestick and sped down the hall with her skirt billowing. "Here be evidence how Ironsides mistreated our property. See the holes." She held the candle close to the wall and gestured to darker-colored rings that left circular gauges. "The manor is riddled with them."

Simon's fingers traced the marred walls. "Bullet holes. Flagrant evidence of brutality. You and your family suffered much during those troubled times. I regret your pain upon returning home to find such loss and destruction."

She huffed in earnest. "Save your sympathy. You need it more than I."

"For what?" The mistrust grated on him. He fought the urge to prove her wrong.

A laugh from Padraig distracted them. "The pair of you bicker like an old married couple."

"I'm glad you're amused. I am not." Roanne glared at Simon and the O'Casey.

"That makes two, m'dear," Simon answered. He wished he could make amends for the destruction his countrymen had performed on her family home. If she had received one kindness from an Englishman, maybe she wouldn't be so bitter against him.

Descending to the next level, Roanne slowed. Braith sniffed at a door. "Murdock and Timothy sleep yonder. Keep your voice down. We'll not disturb their rest."

He nodded toward the next door. "What's in here?"

"Nothing of interest for you," she answered quickly.

Too quick for Simon's way of thinking. She hid something. "This is your bedchamber, is it not?" He took a step forward.

"This way!" She shot across the corridor and opened a different door. "I'm sure you'll find the clan leader's chamber far more interesting."

"I see what interests me—you." Finesse wasn't working. He might as well switch to flattery, only to find his compliment sincere and wished he could shower her with them every day.

A crimson pallor crept up Roanne's neck, and when Braith trotted through the open door, she issued a tiny huff, then trailed the big wolfhound.

That left Padraig and Simon little choice. As they started to enter, a white-haired serving woman scurried to Padraig's side.

"Sir, wait," the servant said.

A frantic Gaelic exchange ensued. Because Simon couldn't understand a word, he used the time to admire Roanne while she listened to the pair. When a frown marred her alluring face, he wondered if there was anything he could do to make her smile.

The conversation ended, and the O'Casey noticeably leaned toward the servant, keen to follow her.

"I'll remain here," Simon said. "After all, we're on the fourth story. Where can I go?"

"Sure, and we've watched you these last days for our health." The clan leader made no attempt to hide his amused grin.

Never willing to lose an opportunity, Simon decided good fortune shined on him. Who was he to refuse a rare chance to be alone with Roanne, a chance to become better acquainted without interference from her family? "My bride can guard me. No harm in that, is there?"

Roanne huffed. "I'll be the judge of that. If you try anything, I'll bring down the house with me screams."

"So dramatic, dear wife. Surely we can come up with a less hostile way to entertain ourselves."

Padraig's eyes narrowed with a hard look. "If you touch my sister, I'll kill you."

Simon took no offense. If he had a beloved wife, sister or daughter, the same protectiveness would have applied to him. "As a gentleman I promise not to seduce her."

The clan leader rubbed his chin in slow motion, seemingly considering the avowal, then nodded. "I'll wake Murdock. You'll not be alone for long."

Simon mentally cursed. So much for engraining himself into Roanne's good graces. Once the antagonistic brother arrived, tension would double, triple. He eyed a tapestry of a woodland scene with a dark green background hanging opposite the bed. When a pair of footfalls echoed down the hallway, he stepped into the chamber.

"The tapestry is a family treasure," Roanne explained next to him as if her animosity had been forgotten. "We hid the tapestry in the cemetery, beneath the coffins of fresh graves. Even if the English desecrated the graves, they'd never think to look beneath them."

He cocked a brow as a salute. "Your notion, I assume, and I'll wager more valuables than one tapestry was saved by your clever thinking. Your harp? It is a prized possession."

"Aye, that too." Delicate features softened at his guess. "This came from one of my ancestors, who shipped it from France over a hundred years ago," she volunteered, her mouth staying opening ever so slightly.

A note in her voice caught his attention. His gaze searched her face and settled on her lips. Those lush, delicious looking lips. So tempting.

Simon didn't care about the consequences. He had to know how she tasted. He didn't think, only acted. Pivoting, he swept her into his arms, catching a whiff of spices and fruit as he coaxed her mouth open to sample the sweetness within.

****

Roanne froze, stunned. Taken off guard, a rush of pleasure hit her. He was a Sassenach. An Englishman. She expected rougher treatment from a man such as him. But his lips were soft, tender upon hers.

Nagging in the back of her mind demanded she push him away.

But she didn't. Couldn't.

His kiss enchanted her. All rational thought vanished. She forgot to breathe as the kiss went on. The sweet taste of his lips intoxicated her. Her arms rose of their own accord to wrap around his neck. His body pressed against hers. In her mind, while she suspected it was wrong to like the way he kissed her, she couldn't stop.

Nor could she stop the conflicting emotions that churned within her. How could she care for him? He was the enemy. Oh sure, a slim chance existed that he might be a lord. Still, she must be insane to let him kiss her. It didn't matter that they were wed. Family counted for everything. Her loyalty belonged to them. No one else.

With that thought, she shook off the spell he cast on her. "Never do that a-again," she pleaded.

"You mean you did not enjoy it?"

She'd never been kissed before. Not like that. Oh sure, lads had stolen a few pecks, but nothing compared to Kirkland's tantalizing kiss. Still, it would be a cold day in hell afore she'd admit that and stoke his inflated vanity.

"Sure, and if you be asking me to rank them, I've had better and worse." She took a deep breath to calm her rapidly beating heart. "I warn you now. There'll be no next time. Tis wrong. You don't understand."

A smile lifted the corners of Kirkland's lush mouth. "It is you who doesn't understand. After all, we are wed. All I want is for you to soften toward me. I never meant to kiss you. It took me by surprise as well. Unless you wish me to…"

"A lie. You'd say whatever you thought I wanted to hear in order to gain your freedom." In spite of her accusation, confusion swamped her mind. She glanced at the giant wolfhound peacefully sleeping on the floor, then out the diamond shaped windows of Padraig's bedchamber as if answers lay in the far beyond.

Kirkland stepped closer. "I would be happy to kiss you again."

"You put yourself in mortal danger by kissing me," she told him. Mayhap she wasn't insane. He was! His behavior courted danger.

"When will the moment be right to kiss you? We are never alone." He brushed his fingers through her hair. "You are very pretty, dear wife."

Roanne watched a fiery curl wrap around his finger and imagined him tugging her breathtakingly closer. She couldn't take her eyes off him, his lips. "I-I am not pretty. You say that—"

"What's going on here? Why'd Padraig leave?" Murdock demanded, his dark gaze taking in every detail.

Roanne's head whipped toward the door, jumping away from Simon with a gasp. "Padraig's minding clan business. As you should be, instead of meddling in mine."

"Where's your head, sister? You are my business."

Her gaze flicked to her husband. Traitorous feelings of affection pinched her lips together. She couldn't denounce him or his actions to her giant brother. She was as much at fault as Kirkland. Murdock was too unpredictable.

What if I am softening toward him?

Until her brothers returned and verified Kirkland's status, she had no business kissing him. Even if, in the eyes of the church, they were legally man and wife. The thought snuck into her head and saddened her. No room existed in her life to be attracted to Simon. If he were not a lord, their marriage could be annulled. Or worse. He could be killed. That thought sent a chill rippling down her spine.

She schooled herself to remain calm and focused on the newcomer.

The expression on Murdock's face might have been a smile, but she knew better. "Ah, I know what I'm talking about," he said.

Kirkland stepped forward. "You're full of yourself, Irishman. Getting worked up over nothing."

"Roanne is nothing? We are bound to protect her. Get away from her, Sassenach. Roanne, hie yourself over here, and be quick about it."

"Don't use that tone with her. She's committed no wrong."

Braith rose from his position on the floor to stare at each person in the room. His long tail dropped lower as their voices climbed. He trotted over to stand beside her.

Murdock's gaze darted from her to Kirkland. Her brother's huge chest puffed out and he charged deeper into Padraig's private chamber, straight for her like an arrow to its target. Roanne back-pedaled to avoid a collision. She knew Murdock wasn't bluffing. He had an infamous temper and sometimes lost control. She had risked Kirkland's life by kissing him. The situation could only get worse.

"You be a fool!" Murdock shouted at the top of his lungs, practically skidding to a stop. "All women are fools."

"I am no fool. You're the fool! You're only being critical because of what happened to Dorinda." Roanne prayed the woman's name distracted her brother. "You've bottled up all your frustration and are taking it on Kirkland because he's English like her."

Murdock paled. "Holy Mother of God! That be a low blow, Roanne. Don't be saying her name in my presence."

Instant regret blossomed in Roanne's chest and shame burned a path up her neck. It wasn't her place to remind her brother of what he lost. At her side the dog whined.

Kirkland stepped forward. "Blast it! I said, 'leave

her alone.' Pick on someone your own size."

"Sure, and a grand idea. I'll begin with you." Fire lit Murdock's dark eyes when he turned back to her. "You're my witness. He's asking for a fight, and a fight he'll receive."

Even though Roanne glared at Kirkland for shredding her loyalty into tiny pieces, she harbored no desire to see him hurt. While both men were equal in height, Murdock had several stones on her husband. The possibility her husband could win seemed highly unlikely.

She glared at her brother. "Fighting will not take away your pain and I doubt Kirkland regrets what he did."

Kirkland edged sideways, working his way around the bigger man. "You fool no one, Murdock. You've had a bone to pick with me even before I wed your sister."

"That's God's truth. Brawling with you gives me a chance to spill English blood."

Murdock stopped speaking and swung. He missed. Kirkland countered, his fist connecting with Murdock's chin. Her brother grunted with pain and staggered backward. He hit the wall with a thud and slid down.

To his credit, Kirkland played fair and didn't pursue the downed man. "Had enough?"

"A lucky punch. Just starting, I am." Murdock climbed to his feet.

Braith whimpered again at her side, clearly disturbed by the brawling.

She patted the dog's head to reassure him. "I hope you're both happy. Your antics have upset Braith."

The mulish pair paid her no mind. They continued

to exchange blows until falling to the floor and rolling across the room with arms and legs tangled together. Loud grunts and curses colored the air. She couldn't tell who was winning.

When they banged against a wall, Murdock landed on top. The vee of his tunic hung limp, brown eyes bright with triumph. Roanne's stomach knotted as he pummeled her husband.

She grabbed a vase, intending to smash it over her brother's head, not trusting Murdock to check his fists. If he hurt Kirkland…

Braith circled the fighters, dodging in and out.

Roanne stopped short. The hound had acted similarly whenever a tussle occurred between her brothers, which happened often. Someone was about to learn a painful lesson. Keeping her smile to herself, she stepped back and waited.

It didn't take long.

Murdock yelped. He twisted off Kirkland to land in a crouch a foot away. He glared at the wolfhound and rubbed his bottom before jumping back into the fray.

The wolfhound continued to skirt the pair, whining with distress at their fighting.

Then her brother lay flat on his back with Kirkland on his knees, grabbing Murdock by his tunic flap. "Never threaten Roanne like that again. Or so help me, I'll thrash you to hell and back."

"You don't scare me. And you don't know her if you think my words intimidate her."

"I don't care who you are. Brother or clan leader. Don't—"

The giant wolfhound trotted closer. Roanne knew the Englishman didn't know what was about to happen, and smiled when Braith nipped Kirkland in the backside.

Yelping, he jerked upright. "What the—"

"What goes on here?" Padraig demanded from the doorway.

Kirkland broke the silence. "That wolfhound bit me. I know he did. Not enough to harm, just enough to distract me."

Murdock snorted. "The Sassenach was trying to escape."

"He was *not* trying to escape. We were kissing." Roanne clamped her hand over her mouth, regretting the utterance the moment she spoke.

The O'Casey's expression crumbled as he entered his bedchamber. "Even worse."

Kirkland erupted with merry laughter. Then Padraig joined him. Even Murdock grinned.

Roanne's cheeks flushed. *Men.* They drove her mad. All of them. "Go ahead. Laugh. We'll see how—"

"Calm yourself." The clan leader held up his hands, his chuckles subsiding. "I thought I could trust you, Simon. It seems I erred."

"Simon, is he?" Roanne hated herself for being defensive. But she didn't know how else to react under the circumstances. The whole family needed to give serious thought about the man being a lord. They couldn't treat him like he belonged in the family.

"Aye, and keep your mouth away from his, Roanne. That can only lead to trouble. If our guest misbehaves again," the clan leader replied, "Murdock can kiss him. That possibility should keep him from running afoul with anyone again."

"I'd rather kiss Rory's pale arse," Murdock said.

The near giant tramped to the door and whirled to face the three for a final time.

"There's been enough trouble for one day, Simon," Padraig said. "After we sup, I'll escort you back to your chamber."

Kirkland turned to her and smiled. "Thank you, madam wife. Despite the interruption, I had a wonderful time."

Recalling his kisses, so had she.

Chapter Six

After three weeks of matrimony, Roanne sat in her favorite chair in the solar. She drew her knees up to her chest, and wrapped her arms over them while soaking up a precious moment of solitude and tranquility. She needed the quiet…or she really would go insane.

Not even playing her harp brought peace of mind. Earlier her fingers trembled as she'd tried to pluck at the strings and felt nothing, which spoke volumes to her sorry state. Normally the music provided perfect relaxation, relieved her of stress.

She closed her eyes and inhaled deeply. Things about Simon Lancaster made her wish the prophecy didn't exist. Granted, the prophecy only pertained to her, but her crazy, loving brothers shouldered the burden of her well-being in all seriousness. They would never forgive themselves if anything harmful befell her.

And, to make matters worse, she found herself becoming attracted to her husband, second son or not. He surprised her with his kindness; that he respected each of her brothers for their own merits meant a great deal to her. Family was all-important to her. She breathed deeply. There was so much to consider.

Of course, his kiss had no bearing on her softening. Ha!

She squeezed her eyes shut and clutched her rosary and began praying to herself until voices beyond the solar drew closer.

"I tell you, my friend, you're wrong. This wasn't a war for social or economic reasons. There was no desire to recast society or redistribute the wealth."

Simon.

Her husband's given name rolled through her mind with a familiarity that came as a complete surprise. She no longer thought of him as Kirkland or even an Englishman. The concept put her at a loss about what to do next.

The voices grew louder.

Her heart stuttered. She gripped her rosary until skin stretched white over bent knuckles, and furiously willed her body to remain calm, to slow her breathing.

"Tell that to the poor devils who lost their homes and loved ones," Rory contested. "Greedy Ironside bastards stole all they owned. Year after year they came to demand the oath of abjuration. Those who didn't cave to the pressure lost two-thirds of all their goods each time until nothing was left. Cromwell's name will forever be a curse to the Irish." He paused and Roanne visualized her tallest brother gathering momentum. Nothing inspired him more than politics and debating invigorated him. "Your countrymen prided themselves on their independent thoughts of cruelty."

Staying concealed, Roanne poked her head around the edge of her chair as two men entered. The only man who interested her stood in the solar. Struck by the rich burgundy velvet of her husband's long doublet, she found his clothing a shocking contrast to the age-dulled tunic and breeches Rory wore.

Then it dawned on her. Once she became a nobleman's wife, she would dress in equal finery. What would silk feel like against her skin? She blushed at the thought.

Pressing into the chair—out of sight, not out of hearing—she vowed to keep it that way. This seemed the perfect opportunity to learn about her husband without him knowing.

"Be sensible, man," Simon said after a pause. "You were blessed."

"Faith! Look about you," Rory's lilting brogue replied within feet of her hiding spot. "D'you see us surrounded by wealth? Are our clothes as fine as yours? Is our table overflowing with sumptuous fare? I would not call us blessed."

"You cannot pull the wool over my eyes. From what I understand, your sister's quick thinking saved many of your treasures."

A pause ensued before Rory spoke. "We grieved along with all of Eire. D'you expect us to be grateful because Roanne saved a few material possessions?"

Roanne nodded as she agreed with her brother. Material items were replaceable. A life was not. Simon must think them fools to fall for his logic.

"Aye, it could be worse," her husband answered. "You could have been among those miserable souls I saw wandering along the roadsides."

"Who says I wasn't?"

Roanne stilled. For more years than she cared to remember, her biggest fear had been discovering one of her brothers among those souls, hungry and cold, always alert for the tromping of Parliamentary soldiers patrolling the countryside.

"Cromwell's fanaticism caused many families to suffer," Simon said. "Not just the Irish. Many English did as well. The people of London grew to hate him and his strict rules. The country people opposed his vision of heaven and hell. It took their joined efforts to bring about Charles' return."

The creak of wood startled her as one of the men sat on the wobbly stool near the hearth. Who was this man she wed? He came from a noble family, yet seemed to empathize with the suffering of lesser beings. Curiosity urged her to peel back the layers instead of merely guessing at his true character.

"The fiend had to die first. It took another whole year before any signs of improvement were seen," Rory countered with emotion lacing his deep voice. "War is always about a difference of ideas, the need to protect a way of life."

"Sometimes the reason is personal, my friend."

Roanne frowned and wondered about the remark, as a shaky calm filled the solar. Eavesdropping might be wrong, but she realized something.

Her husband treated each of her brothers differently.

Rory, he called friend and spoke with him as an equal, as if they could agree or object through a bond of friendship that began years ago, and would remain unbreakable despite difference of opinions.

She recalled how he gave Padraig his due as leader of the O'Caseys, and glad she was of his show of proper respect. Murdock, he seemed to delight in tormenting. Though, in all fairness, her loutish brother usually instigated the argument.

The rest he treated genially, almost agreeably. Since the incident with the lamb, she'd seen more than one offer him a smile of friendship.

"You've got my attention," Rory said. "Get on with your theory."

Deep laughter, without rancor, filled the solar. "Well then, let me see… We live in a better age now, I hope."

Rory huffed. "You don't know the indignities we endured. Our lives might improve, but they will never be the same."

No lie there. Roanne agreed wholeheartedly and believed every decent Irishman would concur.

"Whose will?" came her husband's quick answer. "Open your eyes. Look at me. I am embroiled in your troubles. I married your sister."

A low chuckle came from her brother. "You do stare a-might sheep-eyed at her."

"She is worth admiring."

A hot blush rose up Roanne's neck at the compliment, even though the turf fire heated the room to a cozy temperature.

Rory chuckled. "Thought you might be thinking that way."

"Of graver importance is the spread of science." Kirkland's boots scuffed the floor. "This is England's future. Ireland's, too. Science will improve agriculture, industry, medicine. Everything! We stand on the dawn of a new future."

"Watch it, heretic. You're thinking about our prophecy. I can tell."

"Ah, my friend. That ancient belief doesn't deserve your defense. You must admit something's not right—a mistake was made along the years. It just doesn't make any sense. I'm as superstitious as the next sailor, but my gut tells me your prophecy's not infallible."

Sailor? Roanne perked up. She arched an eyebrow. This was news to her.

"Is it not?" her brother asked with a particular devilish tone.

A queasy sensation rose in her belly. Roanne knew how Rory liked to lead people down the garden path.

"If you doubt its validity," her brother continued, "perchance you are game to defend your view with a simple test of strength?"

"I never turn down a challenge, but what reward do I earn when I win? Time alone with my lovely wife?"

"My undying admiration will have to suffice," Rory said in a tone laced with amusement and seriousness.

A regretful sigh came from one of the men. Roanne couldn't resist the temptation to peek. Kirkland shed his velvet doublet to reveal a snowy white shirt. Nothing in the world could make her look away now. Her heart beat faster.

Rory moved to the stool one of them had vacated earlier. "This'll do just fine for a bit of arm wrestling."

"It won't take me long to beat you," her husband bragged as he knelt next to the stool.

He had his back to her, and Rory faced her direction, though her confidence ran high that neither man suspected her presence. Brightness illuminated the room and a warmth traveled down Roanne's spine. After endless days of rain and drizzle, a triumphant sun broke out from behind layers of clouds.

Simon bent forward. The motion stretched the linen fabric of his shirt tight across his back and arm. His muscles rippled with each slight flexing. How odd they faced the same direction, sharing the identical sensation of warm sun on their backs. It was as though they had become one against her brother. She leaned forward as if to lend him strength.

That surprised her. A wrenching jolt of betrayal struck her chest. Her loyalty felt like that soda bread Simon had ripped apart, being torn between husband and family.

Rory should win. He was her brother. Family.

Yet, she shifted with her husband, leaning farther and farther until half her body extended over the chair.

All of a sudden, her rosary tumbled out of her lap and clattered on the floor. She followed, toppling headfirst.

Both men jumped apart at the unexpected noise.

"What the…" Simon spoke first, then recognizing her, said, "Enjoying the sport, m'dear?"

Mortification burned up her neck and over her cheeks. She clambered to her feet, and came face-to-face with her grinning husband as he offered a hand for her to stand. She considered not accepting his hand, then did. His skin burned into hers. The man had no manners. Didn't he know it was rude to gloat over another's humiliation?

Rory grinned. "Wives and sisters who intrude upon good sport are a bloody nuisance."

"Speak for yourself. I am quite pleased to see the lady."

"Roanne ruined everything. Winning, I was."

"'Twould be a first." She questioned her brother's sanity regarding the budding friendship. "You've never won in your life."

Rory winked. "Against the likes of Murdock and Brian. Aye, you speak the truth. Him, I could have taken blindfolded."

"Simon was winning," she said, going motionless at the utterance. She frowned, considering her admission.

"Why, thank you, m'dear." Simon beamed at her. "Did you learn anything eavesdropping?"

Her heart stopped. She wouldn't lie. "Aye. Since you ask, Rory had it right. What he didn't say, though, was dual loyalty will never happen. While most Irish tried to maintain their religious freedom, it was nigh impossible to remain loyal to a Protestant monarch. The strain is what brought on the Cromwellian government."

Simon arched a dark brow. "You must admit that Charles II is working on tolerance, abolishing many of Cromwell's edicts. His Majesty is broad-minded. It is not his fault that we are not there yet." He turned when Rory retreated to the stool, then brought his attention back to her. "I had no idea you were interested in politics. I would be pleased to continue this discussion and hear more of your opinions on the subject."

Unease forced her to aim a wary glance at Simon. "I have no wish to—"

"Careful what you wish for," he interrupted in a low, seductive tone that caused fairies to flutter their delicate wings in her belly. "It might be granted before the day is over. I know what I desire."

Desire. The word rooted her to the floor, her gaze lingering on his lips. Those marvelous lips. The fairies continued to dance a merry jig as she recalled their magnificent kiss.

When she finally looked higher, a twinkle lit his startling blue eyes. Did he guess her treacherous thoughts? Almost immediately, she banished the notion and stormed out of the solar.

****

Simon admired Roanne's spirit. Always had. Take how she interacted with her brothers. The lucky ingrates had no clue how much she loved and cared for them. No matter how bitterly she argued with them, deep affection showed through.

And today proved no exception. She'd instinctively sided with Rory about governmental dogma.

He had promised himself not to let the image of her innocent face or that fluffy abundance of red hair affect him.

He only fooled himself.

She really was an angel.

Until he'd met her, he had lulled himself into a false sense of serenity. He'd convinced himself that he was happy with his lot in life. Privateering let him build a fortune to match, if not surpass, his brother's. That fact irritated Hugh, but he'd learned long ago not to let his jealousy upset him. The fortune he'd built provided him with all the necessities a man could require in his life. Except for one thing-someone to share it with.

The O'Caseys had something he would never achieve, no matter how much of a Midas he became—a loving family. Money could not purchase devotion, loyalty or love. Look how his own mother deserted him. If what Hugh told him when they were boys was true, even today, the sting remained as sharp and fresh as the day he learned that she had left.

Why think about his childhood now? He was beyond sorrow. That's what he tried to tell himself.

He turned his thoughts sharply. If circumstances

had been different. If Roanne and he had met elsewhere—another time, another place, chances were…

****

"Stay, Roanne," the O'Casey said later that night when she prepared to retire for the evening. The tired tone caught her immediate attention.

Simon and her brothers halted as well.

Padraig gave them a funny look. He waved them away. "Get along with you. I be talking to Roanne alone, not with the likes of all you."

Panic whipped through her. Why in private? She wondered…no, worried. Something bothered the O'Casey. What other setbacks cropped up to distress him?

She waited until the solar emptied. "Sure, and what's turning down your mouth in such a serious frown?" She tried to lift the tension she sensed. "You've got the look of a man who's lost a bet with the devil."

"The devil might have better news," he said in a voice that sent shivers racing down her spine. "I've received word from Finn."

Fear turned into an infernal within her. "Holy Mother, what happened? Is everyone all right?"

"They're fine. They reached Stafford without incident. Mayhap, I was a bit melodramatic, but I wanted you to be the first to learn…" Padraig took an agonizingly long moment to swallow. He lowered his gaze and his voice wavered. "They found the Earl of Kirkland's ancestral home."

Roanne's nerves tangled into a mess. "What news? Tell me quick."

Padraig winced. "Simon spoke true. He was not the earl when he wed you."

Roanne's legs went weak. The real world faded away for several seconds. She suspected her heart already belonged to Simon, but he's wasn't a lord. When her mind cleared, panic clawed its way to the surface. "What are we to do? None of this is his fault."

"Aye, that's God's truth." A shadow passed over Padraig's face. "And now I suspect feelings have developed between the two of you."

Roanne swallowed, unable to deny the possibility.

Age showed on the O'Casey as gray highlights glistened in his hair. "Simon implied he has the power of the throne behind him and probably other well-placed friends, which means he can have your marriage annulled without protests. He considers us…" He waved his arm to take in the solar and tower manor. "…and the prophecy a lark, like a tale to frighten children."

"Could he ask the king for a title? I—I mean, he professes friendship with His Majesty. It would be quicker than seeking an annulment."

Padraig rubbed his chin in deep concentration. "I hadn't thought of that."

Roanne let hope bloom. "I'll speak to him. Perchance an apology will sway him toward leniency." She inhaled a deep breath. "Tomorrow will be a good day to do so. The weather is turning fair. We can tour the garden. A stroll in the sun brightens everyone's spirits." She never realized how long she'd been waiting for the rain to stop until she put her own desire into words.

Padraig slumped into a chair. "Aye, the garden's a

restful spot. Mayhap, see Brian. He's working in the forge tomorrow. Murdock will accompany you. You'll be safe."

Roanne tensed, considering the idea. In all likelihood, it was unwise to put Murdock and Simon together away from the manor. There was no telling what would happen between the pair. "Padraig, this is our failing. We wronged Simon. We have to make it right."

The admission had nothing to do with her budding feelings toward the man. Or so she told herself.

****

Simon stared at the green tinge of the garden beneath the narrow window of his quarters. Nearly a month of imprisonment and he'd made no serious attempt at escaping. However, that was about to change. Surely enough time had passed for Charles II to forgive him or forget what angered him in the first place. The king had brought a return to normality that everyone wanted to enjoy.

In the distance, streaks of a flaming dawn illuminated the sky. An old seafarer's myth popped into his head. *Red sky at night, sailor take delight. Red sky in the morning, sailor take warning.* Was a higher being sending him a message? He shoved the inane thought away, refusing to fall prey to such madness. Being surrounded by the O'Caseys' silly belief in their prophecy was enough foolishness.

Any day the trio who'd traveled to England would return. They would confirm his status.

The reminder caused remorse to worm through him. A noise that sounded like half-frustration, half-sigh surprised him when it slipped from his mouth.

Then he smothered the self-pity with an iron will.

First and foremost, he planned to enjoy the brightness of the new day. With the sun shining, he vowed to persuade his delightfully obstinate wife to give him that promised tour of the grounds.

As he approached his bedchamber door, voices in the hallway caught his attention. He pressed his ear to the thick wood.

"This situation can be easily resolved, and we all know how," proclaimed a high-pitched voice that Simon recognized as Farrell's, the youngest O'Casey. "It might be a grievous sin, but a greater good would be accomplished by breaking the sixth commandant."

Simon tensed at the threat. A chill ran down his spine. He knew the Decalogue and repeated the sixth commandment in his head. *Thou shalt not kill.*

Timothy, his guard for the night, snorted. "You may be young, but worthwhile advice you be giving. Have you spoken with Padraig about this?"

"Not yet. I wanted your opinion aforehand."

Simon heard enough. He set his jaw in a hard line. The youthful O'Casey had figured out what he already knew—an annulment could take years and according to their prophecy, these people had only a set number of months to save their sister. As time went on, they would grow desperate. The quickest way to end the disastrous marriage was for him to die. Not a fate he would willingly surrender to without a fight.

A spurious smile on his face, he stepped into the hallway to find Timothy slumped in a chair and Farrell standing next to him. These two were the youngest O'Caseys. Timothy had ridden beside him in the carriage from Finnigan's. And Roanne claimed he assisted her with their accounts. As if to confirm the statement, Simon spotted a ledger and a gutted candle on the floor. The man must have read long into the night.

Simon had learned little about the gangly, tawny-haired Farrell, but knew the clan leader gave considerable thought to the young man.

"Good morning," he greeted both O'Caseys.

Farrell spun on his heels and left. Clearly, the youngest O'Casey couldn't face him after suggesting murder.

Timothy yawned and stretched. "Eager to be about, are you?"

"What man wouldn't when he expects to spend a glorious day with your lovely sister? The notion makes the sun shine ever brighter."

"Sure, and false flattery trips off your tongue."

Simon kept a straight face. "And I'd say, a night in the chair sours your temperament much like Murdock's. Let's hope Roanne is more appreciative of my presence than you."

A scowl turned Timothy's mouth upside down. "Swallow your tongue, Englishman."

Or else it'll be cut from your head. Simon caught the unsaid threat. He eyed the thin man without an iota of fat to gauge his measure. Simon figured overtaking him would be easy... At least until another O'Casey arrived. And so many crawled these halls. He couldn't take but a few steps without running into one.

Prudence dictated he not push the argument. Moreover, the day had begun on too nice a note to allow an intelligent brother ruin it for him.

His imprisonment was at an end. He pledged to be

gone by nightfall.

****

Roanne awoke by slow degrees, watching dawn fill her bedchamber, determined to enjoy a day too glorious to waste.

It was easy for her to select the low-cut muslin tansy-yellow gown. She owned only two decent gowns-her green wedding one and this-and wanted to appear her best, feel her prettiest for Simon when she told him that they knew the truth and she suggested he ask a boon of the king. If not, this might be the last time she would see him.

Her toilette complete, she swept out of the bedchamber with a swish of skirts and headed for the cellar to fetch a treat everyone in the household would welcome. At the bottom of the steps with darkness surrounding her, she slowed, then stopped dead.

A massive cobweb spread across the space of the last step. She lit a candle and used the flame to burn a path clear. In minutes she filled a bowl with last season's crop of green apples and headed toward the solar.

The sight of Simon approaching with his long stride started her heart pounding. He wore knee-length breeches of dark brown, with a silk waistcoat fitting his large frame perfectly, and gold buttons shaped like lions' heads. His jacket, a lighter brown with black cuffs, collar and lapels, set off his shoulder-length hair, which she had yet to see bound in a queue.

She'd never met a man so…so handsome and so appealing. Every time she laid eyes on him, sinful thoughts filled her head. A wanting melted her insides. She craved to wrap her arms around his neck and smother him with kisses.

She barely noticed Timothy or Padraig walking alongside him. They were ghosts. Invisible. She saw only Simon.

"There you are, m'dear," he greeted her with a smile. "You make a man glad to be up and about on this sunny day."

Padraig and Timothy guffawed like only amused brothers could.

Roanne's breath hitched. Deep down she savored the honeyed praise—a pleasant change from the gruff teasing she usually received from male members of her family. In that instant, she truly wished, *if only he were a lord*.

The admission shook her core. Drawing back on shaky legs, she gaped at her husband in name only. "During the war we had a saying, a dead Englishman was a good Englishman."

He winced as though her words pained him. "Then allow me."

"Allow you what?" she asked in an objectionable tone out of habit.

"To change your mind and have you believe my sincerity. I cannot decide if you're a witch or an angel. Though if I must choose, I'll pick the angel."

Pleasure rippled down her spine. She'd grown to look forward to his compliments. "Sure, and I be the mother of all angels. And you're the father of flattery, driving me crazy trying to understand you."

"Good news to my ears. I like being able to affect you."

She hefted the bowl of apples. "I wish to say something…" She faltered when he took the bowl from her, his warm fingers brushing over her cool ones, and sending a thrill racing up her hand and down to the pit of her belly.

"'Tis not heavy," she managed to utter.

"I insist. They look appetizing."

With his attention focused on the apples, she concentrated on forming the right words. To confess she knew he had told her family the truth.

Unfortunately, each time the confession arose on her tongue, it dissolved like honey in warm water.

They walked into the solar with Padraig and Timothy following in their wake.

"Set the bowl there." She indicated a small table in the sun-filled room. "Would you care for an apple?"

"Faith, Roanne," Timothy said, breaking away from his older brother. "Will you be extending kin the same offer?"

Murdock entered the solar. He stopped to eye the group with a scowl before continuing to the bench seat at the window.

Roanne started cutting an apple into wedges with the knife she kept in the desk. "Eat as many as you like."

"I don't need to be told twice," Padraig said, swiping an apple before Timothy grabbed one for himself. The clan leader bit into the juicy fruit with a twinkle brightening his dark brown eyes.

Not to be bested, Timothy nicked another and tossed one to Murdock. "Best be quick, Sassenach, afore the others arrive and leave you with none."

For a brief moment Simon's expression sobered. "This one, I think." He selected a medium-sized apple.

Roanne's gaze remained glued on him as he sank

his teeth into the apple with a crunch. Muscles rolled his jaw as his lips moved with the same motion.

"Delicious," he murmured, staring at her. "Tart and delicious."

The softly spoken words lured her in like a forbidden fruit. He seemed different. What was on his mind? Did he mean the apple...or her? She'd never make it through the day if the verbal seduction persevered.

Once again, she glanced up. She wished the prophecy held no quarter over her life. But it did and she was powerless to do anything about it. "Glad I am the apple meets with your approval."

"Just like you, m'dear. There is no better food or company to be found hereabouts."

A scoff came from Timothy. "You'll be changing your mind soon enough. *Ack*—"

Padraig slapped his hand when the younger O'Casey reached for a second apple. "Away with you. One is all you get."

"'Tis not what I was going to say. The *Sassen*—"

Padraig stopped Timothy with a glare. "Saints preserve us, d'you hear yourself? I swear lack of sleep is turning you into Murdock's twin."

"Precisely what I told him," Simon added, grinning with pleasure.

"Blessed hell, I'm right here," Murdock said. "And what's wrong with imitating me? A good role model, I am. Ask anyone."

"Ignore them all," Roanne said as way of distraction. "They mean nothing."

"Don't they?" A quizzical expression formed on Simon's countenance. "Why so kind, m'dear? Has your heart changed toward me?"

"I would be remiss not to offer you the best we own. You are our guest, after all."

Shock raised a dark brow. "And this morning you just realized this?"

Roanne muttered under her breath. It irritated her to no end. The man was too quick for his own good. "'Tis the change in the weather. Bright sun and the promise of warmer days improves everyone's appearance…even yours."

"Mayhap 'tis something else. Here." He held out his apple to share with her. "Taste for yourself."

She blinked. "My thanks." She took a dainty nibble before handing back the fruit.

Simon leaned forward, his breath fanning her skin in a warm wave. "I've waited for this moment for a long time."

"Have you now?" She inhaled the scent of soap on his skin. Her heart raced at his closeness. Too close for comfort. "And what have you waited for?"

"You, of course."

His soft avowal fulfilled her fondest dream.

And worst nightmare.

She laughed with nervousness.

His gaze fixed on the window. "The rains have ceased. I think the time has come for that excursion into the grounds. That is, if you're willing."

"Done," she answered without hesitation.

"Your brothers won't object?"

She respected how swiftly he managed to mask his surprise when he glanced at Padraig and Timothy standing nearby. "I fear one will accompany us."

"Too bad," he said as if they formed a binding

pact. "I'd hoped to be alone with you."

Magic filled his words. They floated between them with the gentleness of a lover's promise. Roanne feared to take her eyes off him. The dazzling sun spilling into the solar turned his hair into burnished ink. His angular features were all the more intense by the anticipation spreading across his face.

Holy Mother, give me strength. I know not what I do.

Roanne shook her worries away. A nicer day didn't exist. She couldn't fret. This was her choice. The only one fate allowed her in a string of unfortunate events— Da dying and her marrying a man who turned out not to be the nobleman the prophecy demanded.

"I wish to speak with you. I..." She stopped. Her fingers trailed around the bowl's rim on the table. It had been her brothers' responsibility to determine his status. Yet they rushed the nuptials. She couldn't admit the O'Caseys' mistake. Not here. Not now. "You never really told me anything of yourself."

Simon fixed a steady gaze on her. "What would you like to know?"

"Everything. What month were you born? What was it like growing up in Stafford? How many tutors did you have and what subjects interested you? Did you excel? I am curious."

"December. Awful. Tutors came and went, too many to keep track of. History. Not according to my family. Being a second son meant I wasn't required to shine, and it was best not to outshine my brother. Hugh had a jealous streak in him. He hated that I had freedom to do as I pleased, and he did not. And, to be honest, I did. Though only because I was ignored. I could have been invisible for all my father cared. Only my aunt showed interest in me. She is why I chose the sea."

Roanne followed the rapid answers with a growing empathy. "I'm sorry to hear that. Childhood is a time for innocence."

"Do not apply O'Casey values to my family." A note of indignation sounded in his voice. "Lancasters are not like the O'Caseys."

"Mayhap, they should be," she answered.

With the exception of when he spoke of his aunt, deep-seated aggravation hardened his tone. She wondered what other hardships he suffered as a lad. If his response was any indication, they must have been traumatic. He'd been raised in a horrible way. She quelled her rising curiosity and decided not to press on the personal level. At least not here.

"You mentioned history," she said. "D'you fancy any particular time over others?"

"The Roman era. They owned the world and lost it."

Somehow his answer held little surprise. "A pattern that has occurred more than once."

He quirked an eyebrow. "Have you studied history?"

She nearly choked. "Surely, you jest. Catholics— men and women—were not allowed to educate themselves under Cromwell."

"Yet you became a learned woman and do your sums better than most men."

Pride swelled, but she dared not let his kind words soften her toward him. "*Ack,* first you want me to discuss politics, now history. But I thank you for the compliment. Now, best we start that tour."

Timothy began to rise from his chair where he'd automatically started to run his fingers over the ledger Roanne had returned, as though checking her figures.

Padraig raised his hand to forestall him. "Stay, Timothy. Murdock will accompany our guest today. You'll accomplish far more if you remain here."

Roanne shivered. She did not want to spend her last time with Simon in the company of Murdock. Her brother could turn the brightest day bleak. "I've changed my mind. Mayhap another time."

"Away with you, sister," Padraig chimed in again. "Fresh air will do everyone wonders. You said so yourself."

Simon nodded in agreement. "Have no fear, Roanne. I'm not the monster you believe me to be, and I'm of a mind that few days exist here when the sun bedazzles eyes with its appearance. Tell me true, this is a rare day."

"*Ack*, right you be. Only because it'll likely be a short visit."

The trio walked out of the solar, down the hallway, and descended the stairs. The instant Roanne stepped outdoors, the warm kiss of sun on her face lifted her spirits. The sunshine bathing the property pulled a smile from her. Already, spring flowers dotted the ground with patches of brilliant colors, and dulcet notes drifted on air currents, serenading the newcomers with lyrical ringing.

At her side, Simon cocked his head. "Bells? I hear bells."

"In the willows." She pointed at the branches above his head.

Simon followed her direction. "Pray tell me, why

are bells tied to tree branches?"

Chapter Seven

Roanne couldn't believe Simon's ignorance about fairies. She squashed the flash of mirth as she considered sharing information with him. Maybe the bright sunshine prompted her good mood this morning or maybe the company made her smile. She waved her hand in the air to encompass the garden.

"The bells keep fairies away, of course," she said. "They fear the noise."

Simon raised a brow. "Fairies? Really?"

Murdock snorted. "Everyone knows there are bad fairies. Their wrath can kill," he grumbled. "With Roanne growing up in a household of males, we needed to protect her against all harm."

"Truly?"

Roanne wondered if the man was being deliberately obtuse. Not a wise thing with her brother accompanying them. Murdock wasn't dense and harbored little patience for those who lacked common sense. "You English fear witches, but fairies are worse than them. Witches have a learned magic. Aye, they can cast spells, but you can never trust a fairy. Fairies possess natural magic and are capricious creatures with volatile tempers." She turned toward the manor, eager to end the tour. "Have you seen enough?"

Murdock stomped to a bench seat in the garden.

Simon leaned closer. "Not nearly enough, lovely

mistress. There'll never be sufficient time when I'm with you."

She froze at his intimacy. A manly scent unique to Simon tickled her nose. Why did he tease her? His light-hearted mood certainly threw her off balance. Fairies must live in their garden. One of their jobs was to confuse mortals and trouble their minds.

His warm breath skimmed her cheek and pain twisted in her heart. They accused him of lying, imprisoned him, and yet he showed no sign of holding a grudge.

"It'll be over soon." She snuck a peek at Murdock to ascertain his disposition. He wasn't acting particularly threatening. A good sign. Could her worry be unfounded? "Which path d'you wish to travel?"

"You decide. I daresay you know where they lead better than I. As a ship's captain, I learned long ago to defer to those with more knowledge."

Warmth swirled through her. He offered information about his background to her. The announcement explained a lot about him. No pampered nobleman. A ship's captain deserved respect. The occupation required bravery and cunning. It meant he led men, issued orders, and expected obedience.

And it explained the lines at his eyes, from squinting at the glare on the water, and the muscles she'd seen when he'd arm wrestled Rory.

"A ship's captain?" she replied.

"Aye, for nearly a decade I sailed the ocean as a privateer."

She blinked. It wouldn't do to let admiration show. "A pirate, you mean."

A low chuckle preceded his answer. "No, privateer.

There's a difference. I had a letter of marque empowering me to carry on all forms of hostility permissible at sea. Charles II gave them to me just before he was deposed in '51."

Roanne drew a deep breath. Another reminder of the relationship between him and the new monarch. The dates fit and lent credit to him being a friend to the king.

She eyed the paths before her, one cobbled and rough, or one paved with smooth stones. Did they symbolize the direction of her life? "Which way would you like to go?"

"You pick. I'll follow."

She lifted the hem of her tansy skirt. "The cobblestone path, then. A little adventure appeals to me more than the safe and easy way."

"A woman after my own heart," Simon whispered, tucking her hand on his arm and matching her step for step.

Within minutes they emerged into an open area. Dense foliage overflowed the boundary, tall rose bushes created an intricate maze, their thick silver-blue stalks covered with green shoots of new growth. A massive trellis of slatted timbers bolted to granite blocks stretched from the ground to the fourth story of the tower manor. In the upcoming weeks, the structure would be smothered with climbing roses. Her eyes drifted shut and she imagined perfumed blooms and splashes of color throughout the summer decorating the trellis.

"It's been a long time since I've visited a place this peaceful," Simon said. "The perfect setting for quiet contemplation."

Pleasure brimmed at his appreciation. Her brothers didn't understand her desire to bring the garden to its former glory. They thought her silly. She kept a close eye on Murdock, who followed. He went to another garden seat and sat down. Within moments his eyes closed.

Roanne and Simon stopped to admire tumbling masses of early narcissus.

Both reached for the flowers at the same time. Simon's hand, warm and slightly calloused, brushed over the top of hers. A hot tingle raced up her arm at the contact. Her gaze shot to his.

Simon picked a flower. "Beautiful," he said.

She braced her feet as a spontaneous blush rushed up her neck. "I'm glad you approve. The narcissus means rebirth and new beginnings. It's always nice to see them bloom."

Simon picked another flower and braided the stems together. "They are also a symbol that there is always a chance for things to improve in the future."

Astonished, she eyed him. The man constantly surprised her. Had she misjudged him? "That's what my mother always said. This was her secret hideaway. She loved bringing the garden to life."

He continued picking the bright yellow flowers. "I suspect her daughter does as well."

"I try." Secret delight filled her. Of all the reactions Roanne expected, it wasn't watching his hands snap and pluck the stems. His dexterity made her mull over the purpose of his actions. He wasn't picking her a bouquet of flowers, was he?

They spoke on mundane things, but her body tingled with an anticipation she couldn't explain.

He selected four more flowers, twisting them into a circle. To her wonderment, he made a crown. When he caught her staring at him, he grinned.

"A gift for a lovely lady." He placed his creation on her head, running his finger down the side of her face. "Yellow becomes you."

To her utter embarrassment, a giggle escaped. The earlier blush exploded through her body so intense she thought flames would burst from her body. "I—thank you." She turned away, fighting the unique sensation. "My sister-in-law, Meagan, knows herbs better than any hereabouts. Flowers are more to my liking. Come summer, the plan is to plant wild daisies and a few lilies. Someday flora will bloom all year round."

Simon caught her hands and turned them over as though inspecting them. "If all Irish are like you, no wonder everything is green and ripe."

"Nothing is dearer to an Irishman than his land, because we first have to keep it from those trying to steal it." She stepped away from the flower beds. "Do not the English harbor the same affection for theirs?"

Simon followed. He leaned in and adjusted her crown. "Few lords take genuine interest. Oh, they have their pride to make their properties look good. But they hire others to do the actual work. In fact, 'tis why I journeyed here for my brother. His man of affairs took ill and Hugh was preoccupied with pursuits he considered more enjoyable than bother with his lands. A mistake many nobility make." His tone took on a hard edge.

"And where is your family's estate?"

"West, in Castlebar." He gave her an odd look. "Speaking of family, when did yours lay the responsibility of this prophecy on you?"

A snore told Roanne that Murdock had fallen asleep. She looked over to see him slumped on the bench with his chin resting on his chest. At least they wouldn't be interrupted. "Keep your voice down. We don't want to wake Murdock."

"A little privacy is nice, isn't it?" Simon whispered back.

The sun heated the air to a summer-like temperature.

She dragged her toe through the loose pebbles between them. Expelling a deep sigh, she met his gaze. "You wanted to know when I learned of the prophecy. I was five the first time Da told me."

"So young. What was your reaction?"

"Thrilled, naturally. It meant I was special."

A twinkle sparkled in Simon's blue eyes. "I wager you were special long before that. A precious little girl. Yet, it explains why you accepted the responsibility as your lot in life. They trained you from a young age to put family first. In my opinion, your doting relatives placed an unfair burden upon you."

Roanne pulled her brows down, unsure how to react. His suggestion hinted at blasphemy, yet she loved his compassion. "I did not mind. Sure, and it made me who I am. Now enough about me. Tell me more of your family."

He removed his jacket and draped it over one of the crossbeams of the trellis. "The aunt I mentioned lives in London. She's a writer, but society wouldn't allow her to publish her stories under her own name. Fortunately, my uncle supported her endeavors and she published her stories under his name. He was proud of her accomplishments. She sent me her books. My favorites were ones of the sea. They gave me a glimpse of a different life where individuals who worked hard could achieve whatever they wanted."

Muscles flexed through his loose tunic. The man was telling more than he realized. Roanne wondered if he even knew his frustration showed. "And your mother, father, and brother. What about them?"

A serious expression sobered his face. "My mother died when I was five, maybe six," he said, pain in his voice. "I barely remember her."

Roanne's heart broke. "Oh, Simon, I am so sorry."

"For what?"

"Losing your mother. Every child should know a mother's loving touch. That gentle brush on your forehead to check for fever when ill. The whispered words of encouragement. My own went to heaven while I was young. I still miss her terribly."

A distant expression appeared in Simon's eyes. "I cannot miss what I never knew."

Roanne's heart hitched with a nervous flutter. The answer didn't fool her. She sensed an underlying pain in him. He'd been alone, possibly unloved. Her older brothers had heaped mountains of love on her and their younger brothers to help them overcome the trauma and loss of their mother. "We both know what it's like to live without a mother. We have more in common that you realize."

His eyes widened, then a look of resolve settled on his face. "What child doesn't suffer pangs of guilt when discarded? I used to sneak into her parlor and fantasize about her returning to Hollyhock. That she'd rush over, sweep me into her arms and hug me. Rain kisses down on me. Silly, I know, because it was never going to happen. For years, I could smell her perfume in the air. My father never remarried. He had his heir and neglected me. I survived."

A coldness laced his voice. Anger? Or sadness? Roanne couldn't read between the lines, but she could guess how he suffered. Simon suffered much more than he let on. Her heart melted for him. "And your brother?"

He freed a pent-up sigh. "Some might daresay bad blood existed between us. As children we disagreed constantly. I was two years younger than Hugh, but passed him in height and size. He hated that. Hugh was a sneaky bugger. He stole treats from the kitchen because he thought stuffing himself would make him taller than me. It only made him fatter." He stopped.

Roanne waited, hoping he would continue, then he snorted and did. "Once Hugh released our father's best mare and the neighbor's draft stud covered her. Hugh claimed I did it. No amount of protesting convinced our father of my innocence. Instead of the strap to my backside, though, I was banished to the barn to muck the stables for six months. I lived, ate, and slept there, and enjoyed the freedom and was happy until I returned to the manor to find Hugh had burned my aunt's books."

She reached out and touched his chest. His heart raced liked hers. "How awful for you. He was never caught? Punished?"

Simon shrugged. "Our father preferred to turn a blind eye or take his side. Only once was Hugh held accountable. I caught him torturing a wild animal he'd snared in the woods. I jumped on him to make him stop hurting the creature, but Hugh grabbed a broken branch and began beating me. A farmer caught him red-handed and when the fellow tried to break up the fight, Hugh struck him so hard his leg broke. That upset Father because John was one of his best tenants and the injury left him unable to work his land."

It explained much about Simon, and why he bore the brunt of the fiasco of their marriage without criticism. But Roanne disagreed. Being accustomed to mistreatment didn't mean he should shoulder the responsibility alone. Her huge family constantly squabbled with each other, but never blamed an innocent. "I'm sorry."

"And I'm sorry for you."

Confusion reigned in Roanne's mind. The little insight she'd garnered about his past caused empathy to rise within. She found much to like about Simon. But instead of using the time to confess and right the wrong done to him, she woke Murdock and lead Simon back to the manor.

A smile twitched on her mouth, and she couldn't help wondering if good fairies lived in the garden.

****

At what would have been seven bells aboard ship, Simon went to the window in his bedchamber to peer outside. The rare sight of a twinkling star in the cusp of a new moon heralded an auspicious omen, a clear sign of good luck.

Good Lord, after nearly a month with the O'Caseys, silly childhood myths were popping in his head at all hours. He wondered if Hugh had formed a search party when he disappeared. His brother would have expected a report back by now. He could be looking for him. Or, at least, his fancy carriage.

He frowned. Why had he regaled Roanne with tidbits of his childhood? That was something he seldom shared. He swore compassion flashed over her lovely face more than once. He hadn't been able to get her out of his mind. Some of what he told her had been a half lie. Oh, he'd lost his mother. That was true enough. Only she hadn't died. She'd left. Fled to the new world. Left his father, his brother. And him. He'd been abandoned. The pain had been a constant companion through the years, stirred by Hugh's constant reminders. He couldn't admit that to Roanne. He didn't want her pity.

He shook off his memories to notice silvery light cast shadows over the landscape, shadows capable of hiding a man bent on escape. He studied the ledge protruding from the outer wall, no wider than his foot. He'd discovered the narrow ridge on his first day of imprisonment, yet never considered the shelf a viable avenue of escape. It led to nowhere.

Now he knew differently.

Had Roanne shown him the trellis intentionally? Did she want him to escape? Strange as it seemed, the thought of leaving her tore at him.

Then Farrell's threat of breaking the sixth commandment echoed in his head.

Simon eyed the ledge again. It wrapped around the tower manor, narrow but negotiable. If a man had a destination…

Which now he did—the trellis.

Without a second thought, he squeezed through the window.

Darkened shapes and shadows beckoned from the

grounds below. With an iron will, he cleared his head and steadied his feet. He hugged the wall, letting his fingers slide over coarse stones with few handholds. A touch of moonlight guided his steps in the eerie watery light. The going proved easier than climbing rigging on a moving ship.

He rounded the southwestern-most corner to be greeted by the faint tinkle of bells. The chiming barely covered the sound of voices. He froze.

"Damn him, Padraig. The Englishman is *cunnartach*, dangerous." As crisp and clear as the night air, Murdock's voice reached above the ground where Simon skirted the wall. "You didn't see how Roanne ogled the fellow this afternoon. They thought me asleep and couldn't hear or see them. He acted like a besotted suitor. He wove her a crown of flowers. A crown." Disgust laced the big man's voice. "And-and she tittered like a lovestruck girl."

"Let it go, Murdock. The past is the past. Clinging to your hate affects only you. You'll feel better for doing so."

"Keep my business out of this."

Padraig sneezed, then said. "No matter how much you go about huffing and puffing, we cannot change the past. All Irish have a crying need to hate the English, but not every individual. You, better than any, know that. You do not know all the facts…" His voice trailed off.

Murdock kicked a pebble and Braith bounded after it in the dark. "*Ack*, tell me what you hide."

"Soon. Soon…once everyone gathers together. All will learn at the same time."

Simon tensed when Braith reappeared. The hound

lifted his head to sniff the air. Had the dog caught his scent?

Murdock scooped up another rock and tossed it for the hound to fetch. "Why so mysterious? Does it have any bearing on what you told Roanne the other night?"

"Stop fretting, Murdock. Tis good tidings I'll share."

Simon held his breath, grateful to not inhale dust or sneeze as he flattened himself against the granite side. If either man chanced to look up, he'd be caught for sure. They'd clap him in irons or lock him in a dungeon. And more than likely, throw away the key.

Just ahead lay a window cracked open. He inched along the edge, careful not to make a sound and eased inside.

A tempting combination of oranges and cloves tickled his nose. He inhaled the scent deep into his lungs.

Roanne.

He never imagined the trellis was situated beneath her bedchamber. Fate delivered him the perfect chance to bid his spirited wife farewell, which he felt obligated to take.

****

Roanne watched the shadow slip into her chamber. Sleep had eluded her. Troubling thoughts of Simon had kept her awake long after the noises in the manor house settled down. She'd replayed every step of their walk in the garden. The number of times she'd blushed. The feathery touch when they reached for the same flower. Just thinking about him made her shiver with delight. And that crown he shaped from the flowers and placed on her head…

"Who is it?" she asked as she pulled the covers up to her chin.

"Who else do you expect in the middle of the night?" replied a voice she instantly recognized.

She peered at the silhouette, her heart beating rapidly. "Simon."

"Aye, 'tis I, your husband."

Roanne needed no candle to hear disapproval in his voice. He'd confused her during their outing, though she did appreciate his gift. "What are you doing here?" she asked, going on the defensive. "Begone, if you value your hide."

He remained at the window. "What if I have no wish to leave?"

"Are you mad?" She leaped out of bed and bare-footed stormed over to him. If caught in her chamber, the O'Caseys would demand satisfaction that would not be in Simon's best interest. "You don't belong here."

"My sweet Roanne, someday my fondest wish is to hear my name roll off your lips when you awaken from your dreams."

The honeyed words made her head reel. Heat rushed to her cheeks.

By moonlight his handsome face was a study in perfection. Hair so dark, it shined blue-black touched his wide shoulders. Midnight blue eyes turned black in the night, chiseled cheekbones, and a strong chin caught the moon's glow.

She inhaled a deep breath to gather courage and gush out the string of words she'd meant to speak earlier in the day. "Padraig received word from my brothers. I know you spoke true about not being the Earl of Kirkland."

"Then it's a good thing I am escaping."

This time she snorted with feigned disgust. "Now, that I believe. But you bungled the job. England is that way." She pointed a finger toward the window where a sliver of moonbeam poked through. "For sure, not in my room. Your sense of direction, along with your wits, must be addled."

"Oh, I am perfectly sane."

Then she must be the crazed one, for her arms slid up the hard muscles of his arms to wrap around his neck. "Will you kiss me good-bye?"

Simon held perfectly still. "Are you sure?"

"Aye, very sure."

With a smile, he bent over and nibbled tender kisses on her lips. His hands traveled down her back, tugging her closer against his burning hardness. Warmth surrounded her. The strength of his arms caused a tempest to swirl to life inside her. His soft breath caressed her as he kissed her ears, over her collarbone, across her shoulders. An ache, a bottomless, daring ache, burst within her, and she moaned.

Simon stopped to stare at her in the dim light. "Are you all right?"

She'd never felt this way before, this close to a man. "Oh, aye, if you'll kiss me again."

"With pleasure," he answered, astounding her by sweeping her his arms and carrying her to the bed.

If the first kiss pleased her, the next ones aroused her. The only cloud over her head at the moment—she hated the prophecy and the restriction it placed on her life. This was her chance to experience being with a man of her choosing. Her breath caught at the thought. A man who, if she were brave enough to admit, held a certain fondness in her heart. After all, the future held little chance of her marrying someone she actually admired, much less liked.

Tonight's actions could never be undone. And if they eliminated Sir Percy as a candidate to wed, all the better. She possessed no appeal, if not a virgin.

Who was she to dismiss such an opportunity?

When Simon broke the kiss again, and brushed the back of his fingertips across her cheeks.

She opened her eyes, still feeling the trail of his fingers. "Why'd you stop?"

"To give you a chance to say no." His tongue tickled the seam of her lips.

"Then we'd both lose," she said, before she lost her nerve.

No way could she deny him or herself. She moaned as he nudged her lips open to stroke her tongue with his as his hands, warm and strong, explored her body with infinitely tender touches.

Laughed spilled from Simon before he plunged his tongue inside her mouth. She responded with all her heart, clinging to his hard body, instinct lifting hers in a primal offering.

After a few minutes, Simon stopped again, his voice heavy, his breathing deep. "Pray, listen. We cannot continue."

"Aye, we can. I know exactly what I want—and 'tis you."

Instead of leaping at her suggestion as she half-expected, half-hoped, Simon leaned back to stare at her in the dimness. "Your innocence is still intact. We risk a lot, especially you."

His warning gave Roanne pause, for it held a

measure of truth. Pregnancy. Every woman's fear. So many died in childbirth, her own mother included. For several heartbeats, she searched her mind for a valid reason not to let Simon continue.

She should stop. But her heart wouldn't let her.

Part of her ached for the handsome man, the part that acknowledged she cared for him. That part wanted him and wanted him to make them one.

Another part, the one that knew right from wrong, cringed. If Simon turned out not to be a lord, she very possibly would die. Then again, if their coupling produced a babe, at least a part of her would continue on. This was her decision to make.

None of this was Simon's fault. He was a good man. If he was willing to chance discovery by her family, she could chance pregnancy. In fact, she sent a prayer heavenward that the coupling let her bear his child. She would rather sacrifice herself than go on living without him in her life.

A brazen laugh emerged from her throat as daring as any harlot. "Foolish, foolish man, attend me quick. You be talking about begetting a child. I'm willing to risk it for an evening we should have had on our wedding night."

"I have no French letter."

Roanne merely stared, spellbound. She'd never heard the term used in reference to herself, but knew exactly what it was-sheep's gut to prevent pregnancy.

Once again, the burden of the prophecy pressed down on her like a heavy weight. Yet, stronger feelings drew her to Simon. Dare she follow her heart?

Oh, aye, right or wrong, she dared very much.

Chapter Eight

Simon stretched on the bed beside Roanne. He must have interpreted her silence for apprehension. "Fear naught, m'dear, I promise to protect you." His voice held such seriousness that she studied him for several seconds.

"Ah, Simon, you utter such fine words. Are you sure you're not Irish? I swear you're capable of stealing my heart."

A low chuckle rumbled out of his chest. He took hold of her hand and pressed gentle kisses on her fingertips. "Have I stolen yours? If I'd known sweet words would endear you to me, I would have showered you with them much sooner." He paused to untie the ribbons at her neck and brush aside the open vee of her shift.

Instinctively, Roanne froze when his lips began kissing her shoulder. Then a shiver of delight washed through her body. She glanced down, awed at the sight of his ebony locks contrasting against the paleness of her skin.

Her fingers scraped the beginning of stubble on the strong line of his jaw to his lips. Bolder still, she brushed her palm under his linen shirt, over his chest, feeling his skin ripple as she reveled in the feel of silky swirls and hard muscles. The worst part was that she had no idea what to do next.

Simon groaned her name.

Stilling, Roanne found herself shaking. She liked hearing her name on his lips.

Even more amazingly, Simon's long, muscular frame shook like hers. His reaction made her want to strip off her clothes and dance naked around the room. What would he think of the idea?

Simon adjusted his position on the bed.

"What's wrong?" she asked. "Are you in pain? Have I hurt you?"

"Everything you do is perfect," he whispered in a husky voice.

Encouraged, within seconds, each cast away the flimsy barrier of their clothes.

Intuition told her Simon's broad chest, narrow hips, and long legs were perfect examples of manliness. Roanne suspected few women had the opportunity to lay with such a man. He appealed to her on a level that left her with a wanting—an inborn, undeniable ache for more. She arched against him, his warm body burning her as she offered herself in the only way she knew.

His kisses tasted so good, like the sweetest mead. She loved how he smelled of soap and his own unique scent.

His hand stroked her arms. "Your skin is cool."

"You make me feel toasty warm on the inside."

He answered with a low chuckle. "You make me burn for you."

His comments teased her, tempted her. She knew what happened between a man and woman. He belonged inside her, filling her.

As though sensing her thoughts, Simon gently spread her legs, lifted her hips and eased through her thin virgin's veil. He captured her small cry with a kiss. "Did I hurt you?' His brows drew together with obvious distress. "Forgive me, Roanne. There is pain the first time. Hold me until you are ready. 'Twill get better from now on."

A brazen feeling came over her. "The deed is done, and I am fine. The breaching triggered only a wee bit of pain."

"Oh, my lovely, lovely innocent."

"More," she urged. "I want more."

"Greedy, are we?" he asked, his deep voice laced with teasing.

"Only with you. Only you."

Burning. Quivering. Her body responded to the deep thrusts with an insistence that channeled heat to her apex until spasms of pleasure burst in a rainbow of lights. He transported her to a world of sensations that she'd never experienced before, and knew with all her heart that no man except Simon could make it possible. She uttered his name in a passionate whisper.

Moments later, Simon's long, powerful body shuddered with release. "Roanne," he murmured her name in response.

Neither spoke another word, their breathing labored. She lay still, enjoying the tingles undulating through her body. She was perfectly content to savor the closeness and the intimacy that they had created. And she suspected Simon felt the same.

Then Simon sighed deeply and smiled at her as he sat up. He pulled her into his arms to cradle her against his body like a babe, her head resting on his chest. Roanne listened to the rapid beating of his heart until the sound slowed to normal.

"This feels so right," she purred. "Am I wrong to enjoy being with you?"

"I hope not, dear wife. 'Tis how life should be."

"We're so different." His chuckle made her want to jab his ribs, but she controlled the impulse.

"You're a woman. I am a man. There is supposed to be a difference."

"I meant—I'm Irish. I value life, freedom." She peeked under thick lashes to look up at him through a forest of dark hair. "You're an Englishman. The first I've met who didn't want to pilfer whatever we possessed without permission."

"You noticed?"

She nearly laughed. She couldn't help herself. Being with him made her happy. It was easy to imagine years of teasing each other. "I swear your arm is stretching from all the patting you're giving your back. If you must know, I expected an escape attempt long before now. Though I do confess, I'm glad you stayed."

"As am I." He cradled her closer and stroked her hair.

She squeezed her eyes shut and savored the touch. A twinge of loss stabbed at her. This precious moment wouldn't last. All Roanne wanted were memories to carry with her for as long as she lived. "Tell me more of your family. Your parents."

Simon stiffened beside her. Had she gone too far?

"Talking about my family isn't exactly tales to speak of after making love," he answered.

Roanne didn't press. A hard edge laced his voice. Demons chased her husband. She would gladly take his pain if it would ease his burden.

"Forget I asked. 'Twas my curiosity talking."

Turning, she planted a kiss in the center of his chest. She inhaled deeply to draw in his scent. "You need never be lonely again."

"You know me so well." So saying, he slipped from her side to retrieve his clothes lying on the floor.

Roanne didn't move, not even blink. She sensed a hard curtain drop around Simon and wanted to protest the change that came over him. He moved with the stealth of a hunting cat and intense determination. This time she clutched at the bed linens to keep from reaching out for him. "I-I thought from what you told me about your family. That-that your childhood had been difficult."

His face hardened into an impenetrable mask. "Don't fret about me. What about you? Will you be safe?"

"Why wouldn't I be?"

At the creak of a floorboard, he paused to glance at her. "You sound so positive."

"I know myself, and can keep a secret," she answered, still hoping their union beget her a child.

Reluctance must have shown on her face or the inflection in her voice because he paused in his dressing to smile at her. "I don't want to leave you to face your brothers alone. Come with me, Roanne. I'll take care of you." He raked thick hair out of his eyes. "There's a place on my estate on the southern side of the manor that would be a perfect spot for a flower garden. As my wife you could plant to your heart's content."

"Your offer is tempting." Heat rushed up her neck. She hadn't thought of the future. All she wanted to do was to stay wrapped in his strong arms.

He continued. "I wager you'd like Stafford. I have

a few servants. A bachelor doesn't require many, but we'll hire a maid for you. My manor is located north of Hollyhock. Hugh's estate and mine are connected through a deer park where game is plentiful." He hesitated as though to gather the right words to explain his offer to her as well as himself. "I never expected to wed or have an heir. I always intended to deed the property to my brother's heirs once he wed and begot a family. You change everything."

She scooted higher in bed. "It sounds beautiful." She pursed her lips as though she could keep from speaking the next words. "I wish I could."

"What do you mean? Wish?" His cold tone cut Roanne to the quick. "Nothing is prohibiting you. Leave with me."

Something died inside Roanne. Aware that what they shared changed her life forever, she inhaled a deep, deep sigh. As much as it pained her, the events of tonight would have to last her the rest of her short lifetime. Simon wasn't a lord. Her family would be devastated if she died, especially away from them. "I cannot."

"Cannot? Or will not?"

"Listen, I beg you." Tears burned the back of her eyes as her heart broke. "My family needs me. They take their duty seriously."

Simon shoved his boots on and marched across the floor to the bed. "That idiotic prophecy again! You would rather honor it, than have faith in me to make you happy."

Her heart broke, suspecting how he took her refusal—as another rejection. "I beg you. Simon, please understand. 'Tis what must be done."

He rocked back on the balls of his heels. "I understand all too well. Do as you please. I'm leaving."

The hardness of his words jarred Roanne into silence. She closed her eyes, afraid if she looked at him, saw the pain on his face her rejection caused, she would give in.

At a distinctive clink against wood, she peeked through her lashes. A gold band glimmered in the moonlight on the sill. Da's ring. Her heart squeezed with a new ache. Once a symbol of love and affection, the ring had become a symbol of failure.

Simon slipped through the window without a backward glance.

Pain twisted her insides. The tears she'd held back became a warm trickle escaping down both cheeks. She couldn't stand not seeing him depart and jumped from bed to race toward the window. She searched the darkness for any sign of movement.

A shadow glided through the trees. She stuffed her fist into her mouth, afraid she might call out. The tall figure belonged to only one person. He would never return. It hurt to see him go. It hurt to lose him.

But her family had tricked him into marrying her, held him prisoner. He deserved his freedom.

"Godspeed, Simon Lancaster. My heart goes with you. Hold fast to your memories of me, for I will of you."

****

Simon tramped along the roadway, his sense of guilt and desertion increasing with each rigid step. A primal urge of desertion raged within him. Stopping, he took out his frustration by kicking a rock. It crashed somewhere off the road.

Leaving Roanne had been the hardest thing he'd ever done in his life. She had responded to their lovemaking beyond his wildest dreams. For him to discard her weighed heavily upon him until fear triggered a realization. Was this how his mother felt when she left? Did she regret leaving, even as her heart broke?

Each stomp of his boots carried him farther from the O'Casey manor. Farther from Roanne. What if their coupling produced a child? He'd never felt loved as a boy. Could he do the same to his own offspring? Gritting his teeth until his jaw hurt, he battled the temptation to turn around.

Damn his wife. Damn Roanne. She'd fooled him. For several heartbeats he had actually believed she understood about loneliness since they shared the loss of their mothers.

He'd slipped into her room by accident, an act of desperation, to keep from being discovered by Padraig and Murdock.

The devil hang all O'Caseys. His fingers clenched into fists at his sides until his nails bit into his flesh. He knew the real reason Roanne refused to join him. She cared more for her family than him. The comprehension only heightened his feelings of abandonment.

A night breeze rustled treetops as he trudged forward. Stars glittered in the velvet sky. He pulled his coat tighter to fend off the spring chill and the heartache trying to crush him.

Hours of trekking along the deserted roadway led Simon to Dundalk. Dawn peeked over the low-pitched rooftops. Within another hour he skirted the edges of the awakening town. Entering a street nearest the wharf, gray light began to brighten all the corners, nooks, and crannies. A salty mist hung heavy in the air. He resisted the urge to lick his lips, for salt wasn't the only odor he smelled. Distinctive fish and tar wafted strong in the air currents.

Overhead, seagulls dipped and swooped in the morning sky, their raucous cawing drawing his attention to a frigate moored at the end of a long pier in the deep-water harbor. Simon slowed to take in the view before him. The *Red Dragon*, apply named for its red masts, had been the first ship he'd acquired when he began securing his fortune and to this day, remained a favorite among his fleet.

For one long moment, he yearned to return home and in the next, he ached for the feel of Roanne's arms around him. If only he could inhale her favorite scent of oranges and cloves. Against his will, desire increased with each breath he drew.

Roanne had made her choice.

And he'd made his.

He belonged in England. Alone. Lonely.

"There sits passage home." His words broke the spell his memory created. He'd approach Charles and beg the king's forgiveness. A little humility wasn't beneath him. Surely, enough time had passed for Charles to absolve him. "Good riddance to the O'Caseys and their ludicrous prophecy. Lady Luck is shining on me. England awaits my return."

His pace increased toward the wharf. He skidded to a stop when he spotted a trio of O'Caseys standing upon the deck of the very ship he'd sought with eagerness. Aghast, Simon stared at the familiar group talking with Captain Frazier.

He ducked behind a stack of barrels already unloaded from the ship's hold, and set his attention to the three O'Caseys. They stood near the gangplank. Simon's ears tuned out the clanking rigging and water lapping at the hull and dock to better catch their conversation. Seconds crawled as he waited for one to speak.

"We thank you for the safe crossing, Captain," Sean the Third said in a joyful tone. "A smoother ride we've never enjoyed."

"My pleasure." The well-muscled captain, dark and lean as any Scot, stood erect. He swelled with pride. The long braid in his hair gave him a singular barbaric appearance. Simon knew the *Red Dragon's* crew respected the big Scot and refused to sail under any other captain, for Frazier was considered one of the best. "You are welcome aboard anytime, laddie. Anytime a'tall."

Simon tucked himself back among the barrels when hooves clomped on wooden decking. Two of the O'Caseys led their horses forward, preparing to depart the ship.

"Will you be telling us why your crew shouted with joy at the sight of green clouds?" the youngest Irishman asked.

"Green clouds mean land ho, because they reflect vegetation."

Sean grinned widely. "We'll be returning home now that you've brought us safely back to these cherished shores. Our family will be anxious to hear our tidings."

Finn and Ian pushed off the railing, each leading a shaggy-coated pony down the span of a wobbly gangplank to the pier.

"Best be on our way, Sean," Finn hollered as he mounted. "I have a breeding wife awaiting me. If a sailor you're planning on becoming, you can see the world another day."

"A glorious life I would lead," replied the younger man, sounding unwilling to depart the vessel. "Sail the seas in search of gold and jewels."

"Daydream on your own time," Ian snapped when a horse whinnied. "Traveling we need doing. Faith, these ponies need to stretch their legs on solid ground."

Sean the Third shook Captain Frazier's hand. "Forgive the rudeness of me brothers, Captain. I'll foot the cost of a pint of good Irish ale when next we meet."

"I'll no turn down a free drink." The Scot smiled as the younger O'Casey led his pony down the gangplank. "You got yourself a bargain, laddie."

When the last Irishman mounted, the trio made their way through the hustle and bustle of merchants scurrying here and there, darting like schools of fish, and wharfmen unloading crates and barrels.

Simon waited until they turned a corner before stepping out from behind the barrels. He strode up the gangplank.

"Captain Frazier, good to see you again. You can't imagine my delight upon spying the *Red Dragon* at anchor." Simon stretched out his hand.

The tall Scot accepted it and gave a hearty shake. "I heard tell you visited Ireland, but dinna know you were still here."

"A minor detail delayed me."

"Do tell."

Simon hid his smile. Nothing appealed to the

Scotsman than a good tale, but he refused to oblige him. His life for the last month wasn't up for review.

Frazier frowned, his expression clear that he'd hoped Simon would enlarge upon his meaning. "Well, whatever the cause, you're a sight for sore eyes. I dinna ken the reason why people back in England kept whispering about your whereabouts."

Simon arched a brow, only mildly curious about gossip being spread by loose tongues. "Were they now? Pray tell me, why was that?"

"Dinna know, but speculation ran high."

"Well, I am here now and eager to set sail for home. That's your course, isn't it?"

"Aye, the Pool of London. Unless you have different orders."

A loud bang on the dock drew both men's gazes to the pier. Wharfmen stacking barrels had let one tumble off the top.

"London suits me very well." He indicated the direction the O'Caseys went. "Those three who just left the ship…They appear a happy lot to return to this God-forsaken land."

"You mean the O'Caseys?" Frazier's grin widened. "Nice fellows. Superstitious lot though. Kept going on about a prophecy and luck of the Irish."

"Prophecy, you say?"

"Aye," he said.

"Do tell," he repeated the same phrase the captain used.

"Aye. Every time I made an inquiry, they'd spout this tale of a family prophecy. Couldn't make any sense of it. Is it important?"

"Not likely." Simon refused to pursue the question.

The troublesome clan didn't matter to him. Not anymore. He was homeward bound.

So why did he feel like he was leaving a piece of himself behind?

****

Roanne released a sigh of contentment in the gray light of dawn.

This morning, nestled beneath layers of covers, she burrowed deeper, having no wish to wake, until a tenderness between her thighs reminded her of the night's activities.

Blessed Mary! Realization hit her like a bolt of lightning. She'd come to care for Simon, and worse, she must suffer his loss by herself. He'd become important in her life in such a short while. He meant more than she expected.

Jerking upright, she agonized over what she'd done—lying with him. Her rash actions put her life in danger. She didn't care about herself. It was her brothers who would never forgive themselves for not protecting her. Nay, they would never learn what transpired between her husband and herself. It became their secret.

She must forget Simon. Forget how wonderful he made her feel. *An impossibility*, said a little voice in her head. She touched her heart. It ached with the memory of what they shared. Last night he'd woven himself into a special part of her soul.

She reached for her nightdress, tossed on the floor in the eve's excitement. Drawing the garment over her head, Simon's intoxicating scent clung to the fabric and she vowed to never launder the thin material again.

Her husband. Her lover.

The reminder heated her cheeks as she checked the sheets. A small stain of blood was visual proof of the delights Simon and she had shared. She stripped the sheets, then focused on her morning toilet and plaited her hair. Stepping into a homespun gown, she went outdoors to launder the dirty linens. After hanging the sheets out to dry, she went in search of Meagan.

The odor of drying fish permeated the air as she approached two small huts, one for fish, and one for herbs. Drying was not easy to accomplish in the damp climate, but her ancestors had discovered a stiff breeze from the sea worked nearly as well as the heat of a desert sun.

Inside the smaller hut, Meagan hung rainbow trout on a wooden rack. The older woman reminded Roanne of a doe with her huge brown eyes and gentle manner. "Meagan, can you spare a few moments to talk?"

The brown-haired woman spun around. "You want to talk to me? Whatever for?"

"Silly woman, because your counsel has merit."

Meagan laughed with glee and led Roanne out of the hut to the other. "What blarney is this? You have never sought my guidance in the past." She went to a basket and rubbed her hands with a fistful of rosemary to remove the fishy odor. She wiped her hands on her apron and stepped to another basket.

Roanne's gaze swept over a rough-hewed table covered with baskets teeming with herbs from silver gray to deep green. Shades of red and bronze filled smaller baskets. Many she couldn't identify, though she did recognize the pale purple flowers of chicory, feathery fennel and fragrant oregano. More baskets held willow bark and orange peelings.

Meagan was the real gardener in the family, and an expert on all flora in their region. She derived true enjoyment from her plants and found caring for them neither exacting nor tedious. It was a labor of love.

"Untrue. I recall following your advice about not making stew because you requested I wait for you. And I did," Roanne answered, trying to keep the conversation light. She stepped inside to better watch Meagan work with the herbs. "What are you making?"

"My mixed herbs. Tis cheaper than purchasing those at the market. With coin so few these days, any way I can make ends meet is best."

"Your spice is far better. May I help?"

Meagan tucked a loose strand of brown hair behind her ear. "When isn't another pair of hands welcome? I also found some foxglove. It's toxic, but bless my sainted mother, she taught me to boil it for its oil and mix with beeswax. 'Twill make a good salve against infection. I collected enough to make a batch that should last us up to a year." Meagan pulled long, shallow leaves from her apron. "And look at this."

Roanne stared at leaves that reminded her of parsley. "What is it?"

"Anise! I found it growing near a pond in yonder dale. I was too late to collect the seeds. The leaves will do as bait for mice. I spotted their droppings where our flour is kept, and I will not abide those nasty beasties nibbling at our food stores."

Roanne swept her hand over the long table of baskets. "You collected all this on your last outing for dandelion greens?"

Meagan laughed. "Hardly. Several trips it took. Rain doesn't bother me when I'm out in the freshness of nature."

Roanne picked up a sprig of thyme and followed the other woman's example, crumbling the dry stems into tiny flecks between her fingers. After working in tandem for several minutes, she said, "I never realized how soothing working with herbs could be."

"'Tis the solitude," Meagan said.

"Solitude? What d'you mean?"

"In all my years of wedded bliss to Padraig, I can honestly say he has never ventured here to offer to ease my chores by aiding me. And I don't mind in the least. A little peace and quiet is good for the soul."

Roanne burst out with a laugh. "You know men well?"

A twinkle lit Meagan's brown eyes. "So that's what this visit is about? Men! A fine subject to pass the time."

"You misunderstand," Roanne denied, her heart rate increasing.

"Then explain."

A hot blush of embarrassment crept up Roanne's neck to burn across her cheeks. Did no longer being a maid somehow show on her face? "Being wed causes all types of troubles."

"Ah, not men then. A particular man. Your Englishman. I've seen how the two of you look at each other when you think no one else sees."

"He's not my Englishman." It killed Roanne to lie. "I have no idea what you're talking about. The truth is we quarrel worse than two sows over a single ear of corn."

Meagan chuckled perceptively. "If you say so. Padraig and I dance the best Paphian jig after an argument, even if I say so myself."

The older woman's admission broke the tension, and both laughed softly.

"Feeling better now?" Meagan asked.

"'Tis not easy." Roanne paused. "There are days methinks the O'Caseys' are doomed to be superstitious fools, especially when it comes to our prophecy."

Meagan crossed herself. "Saints protect us. Don't go questioning your heritage. Tis what makes you, you."

"I can't help doubting, Meagan. At least, a little. You believe what you will...as I must."

Suddenly, a crescendo of voices erupted from one of the paths leading to the manor. The two women froze, then glanced at each other.

"I recognize that voice. Tis Sean the Third." A smile broke out on Meagan's face. "And Ian and Finn. Thank the Lord, they've returned."

"At last." Roanne experienced the same joy. She prayed her brothers brought glad tidings, except she held little hope.

In a flurry of skirts, both women barged out the door to race shoulder-to-shoulder down the pathway in the direction of the men.

"What news?" they asked in unison, skidding to a halt in front of a half dozen O'Caseys jostling each other as they trudged toward the manor.

Sean the Third broke away from his brothers. "Come into the solar where our tale can be told in comfort to everyone."

"Good or bad," Roanne demanded, unwilling to wait.

"Depends on who you ask," her brother teased

back. "Good news, I say. The O'Caseys' be the luckiest clan in all of Eire."

Roanne's heart skipped a beat. She stared at Sean the Third and shook her head. No amount of badgering would make him tell until he was ready and willing. She thought about his words-good tidings. That meant only one thing-she was saved. The only way that could happen was for Simon to now hold a title. What else could make her brothers joke with each other, their smiles wide, enjoying themselves? They'd experienced minimal happiness in their lives recently for her to ruin their homecoming.

They entered the solar as a solidified group.

She claimed the chair at her desk, beating back curiosity about her brothers' journey. *Be patient,* she told herself. Everything would come out…in good time. The wait would be worthwhile. In the meantime, being surrounded by family, her happy loving family, felt good. Why should she shatter their good humor?

Though she did wonder about their reaction once they learned the truth.

Simon was gone. Escaped.

Chapter Nine

Roanne studied the newly returned trio in the solar, and knew only one thing would make her brothers so happy. Part of the prophecy had been fulfilled. Simon was a lord.

Sean the Third waited for the group to settle into various chairs around the solar. Then, with the fanfare of a traveling thespian, he announced, "Simon Lancaster *is* a nobleman. He be the fifth Earl of Kirkland."

Her suspicion confirmed, Roanne's head spun until dizziness threatened to engulf her. She'd never swooned in her life and had no intention of starting now. "But—"

"'Tis true," Finn interrupted, his serious expression deepening the wear lines of his face. "We wrote of the circumstances as soon as we arrived."

Sean the Third beamed a grin. "'Twas all the talk in Stafford. The unexpected death of Hugh Lancaster."

Worry snaked through Roanne. "What happened to him? You didn't kill him, did you?"

The newly returned trio exchanged glances with each other. Did she imagine guilt in their expressions? Were they making sure they had their story straight before answering her? She frowned at the thought because she couldn't tell.

"For shame, sister, a mortal sin you be talking

about," Sean the Third denied.

She had to be sure. "You threatened to kill Simon."

"That was wrong of us," Padraig said. "Now let the lads tell their story."

"'Twas a hunting accident," Sean added.

"The local constable found no evidence of foul play. Only a loyal hunting dog remained by his side," Ian added in a low voice. "He was found the very day we arrived. Shot in the back. We didn't know if the earl would live or die. 'Twas a long, suffering death. We stayed until the end. As soon as word reached us of his passing and funeral, we returned posthaste."

"There were no witnesses?" Padraig asked. He stood beside Meagan, his arm draped over her shoulder.

Sean the Third fidgeted in his seat and grinned at everyone. "None came forward as far as we know. Word is, the fellow was a negligent landlord. He made no attempt to maintain the tenants' cottages, offered no improvements, but always demanded his token. The poor devils live in squalor, nearly as bad as we did. He forbade anyone to hunt on his property and they were starving. Few mourned his passing and even fewer tended his funeral. I wager many considered his passing a Godsend. Plus, it be good for us as well."

Several heads nodded in agreement.

"Fetch the new Lord of Kirkland," Padraig announced, beaming. "Today we celebrate."

"Wait!" Roanne jumped to her feet, fighting back panic. "'Twould be unwise."

Face stern, Padraig's brows clustered above his eyes. Meagan put a hand on his arm and shook her head. "Best explain what you mean."

Roanne stood straighter and returned the

147

O'Casey's frown with one of her own. She never considered herself a coward, but confessing knowledge of Simon's departure proved the hardest task she'd ever done in her life. Now she told herself she didn't have a choice.

"Simon's gone," she announced.

The clan leader narrowed his gaze at her. "Gone where?"

She snuck a glance around the room. All present fixed their gazes on her, confusion, anger, and worry clear on each face. "Back to England."

"By all the Saints! What have you done?" Padraig stepped away from his wife and closer to Roanne.

She refused to cower and met the clan leader with her chin raised. "Done? You were going to kill him. Murdock threatened several times. I heard him meself."

Padraig glanced at Timothy, Simon's guard for the night, his expression grave.

The younger O'Casey freed a long breath. "He didn't leave through his door, if that be what you're thinking. I spent the whole night there. Never checked on him when relieved though. Just figured he be still abed."

Padraig's gaze returned to her. "How did he escape?"

"By the trellis." She'd started this revelation, might as well finish. "I gave him that tour yesterday that you agreed to and he risked his neck by walking the ledge to the trellis. Rory's used it often enough to sneak inside."

Murdock growled from his seat.

Rory nodded at the truism. "Aye, 'twas why Da insisted upon climbing roses with thorns on the trellis. He thought that would stop me or another intruder."

Her oldest brother raked back rapidly graying hair. He looked as though he'd aged a whole decade in minutes. "How d'you know he is gone?"

"He bid me farewell."

Sean the Third burst into laughter. "*Ack*, you've done it this time, sister. Wedded to a lord, but none to be seen hereabouts."

Padraig straightened. "'Tis all my fault, I'm thinking. Twice cursed, we are. I was too lenient. I wanted to give you and his lordship time to become acquainted. To become friends afore you became husband and wife in more than name only."

There it was again. *In name only.*

Now even that was false.

"I don't know what all the fuss is about," Roanne said, deciding on the spot not to hide behind a lie. "The marriage was consummated."

****

Dusk came and went. Roanne's eyes burned from the tears she'd shed throughout the day and night. Hours of arguing brought no peace to the manor. No words soothed her brothers or her broken heart.

Midmorning the next day, a cacophony of howls from the wolfhounds broke the silence. The mournful noise sent shivers down Roanne's spine. She flicked a glance at Padraig standing before the fire. The dogs reacted in that manner for only one individual—Sir Percy.

She'd met the golden-brown-eyed woman who'd been his wife, Dorinda, dozens of times when Murdock drove her in a cart to the market in Dundalk. She'd always suspected her brother harbored a fondness for the woman, but never asked. Best not to know. It was the only explanation possible for her brother's animosity toward the pompous lord.

On a more pleasant note, Roanne remembered admiring Dorinda's hair, a medium brown with streaks of honey highlighting curls most women envied. So different from her own bright red.

Nor did Roanne forget the bruises on Dorinda's skin. Not that a complaint or explanation ever came from the petite woman. Roanne suspected the cause and felt anger rise at Sir Percy, another reason she'd offered small kindnesses even though the brunette was English. She deserved a smidgeon of kindness in the cruel world.

The rotund lord swept into the solar, dressed in shimmering emerald green satin. Spotting her, he rushed forward and executed a brief bow, his wig threatening to tip off his head. "Fair Roanne, how are you? I swear you become lovelier each day."

Disgust rose within her. She refused to acknowledge his compliment. "Sir Percy, what do we owe the honor of your visit at this early hour?"

"Have a seat," Padraig said, ever the diplomat, extending a hand to encompass the room.

The man accepted the offer by dragging a chair toward Roanne. "Why, to expedite this awkward situation into which the clan O'Casey find themselves, naturally... I've come to court you, my dear. Everyone in County Louth knows the man you claim as a husband is no lord. I pray you will accept my company on a stroll, so we can become better acquainted."

Roanne's muscles quivered. "I fear you waste your time, Sir Percy. You haven't heard the latest," she answered in the sweetest voice.

His gaze bore into her, clearly suspicious. "What's that?"

"My marriage to Simon Lancaster fulfills the prophecy. His brother suffered a fatal accident and my husband has inherited the title. Twould seem he's been named the fifth Earl of Kirkland."

A greenish tinge and bug-eyed expression changed Sir Percy's face into a frog's. "It cannot be. You lie!"

Roanne clenched her fists to keep a tight hold on her temper. "Tis quite true and easily verified. Now, if you'll excuse me. I have other duties that require my attention."

"Hold!" His tone dripped with authority when she started to leave. "I have colleagues in high places. They'll have this farce of a marriage annulled."

Roanne saw Padraig tense, but remain quiet. He trusted her to handle the situation. "I doubt they'll be successful," was her calculated reply. "I should warn you, though. It would be wise of you to use caution and tread carefully if you have ideas about besmirching my husband's good name or ours. You see, good fortune shines on the O'Caseys. We have connections now, too. My husband is friends with the king himself."

Huffing, the man slurred an unintelligible curse and departed faster than he had entered the solar.

"That felt good," she said to her brother.

Padraig nodded. "I thought you might enjoy putting that toad in his place."

****

Simon believed he did the right thing.

Vengeance hardened his heart as he returned to Dundalk. One of the O'Caseys killed Hugh. No matter how bad a brother Hugh might have been, he deserved justice.

Never did Simon imagine himself controlled by emotions. Rather he'd always considered those consumed by trifling sentiment unstable weaklings.

Yet now, a little more than a sennight after fleeing Ireland, he arrived at first light to stand before the O'Caseys tower manor. He banged on the thick doors and waited for someone to admit him.

Meagan opened the door. Her brown eyes widened, and her mouth puckered like a fish, before a smile brightened her face.

Simon took advantage of her lack of greeting to sweep inside. "Hello, Meagan. I've come to fetch my lovely wife. Is she hereabouts?"

"My—my lord, I'll fetch the O'Casey. He'll be pleased to see you and I'm sure he has much to say to you." The surprised woman scurried off.

Simon merely smiled. He didn't have a grudge against her.

The scent of oranges and clove perfuming the air hit him hard. His wife was nearby. He debated about seeking her out on his own or waiting for the clan leader. Aware of the complex situation, he opted to wait.

Footsteps thundered down the staircase. A half dozen O'Caseys—Padraig, Rory, Sean the Third, Farrell, Timothy, and Brian—raced down the steps. No Roanne. Simon buried the disappointment that swelled like a rogue wave. He wondered if she was avoiding him. If so, it wouldn't last for long. He'd seek her out.

"A sight for sore eyes, you be," Padraig said, wrapping him in a hug.

Simon resisted the urge to break the hold. He

didn't want to cause trouble this soon.

Beside the clan leader, Rory beamed. "I wondered how long it would take you to return." He turned to Sean the Third. "You owe me a six-pence. I was right."

The younger O'Casey beamed. "It be worth it to be wrong."

Padriag raised his arm. "Give his lordship a chance to speak."

"As I told Meagan, I've come to fetch my wife back to Hollyhock with me. That is, if you O'Caseys have no objections. How can I run my affairs without her by my side? Where is she?"

Padraig nodded to Farrell and the tawny-haired lad ran back up the stairs, taking them two at a time.

A sense of uncertainty ate at Simon. Would Roanne even want to see him? If his plan for revenge was to succeed, she must be willing to return home with him. He planned to unmask the brother who murdered Hugh, and she was the bait.

When he spotted her slender form on the upper landing, his heart hitched. She glided down the stairs like an angel descending to earth. A tangle of fiery curls surrounded her face. He couldn't take his gaze off her. The potency of his attraction for his wife produced a burning temptation, yet he refused to waste time or let himself be swayed.

She came to a stop in front of him. "Husband," she said, looking up at him. "You returned. I'm so glad."

"Wife," he responded, breathing slowly to keep his temper in check.

Her joy shone with a huge smile, warmth beaming from her amber-green eyes. Simon recalled the softness of her body. Good Lord, he never realized how much he missed touching her. Unbidden, he traced a finger down the side of her face. Then he remembered his mission and waited to see how she would react next.

All of a sudden, she threw her arms around his neck. "Kiss me."

He flicked a glance at the circle of O'Caseys and tamped down the flash of delight. If nothing else, she seemed grateful he'd come back. As a child he had prayed nightly for his mother's return. She never did. "With pleasure."

When he broke the kiss, O'Caseys stood around them beaming. They wouldn't be so pleased if they suspected the true reason for his appearance.

"That's enough," Padraig said. "Join us for the morning meal."

Simon nodded. "I remember the food. Meagan's seasonings are the best I've ever eaten." As they made their way to the great hall, he said, "I'm glad you harbor no ill will. I've come for Roanne, and would like to invite the entire clan to England for the official wedding at Hollyhock."

"'Twould be an honor, your lordship," Rory answered walking on the other side of Roanne.

Padraig seemed to concentrate as he scratched at his gray hair. "I don't know. There's much to do afore we could leave, I'm thinking. Spring is a busy season."

"We need to do Roanne right," Brian said. "'Tis only fair."

"Make your arrangements," Simon answered, trying to sound nonchalant. "I'm sure Roanne would want all her brothers to share in her happiness."

Roanne squeezed his arm. "How soon do you wish to depart?"

"I was hoping you and I could catch the evening tide."

Simon held his breath and produced a smile he hoped appeared genuine. This was the tricky part. "Preparations will take some time and I want you involved in your own wedding, m'dear."

Roanne leaped to her feet. "I'll pack right away. I'll not take long."

"I'll help," Meagan volunteered.

True to their word, the women finished before noon. Plenty of time to catch the evening tide. A few O'Caseys escorted them to Dundalk, including Sean the Third. The temptation to kidnap the younger O'Casey proved a strong motivator, but he wanted the trio who had gone to England, and Finn and Ian were not present. Best to trap all three, than the wrong one.

The *Black Sheep* rested in the harbor. The vessel had waited for him to select a new captain before joining his merchant fleet. His quartermaster gave the curious O'Caseys' a tour of the ship. Roanne chose to supervise her trunk being hoisted aboard. Then together they bid her brothers farewell and watched them ride out until they disappeared.

He escorted Roanne to the captain's cabin. "I hope this will suit your needs," he said upon entering.

Her smile slipped the tiniest bit. "You were quiet on the journey here. Is something amiss?"

"A twist of fate has fulfilled your idiotic prophecy," he spoke without emotion. "I have come into possession of an earldom. Isn't that what you wanted? Your family appears ecstatic. A nobleman you needed to wed, and so you are."

"Not by choice, but glad I am now."

He jerked her into his arms, harder than he intended, hating the turmoil broiling within himself. Deception wasn't his normal mode of operation. Nor did he approve of taking advantage of weaker individuals, yet he was about to treat his wife worse than the lowest seaman aboard any of his vessels. He steeled himself against weakening.

Then, with a force of will he shoved aside the growing remorse for his behavior. Duty and honor required him to take action. That dullard called Stafford's sheriff had come up empty-handed in finding the culprit involved in Hugh's death.

One of Roanne's brothers killed Hugh.

And Simon was determined to unearth the guilty one and punish the offender.

"You may not think so in the coming weeks." He brushed her lush red hair off her face as if to soften his next words. "Though your family is unaware, when they visit, it'll be to turn over Hugh's killer."

"What gibberish are you talking?" She dropped her hands to her sides.

His hands tingled with the memory of caressing those luscious curves. "Murder, madam. Cold-blooded murder," he said without a thread of warmth. None existed in his brother's grave and he refused to extend any to his murderers. "Hugh is dead, in case you have forgotten, and one of your brothers killed him."

She twisted free of his hold and leapt back to stand in a proud *fianna* stance like the ancient Celtic warriors he'd read about. "I tell you my family had nothing to do with your brother's death. I heard all about it. Twas a sad accident."

Simon snorted. "Accident, my arse. How does one

shoot himself in the back and have it ruled an accident?"

Roanne's mouth opened in protest. "He could have enemies in Stafford. Someone might hold a grudge against him."

"Someone did," he snapped. "Your brothers."

With a squeak of outrage, she raced for the door.

He caught her in two strides and tugged her close to his side. Fear widened her amber and beryl eyes. Despite the warmth in the cabin, she shuddered. He'd always known her intelligence equaled any man's and her sudden silence proved the claim to him.

"Make yourself comfortable," he told her without any warmth in his tone. "You'll remain in here for the crossing."

Spinning around, he locked the cabin door behind him. Misery twisted his insides. He knew he was jumping to conclusions about the Irishmen without proof. Hugh had not been the best landowner, cruel to his tenants, and the way he conducted business was not always honorable. He had enemies throughout the land, but none dared to raise a hand against him.

He refused to believe himself wrong about Roanne's brothers. They were guilty.

****

"Wed or die…" A sennight later, Roanne stood in the oblong room watching her husband take his afternoon meal. A dozen different aromas rose from the sideboard with a host of platters containing paper-thin slices of beef, wedges of ham, oyster patties, potatoes, carrots, loaves of fresh-baked bread and butter. One whiff, and she swayed. How could he eat while she possessed no appetite at all? She swallowed. "…those were my choices."

Simon smacked his fork down on the table. "Your tale makes no difference to me. Surely, those devils in your family taught you to stretch the truth better than that."

Her fingers toyed with the frothy lace around the low-cut neckline of her gown as she fought against the rage building in her. She believed her brothers when they said they had not been involved in Hugh Lancaster's death. She vacillated between wanting Simon and defending her family.

Now all she had to do was convince her stubborn husband. "O'Caseys are many things, but liars they are not. And I for sure have never lied to you or done anything to give you reason to think I have broken a trust."

"Time will tell me whether you lie or not. Now, madam, I grow weary of this discussion."

The dismissal cut deep. His behavior since tricking her into coming to England remained aloof. Why? They both knew he wasn't cold or cruel. She took a deep breath and her head spun. It made her pause, surprised how deep down her belief went.

"The O'Caseys did not kill your brother. My brothers are innocent. Simon, your grief is clouding your judgement. How many times must I tell you before you believe me?" He wasn't listening and her voice trailed to a faint whisper.

Simon's impassive expression showed no sign of compassion. Not a flicker. "Your silence is a welcome change, and much appreciated."

Frustration rippled through her. Her temper flashed. Thoughts of revenge filled his mind, and desperation clung to hope that she would find a way to breach his stubbornness. "Sure, and you'll get it as soon as you remember you have a duty to produce an heir. Or have you forgotten?"

Simon seemed not to hear, or perhaps if he did, just didn't care. Roanne detested the constant arguing. Oh sure, the O'Caseys were a garrulous lot. It was how they communicated, except that wasn't how she wanted to live her life with Simon, and that hurt.

"Don't lecture me about duty," he said at long last. "The earldom can revert to the crown for all I care."

She gasped in shock. What lord willingly gave up an ancestral home? "'Tis why you bar me from your bed?"

Glass crashed in the hallway. Both Simon and Roanne spun toward the sound. Roanne hoped the wind caused the accident, though she seriously doubted that was the cause. Servants saw and heard all that happened within the sprawling manor house. This argument would be no exception.

"Lower your voice," she said. "Our servants—"

"They can be damned, along with you, your family, and me," Simon interrupted, blue eyes glaring at her. "The whole world can be damned as far as I'm concerned."

It crossed her mind that Simon played this twisted game to constantly anger her, to keep her off-balance. And it was working. "Your actions condemn me to die after a year. Are you willing to have my death on your conscience?" Her heart thumped harder, similar to the racket children made when they raced inside the courtyard at Dundalk, dragging a stick behind them. "And my brothers will bear the responsibility with heavy hearts."

"Spare me your concerns. Frankly, I care nothing for those hooligans."

Frigid calm turned his voice icy. His close proximity showed the blue shadow of whiskers on his jaw, even though the fresh scent of soap rose from his skin as if his valet had just shaved him.

Tension became a palpable storm with tingling thunder, but cowering before her husband was not in Roanne's nature. She hadn't survived twelve years under Cromwell's tyrannical rule or in a household of overloud, overbearing men without developing inner strengths of her own. She'd show him her grit.

Her hands clenched at her sides. "If you are bent on revenge, make sure you accuse the right individual. My brothers told me they arrived the same day your brother was found injured. They heard the news in the first pub where they stopped."

"How very convenient. I am done here," Simon growled, walking away.

She followed on his heels. "I'm not. Damn your soul to hell. Turn around and face me."

Simon skidded to a stop. He whirled around. "I'll meet you there, m'dear."

"I know how you feel. If I thought you harmed one of my brothers, I would want vengeance, too. Let me help you find Hugh's true killer. How about a bargain?" she asked, standing midway in the hall. "I'll aid you in uncovering the culprit if you try to get me with child."

"Is that an admission that you know which brother pulled the trigger?"

Fearing for her brothers, her heart sank. "Nay. You deliberately twist my words. I have the utmost faith that my brothers are not murderers. Lock them up if you disbelieve me. Give me time and I will prove it to you, with or without your help."

He whirled around on polished boot heels, so quick she jumped back and lost her balance as her feet tangled together.

Simon grabbed her arm and saved her from a nasty fall.

Just as suddenly, he released her.

Roanne knew by the force of his gaze that Simon declined to heed a word she spoke. She tried to concentrate on the heat of his touch and failed. Real or imagined, enough scorn had laced his words to send a shudder down her spine. She never knew what to expect from him. His coldness broke her heart. Whatever fledgling feelings he whispered on their only night of wedded bliss, those feelings evaporated like a mist burned away by the sun.

Gone before they had a chance to grow into something beautiful.

Gone forever.

And gone with them was her chance to conceive a babe.

Roanne shoved aside regret churning in her belly.

Simon dropped his hold on her and stood glaring at her in disbelief. "You'd not protest if they rotted in a dungeon?"

Roanne refused to panic. Her fingers touched the smooth surface of parchment hidden within the pocket folds of her gown. Millie, the older woman hired as her maid, slipped her a message in Padraig's bold penmanship, a message that combined joy and fear into one emotional ball.

She dare not weaken now, especially since providing Simon with the idea of locking up her family before he killed one of them.

Chapter Ten

Simon glared at the brave redhead with the indomitable will. She reminded him of a storm at sea, one that refused to blow itself out. Today Roanne wore a gown finer than anything he'd seen her wear in Ireland. He remembered thinking how she deserved satins and silks and felt a twinge of pride to have his opinion validated.

But that wasn't enough. A coldness consumed him. "Your brothers don't frighten me. Rather, they should fear me," he said and stomped out of the room without allowing her a chance to respond and headed for the sanctuary of his library.

The patter of Roanne's steps chased after him. "Wait, my lord."

He whipped around. He wasn't willing to hear any more of his tempting wife's pleading. He told himself no amount of arguing would make him change his mind about her brothers, and the thought distressed him. "Stop embarrassing yourself. Cease dogging my footsteps."

Roanne shook her head, making flaming ringlets dance around her face. "Face me, then. Where is your honor? You must heed my pleas."

Whenever he found himself anywhere near his wife, his gaze focused on her mouth. Those well-defined lips hinted of kisses from an angel's mouth.

Every time he closed his eyes, he remembered the scent of her hair and the silky feel of her skin beneath his hands. One night in her arms and he could never forget her.

He suffered as no man. Abandoning his oath to never touch her, he drew Roanne against him and to his chagrin, their bodies molded into a perfect fit. Their eyes met in silent communication as he raised a hand, one finger stretching to trace the curve of her lips.

"Oh, Simon." Soft light gleamed in her eyes. "I vow you won't regret this. I'll do anything to make you happy. Anything."

He blew out a breath, and chose his words with deliberate intent. "Bring back the dead."

She stiffened in his arms. Color drained from her cheeks. "I-I cannot. Grief consumes you. For a man who mistreated you? You must let bygones be bygones."

He wanted to protest. Instead, he dropped his hands, experiencing a loss of epic portions at not touching her. He tried to relax and consider her feelings, but couldn't forget the obvious. "I freely admit many people harbored ill-will toward Hugh, but the O'Caseys had the best motive to seek his death."

Roanne pursed her lips at his claim. "Simon, we consummated our marriage. There can be no annulment. Accept it. We are one."

He stared at her, dumbfounded. "Surely, you jest. You make it sound as if I should just forget Hugh."

"That's grief talking. Of course, you'll always have him in your memories, but you have a new family. One that loves you. Or would, if you would let them do so. I confess at first about having doubts of my brothers' participation, but they swore to me that they weren't involved with your brother's death and I believe them."

Simon's brows furrowed. Trust Roanne to defend her brothers. He knew better than be pulled in by her sweet lies. "Talk is cheap, Roanne. Actions count. Every day I remind myself how beautiful you are…and what a deceitful family spawned you. A babe should be conceived out of love. To create something as wondrous as a child with you would be an admission that I harbor feelings for you, which I cannot. Dare not."

"I see," she whispered.

The little hitch of pain in her voice and flash of defeat that flew across her face slammed him with guilt.

Numerous times Simon had questioned his need for vengeance for a brother who hated him while growing up. He raked his fingers through his hair. Damn, Roanne was right. Hugh's treatment throughout their childhood had taught him to never hurt another without cause. So why punish Roanne? She was blameless.

Simon cringed. He physically desired her, but the idea of forgiving her brothers for Hugh's death chilled him. He held fast in his belief that the guilty deserved punishment. Nonetheless, words tumbled out of his mouth. "Set your mind at ease, m'dear. I have reconsidered your pleas. You'll receive the attention that is your due. Expect me in your chamber when the hour grows late."

She didn't react and that surprised him.

****

Roanne stood frozen while her spirits soared. At first when Simon promised to visit during the night, she suspected a trick. She gathered the hem of skirt and left him standing in the hallway.

All day long, hope had her wishing for nightfall. She went around the manor performing her duties. First, she checked with the gardener and inspected the gardens to see the progress herself. She followed up by writing the next menus for the cook.

A smile curled her lips the whole day. She found it impossible not to. Against her best efforts, she cared for Simon and the thought of him harboring a smidgeon of affection in return thrilled her.

Her breath caught. Did she care more for him than her family?

No. Impossible. That sounded like desperation talking.

It didn't matter what changed Simon's mind, only that he had. She sent a prayer of thanks to the Holy Mother for giving her the strength to persevere.

Millie, a large woman with frizzy graying hair that never stayed in place, lit the candles against the dark. When first engaged as her maid, the older Englishwoman had acted standoffish, cautious about entering her service, but soon warmed to her and became a confidant, almost the mother she lost years before.

That evening Roanne left the security of her favorite chair by the window in her bedchamber to stand in the middle of the room. She loved looking outside at the grounds, admiring the symmetry of trees and lawn. Only seeing her brothers riding up the circular drive would make the scene nicer.

"What was Simon like as a child?" she asked, more than a little curious.

"A good lad in my eyes. Industrious. Always

willing to lend a hand to anyone who needed it. I remember a time he worked from dawn to dusk when a tenant farmer broke his leg and couldn't farm his land. Tried to save the family, he did."

"What happened?"

"The old earl kicked the fellow off the property."

Roanne gasped and shifted her weight. "That's awful."

Millie nodded. "Young master had a terrible row with his lordship over it. He earned the loyalty of almost every servant and tenant at Hollyhock."

Roanne caught the reproach. "Not everyone?"

"I should not be talking about him." Millie busied herself straightening the coverlet. "You should ask him yourself."

"*Ack,* Millie, you know men. They aren't much talkers, especially when it comes to themselves."

"Aye, that's the God's truth." Millie inhaled a deep sigh. "I daresay he was lonely as a lad when it came to family. All he wanted was for them to notice him, perhaps offer him a kernel of love. He tried so hard to please them, only to face ridicule or punishment for wrongs not his doing."

Roanne's heart constricted at how the younger Simon must have suffered. "He mentioned his brother always pointed the blame at him for misdoings that he committed."

"Forgive me for saying so, milady.'Tis bad to speak ill of the dead, but Lord Hugh was rotten to the core. He was the oldest. He should have set a better example to follow. Alas, no, his jealously of young Lord Simon took over. He hated that folks adored him, and tried to get him in trouble at every turn. Lord

Simon deserved better. He only wanted to belong. And as a young lad he idolized Lord Hugh. Took him forever to see the ugly truth about his brother. 'Twas the reason he left Hollyhock. Even so, I can only imagine how hard it affected him to lose his only brother."

Insight into Simon's history did not absolve the problem. While her empathy grew, Roanne could not alter the past. All her attention must be focused on the future, a better one for all concerned.

She headed to the four-poster bed. She reclined on the thick, goose down mattress. The sides rose along her body to wrap against her. Roanne rested one arm on her flat stomach, the other draped across her brow. She drew a deep breath. So much was at stake. Everything had to be perfect for tonight.

"Sounds like you're pleased with his return," Roanne spoke with her eyes closed.

"Aye, that's the truth. Me and everyone hereabouts are happy to see him back. He's already visited every tenant, ordered wagons of building materials for much needed repairs, and is paying the tithe to the church for them."

Roanne offered a smile, pleased, yet not surprised to learn Simon had eased a few burdens for his tenants. "How do I look?" she asked Millie, battling vacillating emotions.

"Like a lamb to slaughter, or have you taken a fever?"

Roanne chuckled and rolled over on her side to prop her head with her hand. "I suppose the position's too obvious. This one is much better, I'm thinking."

Millie stared at Roanne with concern. "Are you tired? Do you wish me to continue lighting the wicks?"

Roanne shook her head. "Oh, Millie. A wondrous thing is happening tonight. Simon is a-visiting me."

This time the older woman snorted. "So I heard. And about time, I say."

Roanne twisted a loose curl on her finger that spilled over her shoulder. "I want to appear my best."

"All he has to do is keep his eyes open to see how lovely you are, child."

Roanne rolled onto her back and stretched her legs. She laid her hands at her sides. Too stiff. That position came across all wrong. "You always say the kindest things to make me feel better." Sitting up, Roanne hugged her knees to her chest. "I'm acting silly. I suppose it's probably unwise to flaunt myself. I should'na appear overly eager."

Her words brought a grin to the soft folds of Millie's pudgy face. "Always works with my Ben. 'Course I takes my loving whenever I can get it these days. Just remember a man likes to think 'tis his idea."

Roanne took the sage advice to heart. "Sure, and a wise woman lets her man take all the credit."

"That's the God's truth." Millie winked at Roanne. "Keep him off-balance, m'lady. His lordship ain't much different from other men. Least not as far as I can tell. Well, except a bit more intimidating and far more handsome. My Ben never knows what he wants or what he's feeling. That is, until I tell him. I think inside their thick skulls, all men are the same."

A surge of confidence rushed through Roanne. "Wiser words have never been spoken."

For a while, the maid shuffled about the room, lighting candles and tidying up. "Trust your instincts, m'lady. If you think the chair best, try it again and see."

"*Ack*, you may be right, Millie. In all honesty, I would rather not look like I'm trying to seduce him…even if I be doing so."

When Millie nodded, Roanne returned to the upholstered chair. She tried various positions—sitting stiff and straight, hunching next—groaning with disapproval at each one. "This isn't working. Perchance, the bed is best."

She stood the exact moment a rap on the door sounded and Millie rushed to open it.

"My lord." Roanne shot Simon a look of interest and delight. "You're early."

"Should I return later?" he asked with the hint of teasing in his voice that she'd heard often in Eire.

He carried a silver tray with a decanter of burgundy wine and two stemmed glasses. She hid a smile, because in spite of all her hopes, she had half feared he might not show. To be wrong felt wonderful. She sputtered, remembering what one of Rory's many ladies had done to keep his attention. She batted her thick lashes in perfect mimicry. "Nay, nay. Enter and be welcome."

Millie stood at the door, silent and watching, shaking her head.

"Leave us, Millie," Simon said, "I shall tend to the rest of my lady's needs for the evening."

"Aye, your lordship." The maid bowed her head, exiting quickly, drawing the door closed with a click.

Simon strode across the room and set the tray on a small table. He turned toward her, and grinned. Happiness flared in Roanne like a stoked fire.

"You look lovely, and I thought we could raise a

toast before we become…engaged," Simon said.

Once again his kindness touched her. He amazed her with it. "How thoughtful, my lord."

He picked up an empty goblet in one hand and the decanter in the other to pour. When he handed her the first glass, a trick of candlelight reflected off the cut glass to sparkle as though he held a fistful of stars. Their fingers touched and sparks exploded in her belly.

"Much appreciated." She took a sip. Cool liquid slipped down her throat. The vintage tasted like the best Hollyhock's cellar offered.

"I hope you are pleased." Simon dropped into the chair by the window where a full moon, a harvest moon—a lover's moon rose in all its glory. Even now, wispy clouds, edges tinted a vibrant pink in the sunset, skittered across the moon as an evening wind shoved them across the sky. Blustery gusts bent treetops to the snapping point.

She remained where she stood. "Immensely. 'Tis very generous of you."

Outside, a blast of wind rattled the pane of glass with a show of force. A shiver rippled down Roanne's spine. A warning? She wasn't superstitious. Not really. Oh, she believed in the prophecy, but that was different. It was fact.

"Are you comfortable, my lord?" she asked.

"I will be shortly," he answered with an evocative grin gracing his handsome face. "Though 'twill go much faster if you aid me."

"Aid you?"

He set his drink down on the table with a dull clatter of crystal on wood, stood, and slipped off his coat. With nimble fingers, he undid the buttons of his silk waistcoat. She counted the buttons—eleven in all. One for each of her brothers. She shook the thought away. The loose-fitting shirt he exposed complimented his dark good looks and black hair. Simon generated a magnetism that made him more handsome, more appealing, and more desirable as never before.

Something else, too. She tried to control her emotions, but shivered with anticipation, eager to please him. She was thrilled to once again feel the strength of his hard-muscled arms wrap around her. Her heart beat a little louder.

Simon's gaze swept over her, his blue eyes caressing her.

A long silence twisted and stretched between them.

Dare she be the aggressor? He'd already implied as much moments ago. She slanted a glance at him, trying to gauge his reaction beforehand. Nothing on his face gave away his state of mind. She admitted to knowing the shape of his powerful body. And what a magnificent one it was.

"Aye, aid me," he repeated. "You must come closer."

Roanne's breath gushed out in short, fast bursts. "What would you have me do?"

"You can begin by sitting on my lap," he told her, claiming the upholstered chair by the window that she favored.

The request seemed harmless enough.

Or so she told herself.

The instant she sat, his strong hands caught her around the waist. Through layers of petticoats, the heat of muscular thighs seared her backside. Her hand shook while she held her glass. She squirmed ever so little.

Simon grinned at her. "Nervous?"

"Aye, a bit." She returned a smile of her own.

"Of me?"

They were beginning anew. She declined to lie. "A little."

A soft chuckle arose, then he retrieved his wine to take a sip. "Fair enough. I deserve that."

Roanne peered over the rim of her glass as she swallowed of the velvety elixir. "I meant no insult."

"None taken."

A sigh of excitement slipped from between her lips and she handed him her wine to set on the table. With her hands free, she encircled his shoulders and closed her eyes. His manly scent swamped her senses. She settled her mouth over his, savoring the taste of wine on his lips with her tongue while he sat motionless. The shock of that first contact proved more exciting than she remembered. Her head spun as if the world tilted on its axis.

Simon shifted. For an instant, worry of him leaving ballooned within her. Roanne leaned into him, her hands tightening on his wide shoulders as if her meager weight could hold him down. He stiffened under the slight pressure, then tense muscles relaxed. She caressed his mouth with whisper-soft kisses.

She released another sigh when his arms traveled up her back, one hand cupping her head and the other pulling her hard against him. The combination of pressure and heat sent waves of awareness though her body. She felt herself melting like the candles in the room.

When his fingers probed her bodice, she arched up, offering herself, her heart, and her love. Warm breath spread over her skin like a blanket.

Simon was reclaiming her as his wife, and she was more than willing to surrender. She clung to his neck, a sense of well-being filling her that defied description.

"Simon," she managed to utter.

"Aye, m'dear?"

"I…" was all she could say when his palm cupped her breasts and his fingers lightly squeezed her nipple before sweeping her into his arms and carrying her to the bed. He set her down in the middle and sat on the edge of the mattress, causing her to roll toward him.

He sat and stared at her. "Tell me what you want."

"You," she whispered, desperate with need.

Grinning, he stripped away her clothes until she lay naked beneath his gaze. "Lord, you're beautiful. So beautiful."

No grain of shame existed within her and she let him look. His dark blue eyes reminded her of Dundalk Bay on a sunny day. Every fiber of her being burned with an unconsumed fire. Only the contact of skin against skin would satisfy her. She reached for the ties on the neckband of his cambric shirt.

Simon trapped her hands between his larger ones. "Go easy, m'dear. Slow and easy. I want you to remember this night for a long while."

"Not too slow, I'm hoping."

"Eager, are you? What would you have me do? Mayhap this…" His fingers moved to her nipple. "Or this…"

****

The small groan of pleasure coming from Roanne induced a soft chuckle from Simon. He inhaled a deep breath, catching the fragrance of orange and clove.

Other times the tangy scent had teased him as he moved about Hollyhock. How like his wife to prefer unique instead of the heavy cloying floral fragrance women of Charles II's court favored.

This night he knew he played with fire as he pressed tiny kisses to every inch of her velvety skin. His hands followed the path of his lips over her body. She moaned with pleasure. It amazed him what a passionate creature he had married.

Somewhere deep inside, her behavior pleased him. He could have enjoyed being married to the spirited, brazen woman for the rest of his life.

He bent his head to brush his lips against her raised nipple. "You feel like warm silk."

"More like scratchy wool."

"You don't have the same appreciation. I say rich, warm silk that makes a man ache to hold it close, smell it, taste it, and caress it with his fingers, his lips. To press his body against the smooth texture." He adjusted his arms tighter. "Now, hush, madam wife."

"It isn't that easy, my lord. I can't help myself. You make me feel strange and wonderful at the same time."

Simon laughed low. Every time she spoke, guilt rose within him. She was a true innocent. He had to constantly remind himself that she needed to be taught a lesson. "Then I'll just have to kiss you into silence." He lowered his head to claim her lips.

Her hands attacked his clothing, and in spite of his resolve to withhold his feelings, he approved of her eagerness. After tonight, though, there would be no doubt in either of their minds who was in control.

His musings ended the instant their bare skin

touched. His body burned against the cool fire of her skin. A savage shudder of yearning rocked him to the core. If he were honest, he reveled in touching her sweet curves, making love to her. When his fingers found the moist slickness of her femininity, he knew she was ready to accept him.

Poised above her, he paused. "Roanne, open your eyes. I want you to look at me when we become one."

Complying, she did, and he found her pupils dilated with passion. His gaze locked on hers and he plunged deep inside her. Instantly, familiarity and oneness filled him like a ship returning to its home port.

He'd forgotten how well they fit together.

No woman made him feel so powerful.

Or powerless.

Blood roared in his ears. His hips dipped and rose in a cadence that left him breathless. A mad logic screamed for him to stop. His plan, part pleasure, part vengeance, suddenly became easier said than done. The rhythm of their movements intoxicated him. His body demanded he stay buried deep within her. The roar in his ears was the sound of his beating heart as the flames of passion labored for completion. If he continued…

"No!" he cried out, abruptly withdrawing.

Roanne struggled to her elbows. "What's wrong? Why did you stop? I thought…you said…"

"I vowed to come to your chamber. That is all. I have kept my word."

The bewilderment faded from Roanne's amber-beryl eyes, then understanding dawned. "You promised."

"No promise, m'dear. Consider this a lesson."

"Lesson?" She sneered at him with loathing. "By

giving me only half of what I want. I need your seed."

"I'll beget no child on you." He wondered who he punished more-her or himself.

Her complexion paled. "You hate me so much?"

"Lord, no." The instant the words escaped, he realized the truth and his mistake. Grief and a heart-wrenching expression danced across Roanne's face so fast he nearly changed his mind.

"Then why?" she asked. "Why be doing this? You place my life in jeopardy. Even your own birthright. All because of a delusion."

"No delusion, m'dear, but murder." Simon's head spun with dizziness. "No wonder England is unable to subdue the fires of rebellion in Ireland. The Irish are the most mutinous lot I've ever met." A sigh escaped before he regained control of his emotions. "Your brothers are the ones who erred. That trio should have hung the instant I learned of Hugh's death. Tis what they deserve."

Roanne sat up, defiance returning to her face. "What proof d'you have of them committing this crime?"

"It's out there. All I have to do is find it." Simon rolled out of bed to reach for his breeches. He wrenched them on. "Think on it. They murdered a lord of the realm. A hanging offense."

All color drained from her lovely face. *Please, God, help him through this fiasco.* He didn't bother to fasten the buttons on the waistband. He grabbed his other clothes off the floor and stomped to the door.

Call him a dunce. It had been a mistake for him to come. He should never have set a foot into Roanne's chamber. Now, the painful throbbing of his manhood

177

reminded him who he really punished with his ill-conceived idea.

And deep down he knew he couldn't help himself. He would return. Again. And again.

His fingers squeezed the knob, twisting slowly, only to glance over his shoulder when Roanne leaped out of the bed to don her chemise and cover her nudity. She raced to a table with toiletry bottles spread over the top in a haphazard order. The disorder reminded him of her desk in the solar. She wrenched open a drawer.

"This will put an end to your cruelty." She waved parchment in the air.

Admiration welled up inside him at her spirit, but he refused to confess the admission. His gaze followed the movement of the crumbled paper. "A piece of paper?"

"Aye. 'Tis from Padraig."

He frowned. "How…"

"*Ack*, I know about withholding my correspondence. But know you now, the O'Caseys are a-coming."

Simon crossed the room in a flash. He never expected Padraig to make preparations so fast. Now, he needed to act. His grandfather had disbanded their private defense force two generations back. The O'Caseys were his enemy. Since Charles had forgiven him for his disobedience, perhaps the king would lend him some soldiers. They'd exchanged correspondence since his return to England. He would send a letter right off. Or maybe he wouldn't.

"Good! About time." The surprise that leapt on her face was worth the revelation. "I was beginning to think they were cowards and had a change of heart."

Roanne opened her mouth to protest, then snapped it shut. Her tangled mass of fiery locks hung in long waves. The glow of their partial lovemaking heightened her porcelain complexion and beneath her chemise the slender contours of her body drove him crazy.

Damnation. He banished the traitorous thoughts to the farthest reaches of his mind, only to realize his attention focused on the rise and fall of her breasts.

Momentarily flummoxed, he snapped, "Don't push me, madam. Which of your accursed brothers are coming? I have the right to know how many guests to expect."

She raised her hand as though to count. "Why, all of them, of course."

Chapter Eleven

Long after morning sunshine spread across an azure sky, Simon jerked awake at the strangled cry of a woman. He shot upright. Male voices boomed in the lower reaches of the manor. The stomping of numerous feet reminded him of a ship being boarded by pirates. His every muscle tensed.

Hollyhock was under attack.

Pure instinct propelled him forward. He wasn't a man to let brigand or noble menace him or his property. He grabbed a sword and dashed out of his chamber.

He charged down the hallway to Roanne's room, his mind full of worry for her.

Empty. She'd been abducted.

A wordless cry of anguish ripped from his throat. *Roanne!* Had the shout that woke him come from her? Was she trying to warn him?

He flew down the stairs two at a time on bare feet, his attention concentrated on finding his wife and defending his home. He'd seen his share of brawls, fought pirates, even a discreet skirmish or two with Ironsides to put Charles II back on the throne, but those times meant nil to him at the moment. Roanne's safety became paramount.

Simon's stomach clenched until the croaking voice of Titus, his elderly butler, spilled out of the room originally part of the great hall when Hollyhock was first built. An upsurge of relief so warm, so immediate, hit him with the force of a gale wind, and he stumbled on the bottom step.

Regaining his footing, he stole across the entry. A chill of iron resolve tore through him. He pressed his spine against a chilled wall to swallow deep breaths and collect his thoughts. In spite of the morning chill, sweat beaded on his brow and rolled into his eyes.

Every muscle between his shoulder blades stiffened. An oath slipped from his lips upon hearing howls of jubilation merging, making it impossible to identify the number of invaders. Did the fools think Hollyhock offered an easy victory? They'd pay for their mistake.

He leaped into the room converted to a modern parlor, ready for a fight, his sword arched high over his head.

Absolute silence greeted him.

A group of nearly a dozen men stared at him in varying degrees of shock. In slow degrees, silly-assed grins and smiles greeted him and grew bigger, one by one.

Simon faced not outlaws, but in-laws. He couldn't decide which was worse.

"'Tis a fine greeting to give weary travelers. That old pisspot wasn't going to admit us," said the closest O'Casey, pointing to the butler.

"Mother of God!" His wife raked him with her gaze, hands on her hips. "You're naked! Cover yourself."

Before Simon could reply, Roanne threw a lap blanket in his face. She left him little option except to knot the blanket around his hips. "What did you expect when awakened to this ruckus? I came as fast as possible. Furthermore, this is how most men prefer to sleep. They find nakedness quite comfortable."

Several O'Caseys nodded in agreement.

Roanne whirled around as though disgusted. The more Simon stared at the back of her head where a mass of fiery curls gave her head a shiny halo, and he inhaled citrusy orange and spicy clove, the faster his heart beat. She filled his senses as much as the potent fragrances filled his nose. The desire to touch her, to confirm for himself that her skin still contained the luxurious feel of silk increased.

And just as suddenly, he recoiled in exasperation.

"'Tis a trap. You must leave," Roanne warned her brothers. "He believes an O'Casey killed his brother."

Denials erupted from every corner of the room.

Padraig held up his hand. "Sweet Jesus, the responsibility is ours."

"I knew it. Sneaking O'Caseys," Simon snarled their name as a curse in the back of his throat. "I recognize a confession when I hear one."

Padraig turned to face him. "Not of your brother's death. Nay. Nay. We be innocent of that crime and I refuse to waste my breath defending ourselves. Nonetheless, we fell for your ruse. Gullible we were, but since we're here, we might as well make the best of it and prove you wrong."

"Aye, a good idea," said another big O'Casey Simon recalled only seeing once before-Sean the Second-sprawled in an upholstered armchair.

Padraig shook his head. "This be the way you make relatives feel welcome, *a chara*. Are we not friends?"

"A dangerous assumption," Simon muttered. He knew any man with a smidgeon of intelligence would fear for his life at the coldness in his tone. He hoped the O'Caseys did.

Brian dropped to the floor and crossed his legs. "If not invited for a celebration, what then?"

"Aye." Padraig stepped forward to take control. "Faith, we hied ourselves over the sea to England as soon as we put our affairs in order."

Roanne's amber and beryl colored eyes blinked in astonishment. "Are you all deaf? He means to hang whoever killed his brother."

"He cannot keep us here against our will," the O'Casey leader said in a calm voice. "We outnumber him."

Simon wasn't in the mood to hear bragging. "I have an army of servants to do my bidding and His Majesty will lend me soldiers, if I ask. I'll find you, no matter where you hide. You cannot escape."

Titus coughed beside Simon. "Shall I summon help to evict these ruffians?"

"Not yet," he replied, positive force wasn't necessary. *Yet.* "Though actual clothing would be welcome."

"But, my lord…"

Simon refused to hear any objection. "No one is being evicted. These men are my lady's relatives."

Titus looked back at Roanne for a second, shamefaced. "Forgive me, my lord. I had me doubts."

Simon's stomach clenched. Poor Titus. "'Tis all right. I'm sure they've endured worse receptions. Now, my clothes."

"Hurry, Titus," Roanne encouraged the elderly

butler, kind to every servant. "We wouldn't want his lordship to catch a fever."

Simon didn't understand the tone in his wife's voice. The concern insinuated far more than anger for his lack of attire. Why? He let his gaze follow hers, only to discover the reason. A little maid stood gaping open-mouthed at him. Roanne's behavior smacked of jealousy.

A most interesting discovery.

A familiar baritone cut his mulling over the situation short. "'Tis a crying shame, if you ask me. Even though you deprive the world of a fine, bragging sight."

Simon turned toward the speaker and almost felt a twinge of friendship. Rory. A twinkle lit his blue-green eyes and a grin lifted the corners of the tall Irishman's mouth.

"Not another word about my appearance or I'll put my fist into your mouth," Simon replied, fighting back his own amusement.

Rory only grinned. "Faith, I'd much rather arm wrestle. You're already one up on me. Another would give me a chance to even the score."

"Drop him, Rory. If you don't, I will." Murdock scowled. "Only respect for Roanne keeps me from removing your head from your shoulders, Sassenach. As far as I'm concerned, 'twas a mistake to bind her to the likes of you."

"For once I whole-heartedly agree with you, Murdock," Simon said. He could easily do without the argumentative O'Casey in his life.

"Progress, I'm hearing," Padraig said, his expression grave. "Long overdue. The prophecy is all that matters."

Simon's blood ran cold. He clenched his fists together as anger surged anew to force its way into his mind. "The clan O'Caseys' prophecy is Irish nonsense. If that's all you can talk about, just turn over the man or men responsible for Hugh's death and begone."

Gasps exploded in the parlor. Outraged O'Caseys surged forward.

"Hold, lads." Deep crows' feet formed at the corners of Padraig's eyes. He turned to face Simon. "I thought you had more sense than to falsely accuse innocents of a wrongdoing."

"You tell him, Padraig," sneered Murdock.

"My lord, please," Roanne said softly. "Heed Padraig. Give him a chance to speak."

"Mayhap you should talk to your sister first," Simon said. He glanced at the door, wondering where Titus was with his clothing. "I wager she'll be only too happy to explain how obstinate I am. It comes from being the second son for so many years. Though the O'Caseys' changed that fact. Now, I do what I want, not what others command. You thrust your sister into my care. That is where she will remain until I say otherwise."

"She be our sister first, last, and always," Murdock ground out. "No piss-faced Englishman is going to scare us away with threats. We won't be leaving until we be assured of her welfare."

"Why would I mistreat any woman, especially my wife?"

"You're English, aren't you?" Murdock shot back.

Damn the O'Caseys. Damn Roanne. Truth be told, with the exception of Murdock, none of the O'Caseys struck him as the murdering sort. And he sincerely believed the big Irishman was full of hot air rather than evil. Of course, that didn't mean one of the trio wouldn't have killed Hugh to fulfill their prophecy. Why must he be saddled with them?

And yet…

He had no choice. He'd trapped himself. Liking these Irishmen didn't mean he believed them. He'd invited them to Hollyhock. Apparently, they'd taken him at his word and here they were—unwelcomed guests, but guests, nonetheless. He would just have to keep in mind these people weren't to be trusted. Not ever.

Sean the Third and Sean the Second wended their way across the room.

The Second won the short race. "Well, has he visited your chamber since he brought you here? Tis not a question we ask lightly."

Roanne's gaze darted to him. Simon held his breath.

"Aye, he has," she whispered.

But Simon heard the lie neatly enfolded within the truth. They had consummated their marriage in Ireland, but he hadn't really done so since returning to Hollyhock. He decided not to refute her, at least not at the moment, and walked over to wrap his arm around her waist.

****

Roanne slapped her hand over her mouth, fuming at her brothers haphazardly lounging in the parlor. It was all she could do to just breathe, with the heat of Simon's naked side pressed against her. He teased and tormented her in so many ways.

While thrilled to see her brothers face-to-face, she couldn't believe she'd been dishonest with her family. It must have been desperation born of guilt. She would have to tell them the truth, eventually.

She convinced herself to do so later because Simon flaunted himself in front of her brothers. Where was Titus? He should be back by now. When he moved and one of his long legs peeked out from under the cover, she hissed. "Blessed Mary, keep yourself covered. An indecent spectacle you be making of yourself."

He leaned closer, setting his chin on her shoulder. "But, madam wife, you are doing such an excellent job of keeping my manhood from view of wandering gazes."

She stomped his bare foot.

Simon hobbled backward.

Both Seans burst out laughing.

The rest of her brothers stared at them with a mixture of amusement and curiosity. No help from that quarter. A sigh rushed from her mouth. They'd probably prefer to watch while Simon performed his husbandly duties like a prized stud.

So would she…but after last night, doubt ran high of that ever happening. She couldn't nullify the fear as a frisson of worry filled her mind.

Sunshine poured through mullioned windows.

Light emphasized the strong angles of Simon's face and clear down his muscular chest with a dusting of dark hair. A modicum of guilt assaulted her upon realizing he must be frozen to the bone with that meager covering around his waist. If Titus did not arrive soon, he would catch a chill.

"That's our Roanne, such a sweet gentle creature,"

said Brian, his voice heavy with irony.

Simon scowled at him, saying, "Churlish fishwives have better dispositions than your sister."

Roanne gasped. What an idiot. "Insults! You are nothing but an *amadan.*"

She wasn't being herself. Outspoken. Independent. Aye, those were part of her nature. But churlish? Nay, that wasn't her.

"Exchanging slurs will not change facts," Rory said, clearly trying to generate a breath of calm in the volatile situation. "It seems to me you are a man who has much to learn about the fairer sex and their ways. They like to be wooed with gentle words, and deeds of affection. Yet you've been wed to our sister these past two months and still haven't figured out that arguing accomplishes naught?"

"Perchance I misspoke," Simon said, not sounding the least bit apologetic.

At that moment, a breathless Titus hurried into the parlor and handed him a pile of neatly folded clothes. Her husband promptly turned his back to don his breeches and another shock knocked the breath out of her. A huge crucifix was tattooed on Simon's skin from his wide shoulders to the small of his back.

"You be full of surprises," Rory spoke before anyone else, curiosity thick in his tone.

Simon spun on bare feet. "What's that supposed to mean?"

"Since when do members of the aristocracy mark their skin?" Roanne questioned. She knew so little about the man she married. Would she ever truly know him?

Simon shrugged into a fine linen shirt with lawn

ruffles on his wrists that fluttered as he tucked the shirt into his breeches. "Oh, the crucifix. Personal safety. On the high seas minor infractions are harshly punished. Tattoos on the back are protection from being flogged. Or at least for a show of leniency when doling out lashes, so as not to deface the crucifix. Unfortunately, that didn't always work."

"Why not?" a curious O'Casey asked.

"Some captains just ordered something not tattooed flogged-buttock, legs."

"A fine tale, but Roanne's breeding is our main concern." Padraig stood in the center of the room to remind everyone in the room about the real purpose of their visit. "Is she or isn't she?"

"'Tis not the time to broach the matter," she said, seeing a familiar glower appear on her husband's face at the sensitive subject.

Padraig frowned. "Methinks I can guess. We have not arrived too late. There still is time."

"Time for what?" Simon demanded, standing straight after jamming on his boots.

Murdock pushed forward. "Let me make him manageable. I be dying for the chance."

Brian leaned forward in his chair. "First, we try to convince him with logic. If that fails, I'll lend you a hand with him."

"Come on," Simon taunted them. "One at a time or all together. Makes no difference to me. What say you, Padraig? You are in control of this motley crew."

Dread raced down Roanne's spine. "Stop it! Every one of you. You're grown men. Act like it."

Everyone in the parlor shot her a look of disbelief. Utter silence filled the room. An icy coldness chilled her bones. Legend said that sudden quiet in a group of talking people meant one of those present would die within a year. In this case, she knew exactly who that was...*her*.

"You know how it is with the lads." Sean the Third drew near her. "They love to argue, drink, and fight. And not necessarily in that order."

Roanne couldn't take it anymore. Making a decisive exit, she never heard Padraig's reply to Simon's challenge. She dashed to her bedchamber where she ripped off her gown and tossed on her riding habit. Why did Simon leave her so confused? It wasn't fair. She needed to clear her head and decided only fresh air would suffice.

She slipped out to the stables on the northern side of the manor. A boy ran around, trying to care for the O'Caseys' ponies.

Requesting a mount, he promptly led out a sleek bay mare fit for a queen. She'd ridden this particular mare a couple times. Time to become better acquainted. Still, Roanne understood the mare liked to gallop and once seated, she gave the horse her head.

Endless miles flew beneath shod hooves. She loved the feeling of the wind tugging at her hair, the way her body became one with the spirited mare. Riding eased the tightness cramping her shoulders and chest. By the time she reined the bay to a walk, a foamy sweat lathered the poor beast across the chest. A looming forest of evergreens surrounded them. Beneath the canopy of branches filtered sunlight reached the ground in uneven patches. Cool, moist air enveloped her and brought a peacefulness to her.

A gray squirrel chattered his objections at being

disturbed somewhere in the upper boughs. The bay snorted a weary breath.

Roanne glanced around with dazed eyes. It had been a mistake to leave without a chaperon accompanying her. She'd never ventured this far from the manor and to make matters worse, she was lost.

"A fine mess I've gotten us into," she said to her mount.

The mare neighed as though in agreement.

She spotted a winding animal trail and prodded the horse onto it. Any trail was better than wandering aimlessly. Even her horse didn't seem to know which direction the barn might be.

After a goodly while passed, she wondered if her company would be missed. Probably not. Her brothers could debate until blue in the face. And Simon appeared cut from the same cloth.

When the sun began to sink below the treetops, she knew nighttime would be upon her soon. Roanne itched to find her way home. She listened for the sound of tumbling water. If she could find a stream, it would lead her somewhere.

She rounded a bend and jerked her reins short at the familiar whoosh of a snare snapping shut. A split second later, the high-pitched squeal of an animal caught by surprise filled the woods. She recognized that sound and if the sudden hush falling over the land meant anything, so did the other inhabitants of the deep woods—a creature had met its doom.

A few meters away, a shallow-faced man with wispy white hair, dressed in well-mended clothes held together with more patches than she could count, limped out of hiding. He made a beeline for the trap marked with a tiny gray feather, bent over the snare, and lifted a dead rabbit free.

On impulse she called out, "Hello, there."

Startled, the man spun around, nearly losing his balance. His gaze darted for an avenue of escape. He started to hobble away.

"Stop!" she cried out, not knowing if he would obey, but felt a rush of gratitude when he did.

His aged face turned guarded. Roanne suspected any misstep on her part and the fellow would disappear into the towering trees faster than illusive fairy folk. She edged her mount forward, slow and careful.

He dropped his prize to the ground and stared at her with wide eyes. "Who are you?"

An honest question. Roanne didn't sense any urgency or imminent danger, but watched for any threat. In her mind, the man was simply trying to put meat on his table. She refused to fault him for that. Starvation had been a constant companion during Cromwell's occupation. For no reason other than spite, his soldiers set fields ablaze, trampled gardens, leaving misery and starvation behind.

"Someone lost," she said.

He peered at her. "Alone?"

"Not anymore," she said, smiling. "I found you, didn't I?"

His hard expression relaxed a bit and he bobbed his head. "Aye, you did. Although, if you came this far off the traveled path, you are lost. You're not from around here."

"Correct you be. I've recently moved into the area. My apologies. I be Ro...I mean Lady Kirkland. And you are?"

A short pause ensued. The man swept off his hat and clutched it to his chest. "Names are best left unsaid in these woods. I'll be on my way." He started to limp off in an uneven gait.

"Wait!" She pointed to the dead rabbit. "'Tis a shame to let good meat go to waste."

His gaze shot to the carcass. "That'd be poaching."

The hunger in the man's rheumy eyes brought tears to hers. The memory of her empty belly grumbling was a sound not easily forgotten and she refused to allow another being to experience the same fate if within her power to correct. "One little rabbit. Skinny, at that."

He shook his head as if he misunderstood her. "The last earl didn't hold with poachers. He hung 'em."

Roanne shuddered and offered a sincere smile. "Well, the last earl has gone to his heavenly bed. This is between you and me. I insist you take it for your table."

Appreciation flashed across his thin face and he licked his lips. The meager rabbit meant survival for him and his family.

A branch broke in the woods.

He twisted in that direction. "And you vouch for the new earl?"

Confused, Roanne recalled how Millie said Simon had provided much needed aid to his tenants, ordering building supplies to repair their homes and barns, and temporarily suspending the tithes. Instinct told her he was a fair man, even while biased toward her.

"No one can give assurances for another," she began, "but I won't tell a soul about what has passed here today, except to give you credit for leading me out of the woods."

Chapter Twelve

Simon almost missed being the black sheep of his family. In those days it gave him an excuse to do what he wanted, without giving a damn about what people thought of him or his behavior. At least that's what he told himself at the time.

He sat atop his stallion a few meters from where Roanne spoke with an elderly man, a peasant by his worn, faded clothes, and watched in silence. For once anger didn't fill him. He wasn't forced to display a coldness that twisted his gut. The scene piqued his interest and amused him. The way the fellow kept tossing covert glances around as though afraid of being caught, Simon would have wagered his last crown the man-far older since he'd last seen him-still poached for a living.

Now the fellow didn't know what to expect from the Irish beauty.

As it turned out, neither did Simon most of the time. He was drawn to Roanne. He swore his fascination with her neared an obsession.

She leaned over her bay. The outing had put a flush on her cheeks and long wisps of red hair escaped confinement to stream alongside her face in crimson waves. On rare occasions, he'd seen a setting sun turn the ocean the same color.

He'd considered himself a fortunate man to have

caressed that mass of silk, weighed the heaviness in his palm. He ached to rake his fingers through her hair, hold a fistful of it and kiss her.

Kiss her.

He rather liked kissing. Especially her. He'd learned a thousand ways to kiss a woman and enjoyed every single one. Any fool could poke a woman, but a kiss…that was another matter altogether. It took skill. It was intimate, and for the best enjoyment, mutual.

Damn. In spite of his best intentions, he wanted to kiss his wife.

It was probably because of the way she smiled at the old poacher, carefree and inviting. A tiny pinch constricted Simon's heart. Around himself, her mouth always seemed tightened with rage. Fury. Or despair. Even so, those full lips enticed him with the memory of when she graced him with smiles.

A noise so small he barely heard it encroached on his introspection. The poacher stepped closer and spoke softly.

She answered him and her answer made the fellow frown. Whatever the conversation, Simon doubted he would win. A second later, his wife held out her hand. The old poacher's frown deepened. He put his hat back on. Roanne wiggled her fingers, refusing to take no for an answer. With a sigh that reached all the way to where Simon hid, he watched the man hand the rabbit to her, accept a gloved hand and climb onto the back of the bay.

Roanne tied the rabbit to her saddle as a smile brightened her face.

Simon winced. While in Ireland he had managed to keep old wounds buried. Or so he thought. Now memories flooded his head, and with them the pain of loneliness returned. He didn't want to remember. Hated the easy comradery the O'Caseys partook with each other. The unity they shared. The way they trusted each other unconditionally.

He nudged the stallion forward to position himself on the trail so Roanne and the poacher would have to pass right in front of him.

Catching the stallion's scent, the mare nickered. His horse replied with his own soft call.

The poacher spotted him first and pointed at Simon. With the stiffness of an old man, he slid off the back of the mare.

Simon wondered if the man would flee. Keeping a stern expression on his face, he grabbed the bay's reins, and leaned in. He brushed Roanne's hair off her face, tipped her chin up to lock his gaze on hers.

"You shouldn't have left," he whispered softly.

While she held still, a quiver ran through her body before answering him. "I refused to stay and listen to you lie to my family."

"Not good enough. Come."

"What about my friend?" She tossed a glance at the fellow who looked poised to bolt.

Simon flicked a glance at the elderly man. "He's free to go his separate way. I'm sure he has his own business to attend to."

"Your lordship." The man swept off his hat a second time. "A pleasure to see you at Hollyhock once again."

Roanne twisted in her saddle to gawk at the poacher.

"'Tis good to be back," Simon said. "Come see me

some time."

The fellow approached from the side that kept Roanne between them. "The name's Langley. John Langley," he said in a low voice. "If you need anything, my lady, you have my word that I'll help. My word is my bond."

Simon groaned. At Hollyhock her very presence made the staff smile, and now in the midst of the woods, even John Langley fell victim to Roanne's charms. "She's my wife. I'll see to her safe return to Hollyhock."

"Aye, Lord Kirkland," the man said, standing firm.

It was small comfort the man recognized him. He had wondered if that would be the case. Decades had passed. Simon acknowledged the man with a nod, trying not to notice how Roanne untied the rabbit and let the animal drop to the ground for John to retrieve once they departed. "We'll return to the manor. There is much to do-the guilty to be revealed."

****

Roanne looked at Simon and her insides contracted. The intensity in his gaze rattled her, but she refused to expose her fear. Her mare sensed the tension and stomped her hooves in response. She patted the horse on the neck to reassure the animal, even as she clutched at the rosary that she'd tucked into her pocket for moral support. She took comfort from the beads warming. Simon's indifferent attitude stemmed from a contingent of O'Caseys' descending upon his home.

To argue was pointless. Still, she refused to buckle under his hard stare. She rejected the belief that her husband would punish an innocent without proper evidence. If she could convince him of their innocence, perhaps hope existed for them.

A gust of wind rustled the heavy branches over her head. Her gaze travelled around the copse of ash, birch, beech, and oak to settle on Simon when the dull thud of his horse being nudged in the sides broke her concentration. Mostly she let the mare find its way behind the stallion.

A rigid Simon sat in the saddle, and though in front of her, it was easy to imagine his expression—all dark and brooding. His anger stemmed from grief turned outward. Before he could heal, he needed to unlock his feelings and set them aside.

She sighed deeply and peered into the woods. "What happens now?"

"We return the Hollyhock."

"That's not what I meant."

"My brother will receive justice. Tell me who murdered him." He twisted in the saddle to face her, a false smile boring into her. "Or I'll take your suggestion and let yours rot in a dungeon."

Despite his smile, she swore pain laced his words. If he was, that encouraged her that she could make him see the error of his way. She stood her ground. "You wouldn't dare imprison my whole family."

"There is little I wouldn't dare. And I always mean what I say."

"If you do as you say, I'll never forgive you."

He issued a low scoff. "First, I must care."

"Harm one, and you'll bring down the wrath of my entire clan. O'Caseys stand together, forever. We always have, always will." Then an idea formed, one she should have thought of much sooner. "I know not all the laws, but if infertility is grounds for divorce, surely an unwilling spouse is a sin as well and cause for an annulment."

The path widened for Simon to rein his horse alongside hers. Her mare flattened her ears when the stallion turned his long neck toward her. The mare nipped at him. Her mount detected her unhappiness and took out her displeasure at the opposite sex.

"You mentioned a bargain," Simon said after a long pause. "What will you barter, dear wife?"

His question cut through Roanne like butter. A profound helplessness engulfed her. "'Tis a little late for that, I'm thinking. Unless you are tryin' to frighten me."

"Am I succeeding?"

She ignored the barb and marshalled her courage. No cowering for her. "Not near enough to make me change my mind. I plan to make inquiries. Many people do not know my identity. They might talk to a stranger. I can start with my new friend. He knows these woods. The wind might have whispered tidings that he's afraid to mention to the authorities."

"You'd trust the word of a poacher?"

So, Simon had known what John Langley's presence in the woods signified. Tears of gratitude leaped into her eyes that he allowed the poacher to go free. It proved he had a heart. "Why not? Clearly, the fellow was in need of nourishment. Being a thief doesn't make him a liar."

"Perception runs the world. It will win over reality every time. Which makes your logic difficult to grasp, much less understand."

Rather than argue, Roanne urged her horse into a trot. Darkness descended over the landscape. Stars twinkled overhead. An owl hooted. Wind ripping through the trees sounded like a person crying. For her? She imagined the fairies of this land were not so different than the fey of Eire and her impossible situation broke their hearts.

They entered the main road to Hollyhock. The manor house sat on a knoll on acres of cultivated land, a lavish garden and a deer park. Clearly, once fortified by a moat, the ditch had been filled in and now a long circular road with aged junipers stood sentry along its edges.

She glanced at Simon with surprise.

"You'd been going in circles," he said. "You were never really very far from the manor."

"I see that now. How long were you watching me?"

"Long enough." He paused. "I learned one needs to have a plan before launching an attack on an enemy in order to succeed."

"And you consider me an enemy?"

"Not necessarily you, madam wife."

In the silence that followed, iron-shod hooves struck pebbles as the two horses maneuvered over the well-traveled path.

"My family, then?" she finally asked.

"There's that bothersome perception again. But you are correct. And, in all fairness, you are involved."

"Me? Since when has anyone considered my feelings in this fiasco?" she asked, totally muddled by his reply. If only she knew the man better. She simply wouldn't be so confused.

"I halfway expect your brothers will try to murder me, then arrange another marriage for you. According to your prophecy there's still time to be rid of one husband and find another." His tone turned curt and harsh.

Thank the Lord she rode, otherwise her legs would have given out. "You don't know them. They are not murderers."

"So you keep saying, but I have no wish to sleep with one eye open for the rest of my life."

As they neared the front of Hollyhock, windows shimmered with candlelight from within. Large iron lanterns cast a glow on the road.

"Roanne! Kirkland!" Sean the Third called from the front steps. "I was just about to give up on the pair of you. Sure, and methought you craved privacy and might not return to a houseful of guests."

"Where is everyone?" Roanne dismounted and handed her mare's reins to a stable boy who rushed out of the darkness.

Sean cast a glance at Simon. "Sorry to say, Murdock, Rory, and Brian found your wine cellar. I suspect they'll crawl out in a day or so after they've drunk their fill."

Roanne sighed, hearing leather creak as Simon dismounted. "And the rest?" She looped her arm over her brother's for him to escort her inside.

"Padraig's composing a letter to Meagan, letting her know of our safe arrival. Sean the Second be catching a few winks. Not sure about Ian or Timothy."

Footfalls sounded behind them to inform her Simon followed. She turned to see him lean against the door jam, stripping off his gloves. He tossed them on the salver and aimed a dark glare at her capable of piercing solid stone.

"Do I tell him or do you?" he asked, stepping forward.

Roanne raised her chin. She'd had enough of this strange man who was her husband. He wasn't acting like the man she had wed. No, deep in her heart, the other man—the teasing one who secretly made her smile was the real Simon Lancaster, the real man—and the one she missed most. "There is no need. Nothing to tell."

"What's going on?" Sean the Third's gaze shot from one to the other.

"Nothing you need be concerned about," she denied, praying Simon would have the decency to remain silent.

A harsh laugh didn't offer much hope.

"You know women and their secrets," he finally said.

Sean the Third missed the tension sparking between them. "Secrets? Faith, I'm to guess? Roanne's breeding. What else could it be? Wait till I tell the others." He gave a whoop of joy and dashed off before either one could deny the assertion.

She halted in her tracks and collapsed to the floor. Ruined. "No... You misled him on purpose."

"Get up, Roanne. You don't want your brothers finding you this way. They'll think you're ill and be concerned."

She didn't stand. Couldn't. Tears ran down her face. Drained by constant arguments, exhausted from lack of sleep, the unpleasant feelings left her little hope.

Simon reached down and lifted her to her feet. He smelled of leather, horse, and the light hint of bay.

"Sure, and you did it on purpose," she sobbed,

angry to her bones.

"We all make choices we regret."

Did she hear an apology in his words? The thought cut through the fog enfolding her and she pushed past him.

In a flash, he caught her and held her fast. For a moment, one long agonizing moment, she swore sadness skidded across his face until the light in his eyes died. He guided her into the library where she caught the whiff of musty books lining three walls. A huge desk constructed of dark wood and clearly from an earlier century sat on a rose-colored rug. Velvet drapes obscured the view from a large window.

The instant the door closed, she slapped Simon.

A crimson imprint formed on his left cheek. Scowling, he covered the mark with his much larger hand. "I might have deserved that, but I suggest you not test me a second time."

Roanne bristled at the emotionless response despite her belly summersaulting on its own. "The devil you say. Giving false impression be as wicked as lying."

"I disagree. Foremost is finding—"

The library door banged open to cut Simon off. He spun around, standing in front of Roanne as though to protect her.

Her brothers, as many as could possibly fit, squeezed under the lintel.

"Is what Sean says true?" Padraig asked in an excited voice. "Roanne be carrying?"

"A miscommunication," Simon answered.

Roanne stood on her tiptoes to speak over his shoulder, trying to make her voice stronger. "I can explain."

The tension in the library unsettled her.

Padraig stepped into the room, followed by a silent crowd. "Now would be a good time."

All her brothers focused on her. She felt the weight of each and everyone's gaze weigh on her. Offering a remorseful smile, she made up a fib. "I took a tumble off my horse and must still be dazed. If Simon hadn't found me, I fear…"

"Faith, sister, take care of your precious self." Padraig grinned as he combed his fingers through graying hair that Roanne swore had turned grayer than the last time she'd seen him.

She tried to edge out the door, but not fast enough. Murdock pushed into the room, his angry voice demanding, "What's happening here?"

Roanne stopped in her tracks. She didn't care for her brother's tone. In spite of their quarrels, deserting Simon to fend for himself against her family was a coward's way out. And she wasn't a coward.

Simon cleared his throat. "What do you mean?"

"Look me in the eye, Sassenach," Murdock said. "She be crying. I see the tracks dried on her cheeks. Furthermore, I was coming from the cellar and heard her-clear. What did you do to me sister?"

"Your threats bore me. But if you insist, I demanded she confess which of you blokes killed my brother, but she refused to provide me with a name due to misplaced loyalty."

"Why browbeat her, in her delicate condition?" Padraig asked, his worried gaze darting between Simon and her.

Her husband took a step forward. "What would you do if someone killed one of your brothers?"

Roanne's mouth opened. Simon's accusation tore her in two. The air in the library pressed down on her chest, hot, suffocating. Taking a deep breath, she discovered she couldn't draw in enough air to fill her lungs.

The O'Casey's gaze snapped in her direction. "You didn't fall off your horse? For shame, Roanne, telling a falsehood and scaring us."

"I say we take Roanne home. Her babe can be born on Irish soil."

Roanne's heart melted a tiny bit at the familiar voice. Ian had spoken. The quiet one. He must be upset to speak out like that.

She straightened, determined to master her own fate. "No one is taking me anywhere."

"Calm yourself, sister," Padraig ordered. "Though I be wondering if you have thrown pebbles over the roof of the house."

The inquiry broke the tension.

A bitter laugh erupted from Simon. "I'm almost afraid to ask. Why would she do that?'"

"To help breed, of course," the O'Casey said with confidence. "I didn't get an answer to my initial question."

"I'm afraid your sister is the only one qualified to respond. Ask her, not me."

A growl came from the left. Clearly Murdock. "Let me at the Sassenach. A few knocks on his head and he'll tell us what we want to know."

"Leave him alone, you fool," Rory said, joining the conversation.

"'Tis better not to fight amongst ourselves." Sean the Third stood at Rory's side with Sean the Second.

The older man's hair was nearly the same shade of gray as Padraig's. "We've just arrived, and I've a mind to experience a bit of this country."

"Then, by all mean, leave," Simon said. "And take your brothers with you. Take them all. I can almost guarantee you'll have a fond experience. The people around Stafford are more than willing to extend kindness to strangers."

"*Ack*, first you invite us," the clan leader said. "Now you're trying to be rid of us. What a fickle fellow."

"As it's been pointed out to me, Padraig, a newly wedded man I am. Mayhap I prefer spending time with my lovely bride rather than her brothers." He winked at her.

Snickers rippled through the book-filled library.

Roanne swore he flirted with her. Why? Besides inappropriate timing, it made no sense. Nor did she believe Simon was a man to jest with an enemy. He was up to something. What? Now, she waited along with her brothers for an explanation.

Silence filled the library when Simon didn't elaborate.

"What have you to say for yourself, Sassenach," Murdock spoke first, shifting from one foot to the other with obvious impatience. "Unless you'd rather I beat it out of you."

Again, Murdock tried to intimidate. Roanne wished he would just stop. No doubt an impossibility. While confident a few opposed his views, she suspected if Simon attacked one, all would rise to the other's defense, even if wrong.

"Spare me further threats. I doubt you'd harm

me… at least not until the prophecy is fulfilled."

Simon had them there.

And, Roanne swore, he was perfectly aware of the fact.

"Don't push me," Murdock growled.

Simon's chin jutted. She'd seen that stubborn angle too often not to recognize it. Stepping forward to intercede, this time the air vanished from her chest.

The world went black.

****

Simon saw the color drain from Roanne's face. He leaped toward her in the blink of an eye and caught her before she hit the floor. Her body seemed hot, her face flushed.

"Roanne," he called his wife's name as if he controlled the power to bring her back to consciousness. Shame for his treatment of her nearly overwhelmed him, which caught him off guard. If something was the matter with her. He didn't want to think about it. He couldn't live without feeling her slender body against his or catching a trace of her scent as he went through the manor.

"What happened?" she asked in a voice barely louder than a whisper.

He carried her to a nearby sofa. "You fainted. You've had enough excitement for one day. I insist you retire to your room. I'll have a meal sent up to you."

She shook her head. "I'll not be ordered away while men discuss my fate."

"Obey your husband," Padraig said. "He has your best welfare at heart."

Simon didn't need the clan leader's help with his wife. He glared at the fellow, then his expression softened when he saw Roanne's complexion pale even more. For once he wanted her to listen to reason.

His heart skipped. She looked so pale, her amber-green eyes huge, haunted. He hated the thought of losing her.

A maid was summoned, and she led Roanne from the room.

As far as he was concerned, this Irish family caused the whole mess. Their belief in that silly prophecy had cost him his brother—a bad brother—but his nonetheless.

Blood was thicker than water.

To be fair, his brother's callous treatment had given him the backbone and determination to succeed. His sense of abandonment that he might not have been good enough had made him stronger.

Now, Simon stared at the Irishmen before him. Half appeared ready to kill him on the spot, and the other half looked ready to bore him to death with their protests of innocence. Either way, the outcome remained the same.

He didn't want them all dead. Just the guilty. Which one?

Sean the Third stuck close to Rory. Safety in numbers? The quiet one, Ian, spent most of his time outdoors. Was it for his own protection? The third member of group, Finn, was suspiciously absent. Had Padraig ordered him to stay behind because of guilt?

Which one killed his brother?

Was Roanne involved? How much did she know? Those questions consumed his every waking moment for the past weeks.

His men searched Stafford for clues. They'd

checked with the tenants, found no real tracks at the scene, and were now making inquiries about strangers being in the area. It took time and hard work to gather evidence.

What about Hugh's rifle? Had it been found and returned? He needed to examine it. To his astonishment, he realized he hadn't considered that fact sooner, and he blamed Roanne. She'd been too much of a distraction.

Simon eased into a chair and grinned at the O'Caseys watching him. "Guess there are some compensations for marrying into such a huge family," he said after a long silence.

"What's that?" Padraig asked.

He had them. He did. "I'll never have to worry about a child of mine not having enough uncles to look after them."

"Good enough," the O'Casey said. "Your answer passes."

Chapter Thirteen

When the O'Caseys dispersed to God knew where and left Simon alone, he welcomed the reprieve. When he spotted Titus pass in the hallway, Simon called out, "Was Hugh's flintlock recovered when he was brought back to the manor?"

A puzzled expression flashed on the butler's aged face. "Aye, my lord. I put it away myself."

"Have it fetched and brought to the library for me."

The hesitation and slight frown told Simon the man wondered why, but discipline kept him from inquiring. In the wait, Simon questioned his own motives. Did he really believe he would uncover evidence from the gun? Or was he grasping at straws?

It didn't matter.

A killer lurked out there somewhere and he vowed to catch the culprit.

A huff of umbrage interrupted his thoughts. He looked up to see Titus holding a flintlock, which from the short distance looked new.

"Thank you," he said. "That'll be all."

His initial assumption proved correct. The weapon dated no more than five years old. Definitely one of the newer breech-loading flintlocks. Hugh always did enjoy owning the latest technology. The barrel had a long thin mark down its side. A scratch. That seemed odd. Hugh preferred his possessions in perfect order.

What caused the scratch? Had the blemish occurred the day Hugh died?

Simon removed the screw plug from the bottom of the barrel, a design that allowed for easier loading compared to muzzle loading. He eyed down the metal cylinder. No blockage. No visible damage. The sporting rifle hadn't misfired.

Now what?

He heaved a sigh and sank into his chair. What really happened in Kirkland Woods on that fateful day? Simon assumed Hugh had been murdered, but could it have been an accident?

****

Roanne clutched her rosary after spending a long, sleepless night waiting to hear Simon's footfalls in the hall outside her bedchamber. All her prayers and waiting paid off in the wee hours of dawn when Simon's familiar gait echoed in the hallway.

She slipped out of bed and hurried on tiptoes to the door to yank it open.

Her husband's dark brows rose in surprise. "You should be asleep."

She snorted. "So should you. However, since you are awake, a moment of your time? This concerns us."

For the longest moment, Simon stared at her, then turned away.

Roanne straightened her shoulders and shouted at him, "You can spare me one moment. It be so little out of your life."

Stopping, he groaned. "Don't presume to know me. I was a privateer. Remember? A pirate in some people's view. Most consider me dangerous, and they would be accurate."

The damn man drove her nuts. No wonder she treated him with the same apathy that he used with her. "You don't frighten me."

"I should. Your thinking is flawed, and I mean to see it corrected." He gave her an intense stare and an odd, little laugh. "I daresay an evening celebration might be a good way to change your opinion. You'll be facing a roomful of English gentry. We're known for our overbearing manner. And many a lady has been crushed by a simple word placed in the right ear and you can trust me when I say, they'll be looking to find fault with you."

"If you're trying to frighten me, you have failed. The O'Caseys have had little to rejoice in our lives, but a celebration with an abundance of food and music is just the thing to make an Irishman happy."

"We'll see," he retorted. "'Tis time to invite the neighbors to rejoice over our nuptials. I should have introduced you sooner. An oversight on my part. With your brothers here, the time is upon us."

Simon was putting on airs. It made no sense. Was this the real man? If so, she didn't like him any better than the argumentative one, but played along. "Good news to my ears."

He quirked a dark brow. "A list of names will be provided and 'twill be your duty to send out invitations."

"As you wish," she replied. No need for him to know the prospect excited her. She'd already said enough. "Thank you for finally understanding."

"Don't be so sure, madam wife. You haven't met our neighbors. Being noble, some are quite boring. And some hold no fondness for me at all. Having an Irish wife and Irish relatives will only prove to them that they were correct in their assumption of me." He paused. "They might attend just to be insulting."

Her heart gave a quick shiver. His words threatened to dampen the tiny spark of happiness growing inside her. "A less than reassuring thought." Then her chin rose, and she said with the same aloofness he used in his tone, "However, being around you, I can assure you that I have learned to let insults roll off my back like a duck does water."

He aimed a bland look at her, appearing unbearably confident. "How reassuring? Do you also vouch for your brothers' behavior? I suspect one or two might not be as open-minded as you."

"O'Caseys are not ruffians. They have traversed halls far grander than these. They know how to behave in society," she defended her family. "When d'you wish to hold this grand celebration?"

"A week from Tuesday will do just fine. I'll send for my tailor to outfit your brothers and a seamstress to provide you with an appropriate gown."

She blinked at his sudden thoughtfulness. She could do this. After all, she'd handled large volumes of people before. Her concern centered around what to prepare for the feast. How finicky were English country nobles? Would they accept hearty Irish dishes? Or would those dishes offend them? "That should give me plenty of time to prepare. I'll do my utmost to please you."

Disbelief flashed across his face. "Don't bother."

Roanne sighed. One battle at a time. She suspected her husband hurt deep inside. He needed time and patience to heal. "Callousness doesn't suit you, Simon.

213

Methinks you'll regret this behavior."

"I very much doubt that."

So much for talking to him in a civil manner. Her temper flared. She would have to try harder. "Blessed Mary, blast you to hell, Simon Lancaster."

She slammed the door in his face. Damn her temper. She'd had a purpose for wishing to speak with him. And now lost the opportunity to mention her suspicions to him.

Her menses were late.

****

Simon stared at the door and frowned. He had hurt her. Deeply. Cruelly. And unjustly. Tears had glistened in his wife's uniquely colored eyes and he had only himself to blame. He felt like a scoundrel, if the ache inside him was any indication.

He had no business tormenting Roanne. She wasn't to blame. The more time he spent with her, the more positive he was of her innocence in the crime he accused her brothers of. His fingers covered the knob to her chamber and silently turned it.

Locked!

That did it. The fiery Irishwoman wasn't the only one with a temper. He shoved his shoulder against the door with all his might, and broke it open to step inside.

Roanne stood in the center of the chamber, cheeks flushing and eyes wide, her mass of fiery curls tumbling over her front. The backdrop of light shone through her chemise to silhouette her long shapely legs. For a moment he squeezed his eyes shut to end the temptation of pulling her onto his arms where he could rid her of the garment.

Thankfully, she had the common sense to back

away from him.

"Never bar your door from me again," he said.

Defiant, as usual, she snapped back, "Why not? You have no intention of visiting my bed."

"You don't know that."

"I hope you rot in hell without a drop of ale to quench your throat."

Why did she have to be so argumentative? It made him behave badly. "Do you mean Hell on earth or Hell? I want everything perfectly clear between us, dear wife."

"Isn't Hell a bit hot to visit regularly?" she asked.

"It can't be any worse than here—perchance better." He stalked out of her room and away from the tempting woman.

Perspiration beaded Simon's forehead. He dreaded facing the smug faces of the aristocracy, but inviting the locals seemed a rational answer when he suggested. He wasn't playing fair and he knew it. Each encounter with Roanne left him tempted to forego his vow of never touching her beautiful body. She'd seemed so vulnerable just now with her flaming hair loose around her shoulders, a vision that enticed him. No, he really hadn't been playing fair with her.

And that made him miserable.

****

Midday the following day, Roanne received a list of a dozen names. She devoted herself to the upcoming event and carefully penned invitations, sealing the flaps with a dollop of wax. Not in her wildest dreams had she expected Simon to introduce his new relatives to his neighbors and friends.

The speed she made ready for the guests surprised

her. Much of the credit belonged to Millie and Hollyhock's numerous and efficient staff.

Only one small matter required attendance-her brothers. They needed to understand she would tolerate no tomfooleries from them. They best be on good behavior for the upcoming event or they'd suffer her wrath.

No more racing down the stairway, sounding like stampeding horses to see who reached the dining room first.

No fighting.

No excessive drinking.

They were to act like gentlemen, even if it killed them.

The clan waited for her in the dining room, the only room with a table long enough to host them when she came downstairs.

"Sleep late, did you?" Sean the Third asked, his expression brightening with an easy smile she knew so well.

"My sleeping habits are none of your concern," she retorted, sharper than necessary, and took a seat at the table.

Brian was eating enough for four, a feat that always amazed her. Yet how else did he maintain his muscled hulk?

"You're our sister," Murdock said. "'Tis our right to know."

"Don't start on her," Padraig said from his chair. "You're hardly an impartial observer. After all, you'd rather be rid of the earl at almost any cost."

For once Murdock failed to respond with a bitter reply.

"No one will be rude to my husband," she cautioned her family. "I'll not have any of you causing nuisance with his guests. They'll not think the Irish are hooligans." She stared at each one, making sure she had their full attention. "This is Simon's home, and thus mine, too. Tis time to set a few rules for you to abide. No insults. No threats. As a matter of fact, best to heap praise upon him for wedding me."

"What?" several voices exclaimed in mock innocence.

Rory stood to face her. "You're taking away all our fun."

"Best you remember," she replied, vesting herself of the idea. "Afore Kirkland came along, I was fated to die."

"Faith, sister. Another lord would have been found," Brian said, his fork poised in front of his mouth.

Her fingers trailed across her belly. "You found Simon first."

"One can only wonder what brings on this display of concern, Roanne," Padraig said, watching her with an anxious expression.

"I have no idea. Nor will I have you...any of you...treat him without respect."

"Don't be getting your feathers ruffled." The clan leader handed a platter of eggs to Timothy.

Sean the Second and Third chuckled, oval faces bright.

Rory leaned against the far wall, munching on a thick slice of bacon.

Murdock's face suffused an angry red.

Brian pushed his empty plate away and grabbed a

winter apple to chew on.

Her brothers drove her mad. She loved them with her whole heart, but she'd never find a moment of peace with them around. Never have a chance to win her husband's affection.

Leaping off the chair, fists clenched at her sides, she declared, "Consider this your one and only warning. How can I make my husband look favorably on me if he believes one of you killed his brother?"

****

The night of the grand dinner arrived without undue fuss or turmoil. Roanne had gathered the army of servants to bring Hollyhock up to the proper standards and they had not disappointed. A massive evergreen and holly arrangement held a place of honor in the center of a round table in the middle of the foyer. Hired musicians practiced in the stately ballroom upstairs where guests would gather after the feast. The aroma of salmon, beef, and mutton being prepared by the manor's cook teased the collected guests' noses.

She had selected a gown of dark red chintz with Brussels lace, cut to display her figure and complexion to perfection. Even her brothers appeared garbed in new breeches and coats that flattered them, thanks to Simon's tailor. They stood around, pretending to be inconspicuous, a near impossibility for her rowdy family.

When an opening in the crowd occurred and Simon emerged, her heart cartwheeled at his dashing good looks, with a lacy cravat at his throat and wrists that contrasted with his smoldering expression. A long, fairly tight-fitting coat reached his knees and his breeches were decorated with ribbons at the knees.

Guests began arriving as dusk fell, appearing in carriages and on horseback.

"I am very glad you accepted our invitation, Lady Hartmon. I be delighted to meet you," Roanne greeted the woman in the entry. Millie, behind her, whispered each individual's name and title or station in society as they entered the manor. "Tonight would have been incomplete without your presence, your ladyship."

A mountain of a woman wielded a feathered fan. "You honor me. Would have come sooner if I'd known Kirkland had returned. Fellow's too wild for his own good. About time he got himself wed."

"I hope you still feel that way after you get to know me. I plan to make him very, very happy." Roanne stopped when Simon approached.

"Who are you talking about, madam wife?"

"Why you, of course, my lord. Everyone is dying to know how we met."

"Are they now?" Simon said. "More likely they're looking for gossip to carry back to town once they leave here."

Lady Hartmon fluttered her fan like a hummingbird. "I can tell you're from Ireland, m'dear. What part?"

Roanne hesitated a moment. Her husband's blue gaze dared her, and his snide smile made her all the more determined to make the ball a success. "Dundalk Bay."

"A free city is your ancestral home?"

Roanne hid her surprise of the woman's knowledge. No need to stir the gossip pot. After tonight, tongues would wag enough on their own. "Aye, since St. Patrick chased snakes from Ireland. And 'twill always hold a special place in my heart until the sea dries up and the wind blows away the dust."

A twinkle appeared in the woman's eye. "Being devoted to your native land is an admirable trait."

Roanne's chin came up. Then she remembered, best to play the simpering wife. "Hollyhock is my home now. My loyalty belongs to my husband and is his alone."

With a laugh, Lady Hartmon turned to Simon. "She doesn't fool me, Kirkland. Despite her best effort to make me believe she'll be a docile wife, the chit has a mind of her own. I say good for her and suspect she'll make you work hard for her devotion. Here's hoping she gives you a merry chase. That'll be an event I plan to enjoy watching."

Heat burned Roanne's cheeks. So much for fooling the aristocracy.

****

Simon chuckled and stepped to the elderly matron's side. "You never disappoint, my lady." He picked up her gloved hand and brought it to his lips. "Thank you," he murmured against the back of her hand. No matter what happened, he was glad this harridan put her stamp of approval on Roanne.

Guests continued to arrive. He remembered now why he didn't care for these functions-stuffy aristocrats always full of themselves.

If not for Roanne, he would have liked nothing better than slipping away. But she surprised him again. For someone who'd never entertained English society, Roanne excelled in the endeavor. He hadn't thought far enough ahead to consider how he would react if anyone of the nobility insulted his wife. All he knew was he would not tolerate her being hurt by anyone…but him.

Despite his vow to remain distant, something about Roanne called to him on a primal level, and the yearning unsettled him thoroughly. Every time he closed his eyes, the image of her golden-green eyes and sweet voice obsessed him. She'd taken over running the household with the skill of a chief mate. The servants gushed with praise for her. He'd seen her in the garden a few times with the head gardener and assumed she discussed plans to improve the grounds. The man had bobbed his head, smiling and nodding with approval.

He just had to remember he could not trust her.

Finding Hugh's killer and dispensing justice came before all else. Yet at the same time, he had never met such a compelling woman. She plundered his heart like a pirate after sunken treasure.

Next to arrive was Squire Matthews, whose only claim to fame was a distant relative who'd served a knight during the last crusades. A true snob, Matthews' beady eyes rounded into circles of shock at the O'Caseys. In his powdered wig and a simple coat-sleeve with the shirt puffed out to hide his bulging stomach, he resembled a glorified rooster, much like that pompous Irishman who had called on Roanne while he'd been there.

Alongside him stood a young woman twenty years his junior bedecked in a deep purple gown that contrasted with a creamy complexion and blonde coiffeur that needed no wig.

The woman, Simon noticed, stared back at the O'Caseys in wonder—Sean the Third in particular. The young Irishman did some hard looking himself.

"See there," Sean the Third swept up to announce

in a bold voice, "I be right about the English, lads. I told you we'd be welcome. Sure, and look at the lovely flower they brought to make us smile."

"Aye, you can look, runt. But don't be touching something that fair and pretty," Murdock warned alongside him.

Simon tensed. He hoped the unpredictable O'Caseys had enough sense to censure themselves and behave civilly.

Laughter from Rory made Simon eye the tall redhead. "That might be the way *you* woo a woman, Murdock, but I've a mind that action speaks louder than words." He followed Sean the Third, whose boots heels clicked as he strode across the foyer and extended a finely-hosed leg in a bow before the girl, whose cheeks blushed scarlet.

The squire inched closer to his companion. "What are you looking at?"

"Your sweet daughter," Sean the Third said, coming up and winking at the stunned lady. "Will you be making introductions, or should I be doing it myself?"

Another blush colored the lady's face. She held a fan with one of those perfumed gloves imported from France. As she fluttered the fan, the sharpness of Simon's nose picked up underlying body odors. Not from the O'Caseys or him. All had bathed beforehand.

Lowering her fan, she said, "I am Mrs. Matthews, the squire's wife."

Padraig stepped forward, scowling at his family. "Forgive me brothers for embarrassing the poor, wee thing, Squire. They'll not bother you or your wife again."

Simon almost thanked his oldest brother-in-law. In spite of their differences, both simply desired harmony within their domiciles.

A sudden commotion at the door directed everyone's attention toward it. His childhood friend, Addison Humphrey, Duke of Denton and his younger sister, Lady D, were handing their cloaks to Titus. Fond memories of playing hide and seek and getting into trouble while growing up rushed to the forefront of his mind. The pair had defied his father and befriended him. To Simon's delight, because of Denton's higher rank, his father was at a loss to control or punish the brother and sister. How he'd missed them. He'd been at sea when Lady D wed, but rumor claimed she'd returned without explanation.

Simon started forward, eager to catch up on old times.

When Addison spotted him, he waved across the wide expanse of the foyer and took his sister by the arm to lead her forward.

A male voice bellowed over the din of voices.

"Dorinda!"

Chapter Fourteen

Roanne recognized Murdock's stunned cry and whirled around from speaking with a servant to spy her huge brother rushing forward with the strength of a charging bull, knocking new arrivals aside like chickens in a barnyard in his eagerness to reach the entry.

A dead woman had walked into Hollyhock.

Roanne wasn't exaggerating. She had to see it with her own eyes to believe it. Dorinda was alive. All of County Louth assumed the brown-haired woman had drowned, committing suicide to be free of her husband's tyranny.

And Murdock loved her. It had taken Roanne a while to make the connection. Her family had been blind to the relationship between the love-struck couple and she'd vowed to never reveal their secret. As far as she was concerned, it was no one else's concern.

Because Dorinda had been wed to another—Sir Percy.

A touch at her elbow broke her concentration.

Simon gripped her arm. "I don't know what's happening, but let's intercede before your brother starts a feud with my best friend's family."

Roanne couldn't agree more. Especially since she was positive Dorinda had a very interesting tale to spin, and she wanted to hear every single word from beginning to end.

Murdock reached the couple first. Joy and disbelief enveloped his broad face as he grabbed the petite woman at the waist, lifted her into the air, and spun her around. The happy reunion meant the world to Roanne and she tried not to laugh.

Dorinda clung to Murdock, crying giant tears and laughing at the same time.

His Grace's golden-brown eyes looked on with amused interest, but he did not protest the manhandling of his sister or take a step to interfere.

"Put me down, you fool," Dorinda said, without any real bite behind her statement. "What will people say?"

Murdock complied, his massive hands remaining on her shoulders as if afraid she might disappear. "I don't care what others think. Blessed Mary. I can't believe you're alive. What happened? Where have you been?"

"I'm sorry, my love. Fear kept me from telling you my plans. I—"

Murdock didn't hide his quick sadness before speaking. "Ye had nothing to fear. Not from me."

Dorinda touched his chest. "I know, Murdock. But I did what I thought was best for all parties concerned."

Before anyone else could speak Simon nodded toward the hallway. "Shall we all retire into the library? People are starting to gawk at us, and I suspect this tale requires privacy."

"Let me speak with Murdock alone," Dorinda said before tossing a beseeching look at her brother. "We'll not be long. He deserves to hear the whole truth first."

"Fair enough. Let them have their privacy." Denton's expression softened and he showed a slightly crooked grin. "We'll wait for you to join us in the library."

The tall duke made sense. By the look of affection he shot in his sister's direction, the man considered her welfare before what the gossipmongers would say. Roanne hadn't met him until this very moment. Instinct told her he was a rational man. Obviously, the man knew more about the situation than they did.

She accepted her husband's arm when he held it out for her. Nearly as one, the O'Caseys, Lord Denton and they flowed down the hallway to squeeze into the library. Simon led her to the divan that faced the fireplace and hovered nearby.

A buzz permeated the room loud enough to drown out the sound of crackling wood within the hearth. Roanne could only guess at the speculation everyone imagined.

"You know what's going on," Simon said to Denton. "What is it?"

The duke shook his head. "Wait for Dorinda."

Roanne remained quiet. Clearly, the duke believed it was Dorinda's tale to relay. Minutes ticked by before Murdock and Dorinda entered arm-in-arm. He led her to the divan. Roanne offered a smile and received one in return as the golden-eyed woman took a seat beside her.

Lord Denton and Simon remained standing next to each other. The rest of her family spaced themselves throughout the library. They reminded Roanne of a flock of buzzards circling for an opportunity to descend and scoop up a morsel.

A flicker of sadness flashed in Dorinda's eyes. She squeezed them shut for a moment, then blinked them open to look at each person in the room. "I suppose I should begin."

"Take your time," Murdock said with more patience than Roanne had ever heard him utter. "If this is hard for you, I can tell them."

"I can do it," Dorinda responded. "It's best coming from me. I can answer questions."

Roanne patted her hand. "No one wants to make you feel uncomfortable."

"My thanks," Dorinda said, then exhaled a deep sigh as she glanced at Murdock. "I had to disappear. A drowning accident seemed the best way to achieve that- no body to recover, only a capsized boat. People would draw their own conclusions."

"Most thought you committed suicide," Roanne said.

"Good. 'Tis what I wanted." Dorinda kept her gaze on Murdock. "I regret I didn't confide in you, but feared the repercussions if you learned the truth."

"You could have told me anything, my love," the giant O'Casey replied. He dropped to his knees. "You could commit no wrong in my eyes."

Dorinda inhaled deeply. "You're too kind, but your temper's reputation is well-known. If you had known that Percy beat me, you would—"

Murdock leapt to his feet and slammed his fist into his palm. "After you disappeared, I heard rumors. Faith, I nearly confronted the fiend to demand the truth. What man mistreats an angel? You should have confided in me. I would have protected you with my life. When I return to Eire, I'm going to tear the bastard limb from limb."

"Stand in line, Irishman." A frown marred

Denton's even features. "I get first crack at that pompous toad."

Murdock sank down to reclaim Dorinda's hand. "I remember those bruises…You told me that you tripped. If I had suspected…"

Dorinda laid her hand on his arm. "As I told you, I did it for your own safety."

"I was a fool to believe you."

The pain in her brother's voice broke Roanne's heart. He sounded so defeated, which increased her own guilt for not aiding the defenseless woman. "You took a bold and courageous step to seek freedom from abuse."

Dorinda tried to smile, only for sadness to fill the eyes that matched her brother's. "I'll never forget how you befriended me in the market. Each time our paths crossed, you brightened my day. It gave me hope when I felt so helpless."

Roanne edged closer to Dorinda. "Common practice or not, no one should have the right to mistreat another. Only a person with a warped sense of perception would deem it acceptable."

A growl rumbled out of Murdock's giant chest.

Dorinda's gaze flicked to him. "If I left my husband, he would have considered it a betrayal or rejection and the church would have sided with him. That's why I couldn't let anyone know my plans. If Percy somehow found out about us, he would have turned you over to Cromwell for treason and you would have hung. That would have killed me. How was I to know Cromwell would die right after I left?"

"'Tis been two years," Murdock said. "Why didn't you send word that you were alive? We could have run off together."

This time Dorinda smiled. "I know, my love, but people gossip. Word would have gotten out, and Percy would have found a way to punish your family for our transgression. Even without Cromwell's backing, too many owed him favors. He would have called in debts and penalized anyone who had prior knowledge. I couldn't allow that to occur to innocent people. By you remaining in Ireland, he wouldn't suspect you or my duplicity."

Roanne twisted her hands together. She checked Simon for his reaction. Her heart ached when a quick peek at his face revealed no sign of emotion. He was good at hiding his feelings. Something she wished she did better.

Murdock shook his head. "I could have aided you and known you were safe. Alive. Once sufficient time had lapsed, I'd have joined you. We could have gone to the Americas, or the Continent. Anywhere as long as we were together."

The heartfelt plea made Dorinda cover her face and sob. "'Tis all my fault. I was a coward. Everyone had to believe I drowned. Otherwise Percy would have tracked us down. Destroyed you, your family. I couldn't bear that on my conscience."

Murdock gathered the weeping woman into his arms and brushed her hair, making soothing noises. "'Tis all right, my love. You're alive and returned to me. We are together now. I don't care if you're still married to that pig. We'll live in sin. I'll never let you go."

Roanne studied the people surrounding them. Everyone was affected by the tale. Sympathy reflected in their expressions and mirrored the same deep sorrow twisting her insides. Life wasn't fair. Dorinda had suffered at the hands of Sir Percy, a miserable specimen of a man. Murdock had suffered because he believed the love of his life had taken her own.

Denton patted Murdock on the back. "My sister told me everything upon her return. Soon, justice will right the wrong done to her. The machinations of divorce move with a slowness that drives a man insane. Fortunately, Dorinda's will be complete within days. It's a good thing I'm filthy rich. With money, doors always open. And those same doors will remain open until the proper results are finalized."

Padraig stepped forward. "What about Percy? Shouldn't punishment be meted out for what he did to the young lady?"

"Never fear on that account." The duke nodded. "He surely will be. Dorinda is too kind-hearted. She didn't want to extract revenge for his treatment. Me, I am not so kindly."

He stopped when Murdock growled. "I'll take care of him. I'll break every bone in his worthless body."

"Nay!" Dorinda grabbed his arm. "I beg you. Please. Don't confront him. He still wields power in Ireland. I would absolutely perish if you were killed or thrown in prison or deported. Knowing that you were safe is what kept me from going insane."

Grumblings from the other O'Caseys echoed in the crowded room.

"Quiet, everyone." Denton held up his hands. "All has been taken of. Like I said, wealth has its privileges. As far as the fiend is concerned, once the divorce is finalized, financial ruin will rain down on Percy. I've made sure all his funds are tied up in various schemes.

Schemes, his greedy soul expected to make him as rich as Midas. Those same investments he thought foolproof are going to fail one after another."

Padraig offered his hand to the duke. "A sister should always be protected."

Roanne's head snapped up. She'd been concentrating on the tale so hard, that she hadn't considered how her life paralleled Dorinda's in a small way, married to a man who was a stranger, and swept away from all the people she knew. True, while Simon had made her life miserable the last few weeks, he hadn't beaten her. Not once. Nor had he ever threatened to do so.

To admit an error was difficult for her, but she had to try. She reached out to place her hand on Simon's. For one long moment, he rested his other hand on hers. The contact made her melt and let hope grow like a seed ready to sprout. Then he eased his hand away and her heart broke.

She closed her eyes and wished she could make Simon look at her like Murdock and Dorinda did, with true affection reflected in their eyes. Both had suffered and endured in the name of love.

As would she. She vowed to find Hugh's killer and meant to keep her word. She would prove to Simon that no one in her family committed the crime. Then Simon and she could start over with each other. She would find a way to make their life together worthwhile.

And she would start with John Langley.

****

Early the next day, while mulling over how happy Murdock and Dorinda were, Roanne headed for the stables with dew still moistening the ground. Something good had occurred because her family visited England—Murdock and Dorinda had found each other.

She discovered Ian at the stables admiring the horses. Given a choice, he always preferred animals over people.

"Your husband knows his horseflesh. Many have the look of hot blood in their veins. They appear light and swift, excellent candidates for flat racing. Their sleek lines suggest Hobby runs through their veins," he greeted her with a smidgeon of pride, for the breed he mentioned was pure Irish.

Roanne loved seeing her brothers happy and this occasion proved no exception. "Horses are your area of expertise. I'm sure my husband would appreciate any suggestions you offer."

"*Ack*, from what I've seen, he isn't thrilled about the Irish. 'Sides, there be nothing here that needs improvement."

She asked the stable boy to fetch her bay. "Look around. There is always something to improve upon."

Ian walked over to inspect the mare being led out of the barn. He ran his hands down the animal's graceful neck, high withers, over her long legs before trailing his hand along her back. Then he faced the mare, looking deep in her eyes.

"Cromwell might have banned horse racing, but this mare's been bred for running," he said, looking over his shoulder at her. "I can see she has heart, much like you."

A rush of warmth sped through Roanne at the compliment. Ian rarely criticized, and even rarer uttered compliments. Perhaps he did so now because he was full of excitement about the horses. "You be right, Ian.

The moment we laid eyes on each other, we shared an affinity. I've renamed her Bridget for her high spirits."

Ian chuckled. "Bridget fits. The sainted lady would be pleased, I'm thinking."

Roanne tied a small bundle to the saddle, received a leg up and waved farewell. She set off on a beautiful late spring day with the hint of summer in the air. Going slow, she took in her surroundings, memorizing landmarks along the way. Deciduous trees had flowered, and the various leaves colored the woods with assorted shades of green. Grasses and plants turned the ground into a verdant carpet. Birds chirped in the branches, and squirrels chattered to each other.

Bridget's hooves crushed detritus as she pranced over the forest floor.

Roanne kept an eye open for snares. After two hours of searching, she spotted the first trap. It hadn't been sprung. She kept going.

A second one was set as well.

If these were John Langley's, which she suspected, for each were marked with a small gray feather, he was somewhere nearby.

Dismounting, she tied Bridget to a tree and sat on a fallen log.

Within the hour, the trap sprung on its prey. Not much later, a twig snapped in the woods. Roanne climbed to her feet, slowly, quietly.

Sure enough, John Langley emerged with a limp from the woods and headed straight for the sprung trap. He removed a bushy-tailed squirrel and held it before him for inspection.

"Good day, John." Roanne stood and stepped forward. "I was hoping to find you this fine day."

"Glad to see you, too, my lady." He removed his hat and gave her a puzzled look. "Might I ask why you were looking for me?"

"I brought you some winter onions. The garden at Hollyhock has an overabundance of them. Methought to share the bounty." She turned toward Bridget and the sack she tied to the saddle. "Also, some salt and pepper. You can use them, I'm hoping."

John's eyes widened. Seasonings were scarce and invaluable. "Must be important, if you're bribing me. Though I already feel indebted to you."

Roanne should have realized the gesture wouldn't fool the wily man, even if intended with all sincerity. "We owe each other, I'm thinking. Best call us even." She led him to the log where she'd sat earlier and resumed her place.

"What can I do for you, my lady?" He remained standing.

She pressed her lips together for an instant. She needed to get to the bottom of Hugh's death. "The previous earl...Lord Hugh. What was he like? Did he merit loyalty from his tenants?"

John spit on the ground. "The fellow's gone and is reaping his just desserts, whatever they might be."

"A fair answer for a man who I suspect did little for his tenants." She got right to the point. "Hugh Lancaster died in these woods. My husband believes my brothers killed him and I aim to prove him wrong."

"Might I ask how you'll do that?"

"By making inquiries, and who better than you, to start with?" Roanne answered in a level voice. She pretended not to see his surprise. "You have spent many hours here and even if you don't know first-hand what happened, you might have heard who has."

The poacher tightened his mouth.

Roanne held up her hand. "Hear me out. I suspect you're not the only person who uses these woods to supplement their table, which be fine with me. Being hungry isn't unknown to me and my family. Eire suffered grave depravity the previous decade. Food was so scarce many a time that our bellies woke us from our sleep with their rumblings."

Compassion softened the crags and valleys on the man's face. "Shit," he said softly, then hurried on. "Beggin' your pardon, m'lady. Aye, I know the sound."

The common bond proved more valuable than any gift she could have offered. "I beg you, John, what d'you know about Hugh's death?"

Nerve-wracking silence followed her plea. Roanne refused to show impatience. She waited. Sometimes patience reaped rewards.

John twisted the hat caught in his hands. "The trees see things."

Roanne didn't doubt that at all. But instinct told her John referred to himself. He practically lived in the forest. She wouldn't be surprised to discover he resided in a hut deep within the woods. "Tell me more."

John fidgeted. "It would be rumor only."

"A grain of truth is worth more than a bucket of lies."

"'Twas an accident," he said, crossing himself. "I swear to God."

It seemed the woods fell silent. The air grew heavy.

Her heart raced with excitement. At last she had a clue. Albeit, a small one. Roanne began to process the good news. If an accident…

Wait! Simon claimed the previous earl had been shot in the back. How could that be an accident? "Were you there? Did you see it happen?"

"I—I just know." John started to turn, but Roanne grabbed his sleeve.

"That's not enough to bring to the earl, John. He won't believe me, I'm afraid. I need proof. Something concrete. Perchance you know of an eyewitness. Faith, his lordship blames my brothers. He won't stop until the truth is revealed. He'll only believe someone with roots in Stafford." She paused, squeezed his bony arm, then continued. "Someone like you."

"That'll prove difficult, my lady. The previous earl didn't allow people in Kirkland Woods. There are consequences. It would mean admitting to trespassing. Or worse, poaching. People like their necks not being stretched."

Roanne inhaled deeply. The situation required deft maneuvers through twists and turns of what wasn't being said. She knew John, and surely others in the district, poached. "Bring whoever you discover to me. Let me speak with them, first. Perchance I can convince them that they would be doing me a great service. Saving innocent people."

"No offense, Lady Kirkland. Rumor has it the new earl is obstinate in his belief."

"No need to stand on ceremony, not between friends. Call me Roanne," she replied first. "So, word of my predicament is public knowledge. Oh, please, John. If you know anything, I beg you. Tell me. I vow to make it worthwhile."

"I make no promise," he answered. "Let me think on it."

Roanne's shoulders slumped. She had to accept the man's statement. A hard knot of defeat formed, but she offered a sad smile to show acceptance. "That's all I can ask. I trust you'll make the correct decision."

****

Right now, for a split second, Simon considered being wrong about the O'Caseys' involvement in Hugh's death. Aye. The tenants who labored on his land possessed an understandable grudge against his brother. They were decent people, forced to become poachers, taking to the shadows in order to survive. The logic confused him and left him restless.

Look at how Murdock changed. His eternal scowl literally disappeared over night. In its place a smile beamed that blinded all who glimpsed it. Of course, the fellow wasn't underfoot as much now. His days and hours long into the night were spent with Dorinda. Let Addison handle the love-struck Irishman.

If only Simon's life could change as easily.

He stood in the library and peered out the window at the rolling hills of Hollyhock. A knot tightened in his chest. Stubbornness mutinied at the notion of being married to the killer's sister. Oh sure, doubts churned and bubbled within him, but until they were verified…

Roanne dared to suggest someone held a grudge against Hugh. After inspecting the sorry conditions of the holdings, the suggestion wasn't as far-fetched as it first seemed. He would be hard pressed to find a single soul willing to defend Hugh. Worse, it meant the O'Caseys weren't the only ones eager for Hugh's death. Which left Simon suspecting a tenant, a neighbor, or a friend.

Staring at the estate's vastness, a spot appeared

atop the crest of a far hill. It moved closer at a steady pace. A horse and rider. He recognized the bay mare immediately and guessed the rider's identity. Laughter bubbled up as delight lit his insides.

On impulse, he headed for the stables to intercept the pair upon their return.

When they trotted into the courtyard, he stepped out of the shadows. "Riding again?"

"I find the solitude soothing," Roanne answered him. "Are you going out?"

"I was hoping for a stroll in the garden with you."

"Faith, why wish for my company when all you've done since we arrived at Hollyhock was avoid me?"

"A mistake I am eager to correct." He didn't know why he wanted to spend time with his wife, but he did. "Forgive me."

"And if I do?"

"Am I not already being punished with so many O'Caseys crawling within my home? Discretion is nigh impossible. I wish to spend time with you without interruption from your family."

The corners of Roanne's mouth lifted ever so little. "They can be overwhelming if one is unaccustomed to them."

He let a smile of his own show. "I daresay I'm surprised not to find them going barefoot outdoors."

Roanne must have approved of his reply for she volunteered one of those smiles he deeply craved. "O'Caseys do just that upon occasion. All Irish believe that one should touch the earth. Toes should wiggle in the grass and feel mud ooze between them. Shoes be such a hindrance."

Simon imagined his wife running barefoot over the

manicured lawns of Hollyhock, her red hair flying loose. A sight he willingly looked forward to seeing one day. "Will I ever be rid of them?" he asked in a dry enough tone to be burnt toast.

"You invited them. Remember?" Roanne batted her eyelashes at him.

He didn't reply. Was she flirting with him? He hadn't expected that.

Rather than ponder the situation, he escorted her to one of the three wrought-iron entrances of a walled garden. As far as the eye could see trees, shrubs, and stoned terraces covered the ground.

Her eyes widened at the display. "This is beautiful."

"The Irish do not have a hold on all superstitions, madam wife," he began, deciding he enjoyed his time in her company. "We English have a few of our own. This garden, for instance, was designed to keep the fairy kingdom happy. First we enclosed it, then planted a different tree in each corner for protection. My grandfather chose an apple for one because it is a traditional luck-bringer, and a mountain ash to keep witches away. A Glastonbury tree for religious significance. And last, but not least, an oak tree to act as a lightning deflector. When young, I collected acorns and put them on my windowsill to protect me from evil spirits."

"Me, too. Acorns are powerful protectors. I kept mine in a bowl at home. I even tucked a fistful in my pocket the night we wed," she told him with the hint of another smile. "D'you have many flower beds here?"

"In all honesty, I know not." He smiled at her, deeply enjoying this time with her. He recalled the crown of yellow flowers he'd woven for her. "I preferred climbing trees and spent little time within the actual garden."

"You were a boy, playing boy games."

Such a simple explanation. "I suppose."

"White flowers are thought to be clean and pure," Roanne went on. "It be said red and pink bring passion and romance to a household."

He hadn't considered the meaning of flowers, but was willing to listen. "My new favorite colors. The garden needs a woman's touch. Your touch. You could do whatever you desire. Perchance plant red and pink roses everywhere." He paused. Whatever made him say that?

"Legend says you must never mix red and white together for it will bring misfortune." She eyed the garden as though visualizing the placement of new plants. "Some claim yellow in a garden angers the fey, but me ma had a fondness for the color and put a few tulips on the sunniest side of our land."

"I remember them," he said, pleased with the easy conversation. He liked this change, rather than the arguing. "That'll be your responsibility. I've seen you talking with the head gardener and assumed you were presenting your ideas to him. You said you preferred flowers over herbs."

Her green-gold eyes swept up. "Aye, my lord husband."

Her reply, so soft, so sweet, drew him in with an allure that could not be denied.

He leaned and kissed her. And didn't regret it in the least.

Chapter Fifteen

"You have a caller, my lady," Titus announced a few days later when Roanne came down to break her morning fast. She'd been feeling mellow since her walk in the garden with Simon, and hoped that they had made progress in their relationship. Of course, his sweet kiss lent weight to the idea.

Now, her heart skipped a tiny bit and she swallowed down the inquisitiveness wrapping around her chest as tightly as any bonds on her wrists and ankles. This was her first official caller since the gala.

"Where are they?" she asked, trying to contain her excitement.

"In the small drawing room."

"Thank you." She headed toward the room designated as a lady's parlor with a light-hearted step.

She opened the door and entered a heavily paneled room. Her gaze swept over the room left over from a different time. A musty smell filled the room, in spite of the fact that the windows had been left open to air the place out, and a servant had placed a small vase of purple crocus on a table. The spot of color brightened the obviously neglected space.

Dorinda rose from a divan that looked like it hadn't been sat in for decades.

Roanne glanced about, fully expecting to find Murdock, but he was nowhere in sight. Probably a good thing. This gave her and Dorinda a chance to speak freely without him hanging on every word.

She rushed forward. Roanne wished she had done more while Dorinda lived in Ireland. Now, all she could do was hug the petite brunette.

"I'm still whirling from your epic tale. It merits being written down for the ages." Roanne indicated they both sit. "I can't tell you how happy it makes me to know you didn't die."

Dorinda chuckled. "As am I. You were the only person, besides Murdock, who showed me kindness. Most were afraid of Percy's reaction. I cherished our exchanges."

Guilt threatened to overwhelm Roanne. "I should have done more."

"A friendly smile was worth more than gold when I thought my world was ending." Dorinda chuckled softly. "Remember when you chided that merchant for trying to cheat me? And what about the time you aided me in purchasing that wool? I had no clue how to barter. Those times, after I returned home, I repeated your words and memorized our interplay. I could hardly wait for the week for my next trip to the market. 'Twas the only time Percy allowed me out."

"As I recall, a maid always accompanied you."

Dorinda shrugged. "Also under Percy's thumb. She'd been tasked with reporting every detail of my outings. Refusal was forbidden. The poor child had to obey. She was terrified of him. He threatened her with being discharged and her whole family with expulsion from his land if she disobeyed."

Roanne shook her head. She couldn't help herself. "If I may be so bold...how did you come to meet

Murdock?"

This time Dorinda beamed a grin. "One day our carriage wheel came loose after leaving the market. He came along and lifted the axle all by himself to put the wheel back on. I'd never seen such a strong man. Yet when he spoke, it was in such a soothing voice, reassuring me that everything would be all right. At first, he frightened me because he was so big and strong, yet appealed to me at the same time. Then he started showing up at the market."

Roanne raised an eyebrow. "That explained his sudden interest in being the one to drive me there. He was searching for you."

Genuine embarrassment colored Dorinda's cheeks pink. "I fear we were drawn to each other immediately. I was lonely and so was he. Loneliness is a powerful lure. We sensed our mutual need and could be ourselves while together. At first, we talked about little things-the weather, our mutual neighbors. He spoke of his family. I told him about my brother. We became friends, but as the months passed, our friendship grew into something stronger."

Roanne found the tale bittersweet. She couldn't help wondering how lonely Simon had been growing up. Or how her brother and the woman before her were able to fight temptation with such a strong attraction. "Blessed Mary, 'twas a problem."

"Aye, and we knew it was wrong. The first time Murdock saw a bruise on my cheek, his concern for my well-being melted my heart. He brushed his hand over my face with the gentlest touch and my stomach fluttered. I couldn't dare confess my husband struck me. Besides, I thought it was my fault, that I merited the punishment. Percy apologized, begged my forgiveness. Claimed it was an accident."

"Hogwash!" Roanne snapped. As combative as her family were, they never struck a weaker person. "Excuses. Or worse, outright lies. Spoken to keep you quiet and from exposing him as a fiend. I'm wagering he wanted to stay in your brother's good graces." Roanne wished she had ordered tea and biscuits for them. She suspected a long day lay ahead, and both could use the nourishment.

Dorinda's chest shuddered with a deep sigh. "Aye, 'twas common knowledge Addison did not condone violence against women. Percy even accompanied him once when he spoke in the House of Lords about stricter punishment for those who mistreated their spouses. Even so, the law gave Percy the right to beat me. And the church placed great emphasis on the sacredness of marriage. Murdock and I were caught in a pickle. Neither one of us was willing to commit adultery."

"And Percy beat you again. And again," Roanne voiced her suspicions.

"True." Dorinda stared at the far wall.

Roanne ached for the woman. What she wouldn't give for a few minutes with the fiend. "I wager you never gave the man cause for his actions."

Fidgeting, Dorinda turned back to face her. "When I realized Percy would never stop hitting me, I began to plan. During those weeks, the only bright light in my life was meeting Murdock at the market. I'd send my maid off on a silly errand. She was a sweet little thing and that way she never had to lie about my activities. I didn't want her involved. Murdock and I would stroll along the booths and talk. He made me laugh. His sense of humor tickles me."

Roanne recalled how Murdock used to disappear the instant they arrived at the market. She assumed he went to the nearest ale house. Only once did she tease him about meeting a mistress. He had blushed and stormed away. She never realized until today, she'd hit the mark. "Not exactly the image I have of my brother."

"He truly sees humor in many things," Dorinda whispered. "His kindness made me pine for him while married to a monster. I couldn't divorce Percy. The difference between the two men made me wish I was a widow."

Anguish curled her insides. Roanne couldn't wait any longer to speak her mind. "Your reported death nearly destroyed Murdock, and yet he never told a soul. In a twisted way it explains the dislike he developed against Sir Percy. Losing you devastated him. I suspect the only way he could handle his grief was to blame all things English, including Simon."

"My poor Murdock. Love is a prized emotion and he mourned for me and his loss. I never meant for him to suffer. Over the last few days we have talked and talked on nearly every subject we could think of to catch up with each other." Dorinda sighed as though she possessed a guilty conscience, which Roanne swore was ridiculous. "He has confided in me that he's been unjustly hard on Simon, hoping for a blunder to have an excuse to take out his frustration on the man. I've berated Murdock for his shameless treatment. 'Twas wrong of him. And poor Simon. Under the strictest confidence, I told him how Simon suffered as a child. He was defenseless and blamed for many wrongs that he was not guilty of committing.

"Murdock knows better now and regrets his behavior. 'Tis why I came today," Dorinda went on. "I'm here to offer my support. In Ireland you tendered me your friendship when I believed myself all alone. It made all the difference in the world. Your kindnesses and Murdock's love gave me the courage to keep going. It's my turn to return the favor. You need someone you can depend upon."

Surprised, Roanne wondered how much to reveal. "I have my brothers."

"All males. Come, Roanne, you need another woman who has been through a similar ordeal, a friend to confide in, someone who understands and empathizes. You need not say anything today. Just-when you're ready. Please...consider me." Dorinda straightened on her seat, a spark of determination gleaming in her golden-brown eyes. "I've known Simon all my life. He and Addison were my heroes growing up. They let me tag along with them, protected me, tormented me, but always loved me. Neither one would have let harm come to me. Simon can be obstinate and bull-headed with the best of men. He can't be making life easy for you."

Roanne breathed a sigh of relief. Kinder words had never been spoken to her. "I daresay the circumstances regarding Hugh's death are suspicious. Reason eluded Simon and he blames one of my brothers for the deed. He doesn't hold me responsible, but insists I know the culprit's name and need to divulge it." She took hold of Dorinda's hands and squeezed. "They didn't. I swear on me blessed mother's grave."

"I believe you. I do. All we have to do is convince

Simon of the same. He'll come around. You'll see." Dorinda took in the small drawing room, her brows pulling together in concentration before relaxing. "You know, I've never seen the inside of this room before. It was closed off when I was young. I believe this was Simon's mother's favorite. The old lord forbade letting anyone inside."

Roanne leaned forward, eager to learn any tidbit about Simon's past. "Simon told me he used to sneak in."

A thoughtful expression passed over Dorinda's face. "Did he now? I'm glad. My brother and I tried to fill the gap in his life. His father ignored Simon because his mother died giving birth to him. Which is such a shame…because 'tis untrue."

Roanne's head snapped up. Her heart raced. "What d'you mean?"

"Lord Kirkland showered Hugh with all his affection and snubbed Simon. Some say his rejection was cruel. Not physically, mind you. He never raised a hand to him. His disregard crushed Lady Kirkland. Her baby deserved better treatment—love and affection. After four or five years, she ran away. Some say his lordship's stony behavior drove her into a lover's arms. 'Twas the old earl himself who put out the rumor that she died. A few in the aristocracy knew the truth about her running away. They let him perpetuate the lie. 'Twas what gave me the idea to fake my own death."

Roanne glanced around the room, trying to visualize the woman whose actions affected so many lives. "If she felt that way, why not take Simon with her? A little one has no way to protect themselves against injustices and from what little I've heard, he suffered greatly and unjustly."

"I know not the answer. The aristocracy is very touchy about heirs and spares."

Roanne slumped onto the cushions. So much to mull over. "And Simon never knew? No one told him?"

Dorinda shook her head. "'Twould only have added to his burden."

Oh, Simon.

Her heart broke. She could only imagine his wretched childhood.

She tried not to dwell on his suffering. If she did, empathy would rise and cloud her judgement. Every instinct she possessed told her Simon ached from grief infiltrating his very bones, that it controlled his emotions. Vengeance and grief consumed him. He couldn't see beyond either one.

Simon deserved the truth. A secret of such importance should not be kept hidden from him. "In some ways, that explains his behavior. He's acting like his father, trying to keep me at arms' length. Afraid to show any tenderness."

Dorinda reached out to touch her hand. "Sometimes knowing the reason makes acceptance of another's behavior easier, but it doesn't forgive a mistreatment. Never."

"Simon has never raised a hand to me, if that is what you're implying. Nor do I believe he ever would. I saw his expression while you relayed your tale. His face turned black with rage."

"Oh, thank heaven," Dorinda gushed with relief. "I cannot tell you how relieved that makes me feel. Friend or not, after what happened to me, Addison would have been livid to discover another woman being abused.

Especially by a friend. He would have challenged Simon to a duel and he's a deadly shot."

Fear leaped to Roanne's chest. "Don't tittle-tattle about this to anyone. Promise me, Dorinda. Please. I am conducting my own investigation into Hugh's death. I have vowed to hunt down the real culprit. I will prove to Simon that my brothers are innocent."

"May I help?"

"Nay, nay. My thanks for your offer. I must tread carefully. Simon is aware of my intention, and thus far hasn't fully given his blessings."

"As if that would stop you," the brunette said with a smile.

Roanne slanted a glance at her. "I refuse to sit idle and am doing so covertly. Best I not involve another."

"If there is anything I can do, just ask and it will be done."

Make my husband love me.

****

Simon knew he had to take action. Uncomplicating his life soared high on his priorities.

When he found Padraig alone in the front parlor, he jumped at the opportunity to have a man-to-man with the clan leader. Time to bring the mess plaguing his life to an end. Then, perhaps, easier decisions could be made.

"Glad you're here, Padraig," he opened. "I daresay we need to talk."

"*Ack*, I've been wondering when you would approach me."

Simon kept his surprise to himself. "What do you mean? If something was amiss, you should have informed me."

"Not my place."

Still puzzled, Simon asked, "Then what's on your mind?"

"Roanne," her brother said.

Simon's heart leapt. The name packed a swift punch to his gut. He instantly went on guard. "What about her?"

Padraig swiped back graying hair as he adjusted his position in the chair. "I be speaking as a man wed nearly two decades, a roundabout way of saying I have some experience. The tension between you and me sister is palpable. Methought you could use a bit of advice or would like to speak to another man." He looked at Simon and wiggled his eyebrows ever so little.

Simon snorted. "I daresay any man would be honored to have Roanne as his spouse, but the circumstances which brought us together leave a lot to be desired. Wedding her while drunk, being kept prisoner—" He raised his hands with his palms skyward when Padraig started to protest. "Aye, it's true. You know it, I know it, and so does Roanne. Just hear me out."

"Mayhap I objected too soon. Go on."

"After I decided to escape Ireland, I asked Roanne to accompany me. She refused. I didn't hold that against her. Oh, I wanted to, but believe me, the temptation to kidnap my bride proved monumental." He stopped to study the clan leader before continuing. "Because I harbored a certain fondness for her."

Padraig chuckled low. "Affection for a spouse be a good start in a marriage."

"Let me finish," Simon replied, trying to maintain

control over the conversation. "Upon reaching Hollyhock and learning of Hugh's death, everything changed. While we barely tolerated each other, his manner of death raised suspicions. Alone in the woods with only a hunting dog for company. Shot in the back. Tis my responsibility to uncover the truth. Nor can you fault me for believing an O'Casey was behind the deed. I—"

The clan leader tensed. "We had nothing to do with your brother's death. You do us a disservice to falsely accuse any member of our clan."

Simon respected Padraig's defense of his family. "I daresay it is very suspect for three of your brothers to arrive in Stafford on the very day Hugh was found wounded. Granted, no witnesses stepped forward. Convenient for them, although I doubt they would commit the crime in front of others. Who's to say they didn't take advantage of finding Hugh alone." He let the accusation hang in the air.

Padraig's face turned bright red. "They be God-fearing men."

"God-fearing men commit sins all the time. All you have to do is tell me which brother—Sean the Third, Ian or Finn—pulled the trigger, and I promise not to punish the rest."

Padraig climbed to his feet like an old man with the weight of the world bearing down on his shoulders. "You don't think I questioned those three? They swore on the memory of our dear departed Da that the accident had already happened upon their arrival at the public house. That's where they first heard of the mishap."

"They could have shot him in the woods, and then

gone there to establish their alibi."

"*Ack*, you think I be a fool. At court lies are woven like tapestries. I like to credit myself with a measure of skill to maneuver through falsehoods to uncover the truth. I would not condone murder and believe my brothers committed no wrong."

Simon found it annoying how well the clan leader made sense. Against his better judgement, this conversation drove a bigger crack in his initial misgivings. Could he be wrong about the O'Caseys? Could his aloof treatment of Roanne been misplaced? Was he of the same ilk as Percy—a heartless man who preyed on weaker individuals because he could? The thought sickened him.

"I can't explain it," he answered Padraig. "I want to believe you, I do. Although until tangible proof is provided, I simply can't."

Padraig waved off his rebuff. "Question the two who be here. Speak with them. I'm sure they'll change your mind."

He doubted that. "Only if I can do so alone."

"I will arrange it."

"Your cooperation is much appreciated." Simon released a deep sigh. The conversation could have taken a very different turn.

"*Ack*, would it matter? I would insist you speak with the devil himself, if it helped change your mind. Best to keep the peace and cooperate. All I desire is for the anger in your eyes and the sadness in Roanne's to be gone. You two look at each other with such longing it hurts me heart, yet both of you be too proud to make the first move."

Simon almost smiled. Tension seemed to melt off

him with the clan leader's words. Was it because they were what he wanted to hear? Or something else? He gave the man a steady look and nodded.

"Make it so," he said. "I'd like to start with Ian. Sometimes the quiet ones have the most to say."

"In all likelihood he's wandering the grounds this morning, getting the lay of the land. I'll find him and send him to you. Then Sean the Third." Padraig studied him for a long moment. "You do understand Finn stayed behind because his wife just gave birth, and not because of any guilty feelings."

Simon doubted the O'Caseys would disclose a vital clue. But the hope that he might catch one in a lie or an inconsistency remained high. "I assumed as much, but if Ian or Sean don't provide satisfactory answers, I'll want to question him as well. Send Ian to the library. I'm using it as my office."

Padraig raised a graying brow. "Have you considered someone from Stafford?"

Simon forced himself to maintain eye contact. "I've considered it. And must admit Roanne suggested the very same."

"I'm not surprised. She be clever and unafraid to speak her mind."

"So I'm learning. I wonder if I will ever understand her." *Or trust.*

"What's to understand? She be a woman. Best remember the road to a happy life is a happy wife."

"Onto other matters." Simon had no desire to foster a discussion about his wife or his treatment of her, especially with her eldest brother. "I confess that my brother's treatment of those here shames me. He scorned his duties for the people he was responsible for, selfishly putting his own desires before those less able to care for themselves. My only regret is that I wasn't here to stop him. Though, in all honesty, I am not sure what I could have done."

Padraig huffed. "You be here now. And, evidence of improvements abound. That be your doing, I'm thinking."

For the second time Simon paused. He liked receiving compliments from the man he respected. What if Padraig was right? The stakes ran high. His future. His happiness.

And Roanne's. Visualizing the tall, feisty redhead, he couldn't forget about her.

****

Three-quarters of an hour passed before a knock on the library door sounded.

"Enter," Simon called from behind the giant desk.

Ian O'Casey stepped into the room. The Irishman was not as tall as Rory, nor as gray as Padraig, which made Simon estimate his age a decade or so older than him. Yet, there was no mistaking the kinship. Something in the eyes revealed him as an O'Casey through and through.

"Padraig said you wanted to see me," Ian said, dark brown gaze looking about.

Simon did not smile in return. He indicated a chair before the desk. "I do. Sit down. I don't know how long this will take. I would like to ask a few questions about your first visit to Stafford."

Ian shrugged. "Not much to tell. Took three days of travel to reach here after sailing across the sea."

"Let's start at the beginning. What ship brought you to England?"

"The *Hollandsche Tuin*. Rough seas prevented us from disembarking for a whole day. The captain declined to put down a tender. Worried about capsizing the rowboat. And then there were the ponies to consider. They'd have to swim to shore."

Simon knew the ship, a Dutch vessel with a captain who didn't hurry. He also knew it had arrived at Blackpool, which meant the O'Caseys would have had a hundred-mile journey ahead of them. The events and timing could easily be verified. "Did you happen to see anyone along the way?"

"A fancy carriage passed us, heading south. The curtains were drawn so we never saw the occupant. There were wagons coming and going on the road. Merchants and farmers. A few foot-travelers. We didn't stop to prattle. I don't much care for people. Prefer animals over them. Less conflict."

Made sense to Simon. The O'Caseys would have been in a rush to reach Stafford. "What did you do upon reaching Stafford?"

"Went straight to a pub in search of lodging. That'd be Tuesday. The place was abuzz with news of your brother's injury."

Simon relaxed during the exchange. Ian's calm demeanor gave the impression of an honest man, and the open, direct answers cemented that idea. "So, he wasn't dead when you arrived?"

"Nay, 'tis why we extended our stay. Most believed his injury was fatal. Turned out they were right." Ian crossed himself when he stopped speaking.

A knot twisted Simon's gut. Hugh had gone hunting Monday at first light and didn't return to Hollyhock that night. A search party had set out the next morning, finding him wounded in the deer park. He languished unconscious for six long days before succumbing to his wound.

The O'Caseys arrival appeared very circumstantial. They could have reached the area Monday, but that meant pushing horses to their limits or changing mounts along the way. Somehow, he doubted Ian allowed mistreatment of their mounts, or that the fellow would trade his precious Irish ponies for inferior English ones. "What time did you arrive?"

"Dusk had fallen, but the stars hadn't come out totally. Owls screeched in the woods."

The news gave Simon pause. By all accounts, Hugh had been shot the previous morning. "Which pub did you stop at in Stafford?"

"The Crowing Rooster."

The closest one to Kirkland Woods. Confirmation of Ian's story with the proprietor would be a simple matter. "Why did you pick that particular establishment?"

"It be the first we came across in the area. After three days spent under the stars, we were ready for a bed to cushion our bodies."

Quick calculations left Simon without answers. The timing fit. Even with hard riding, no way could they have reached Stafford in time. A sinking feeling settled in his gut.

If the O'Caseys didn't murder Hugh, who did?

Chapter Sixteen

In the silence, Ian stood to face the library desk which Simon sat behind. "That be all?"

Simon crossed his arms. No reason to appear pleased, even though the exchange had gone well. Better than anticipated. "I believe so. I daresay I could do with a spot of fresh air."

The older man cocked a weathered brow in surprise. "You share my enthusiasm for the outdoors?"

Simon stood and signaled for them to head for the main entrance of Hollyhock. "I'm a landlocked sailor. I daresay many years on the high seas gave me an appreciation for wide open spaces and fresh air. The enjoyment does not vanish just because I'm on solid ground."

Ian huffed with approval. "A man after my own heart. Mayhap we have more in common than I first suspected."

Simon's stomach knotted in confusion. Here was another O'Casey he could have liked under different circumstances. Damn. It wasn't fair.

****

Roanne loved roaming Hollyhock's grounds. After yesterday and Dorinda's visit, she walked with a spring in her step. Here and there, she noticed signs of bulbs being planted, per her instructions. She could hardly wait to see them bloom.

Her kindness to the petite Englishwoman in Eire was being repaid a hundredfold now in the form of an ally, someone she felt confident would become a true friend as time went on. If such a luxury existed for her.

Today a heavy fog moistened the earth. She enjoyed being out in the cool, damp weather with visibility less than a foot before her. It reminded her of home.

Rather than chancing a tumble, she took a seat on a bench to watch the fog curl thick and thin. The temperature rose to a comfortable level. After a while, being alone, she removed her shoes and stockings. What she'd told Simon about Irish men and women needing to contact the earth had been the truth.

With her toes free, Roanne wiggled them before digging them into the wet ground. The mud beneath her feet heightened her homesickness for the green hills of Eire. She could almost see Meagan in her straw hat, carrying a wooden *bascauda*, and trekking the hills to collect plants, the smoke curling from Brian's forge, and Ian working with the ponies he so adored. With a sigh, she envisioned white dots of sheep grazing on the far hills with lambs frolicking like all newborns were prone to do. The happy memories would have to carry her through to the future.

She drew a long woolen cloak tighter around her shoulders. Courage she had plenty. But she needed more. Standing as the fog lifted, she tucked her boots and stockings under the bench and traversed the garden path, mulling over her life and what to expect next. As she went, she took mental note of barren patches of ground crying for spots of color to be added. Tulips like her mother planted in a sunny corner here, a trellis for climbing roses there. Pink and red flowers for Simon, she added as an afterthought. Lost in her thoughts, she nearly missed a voice hailing her in an urgent whisper.

"M'lady," a male voice softly called.

Her gaze darted around the garden area for the speaker. "Who's there? Step forward so I can see you."

John Langley sidled into view. He swept off his hat and clutched it in his hands. "I've given what you asked some thought."

Roanne's heart leaped. "And?"

"I might know something."

She held her breath, afraid to breathe as she absorbed the news. "How? I mean, 'tis wonderful. Come with me to the manor house. We must inform his lordship."

"Nay." John hesitated, his gaze fitted around the garden as though undergoing second thoughts. "What I have to say is for your ears alone, m'lady."

That wouldn't do at all. If the old poacher relayed news vital to the investigation, Simon must hear the tidings as well. Otherwise he'd reject whatever she told him outright. She swallowed her pride.

She was his wife. He should take her word. But he wouldn't. And that would only lead to arguing,something she feared happened far too often. The bitter exchange of harsh words was nibbling away at their very chance of finding happiness together. How could she convince John to trust her enough to face Simon?

And if she did—what then? Would Simon believe the word of a poacher?

Questions filled her head.

She decided to take one step at a time. "We'll sit

on the bench and you can tell me first. Afterward, we'll decide together what our next course of action will be."

"Fair enough," he said. "Though I don't know what good it'll do, if I have to repeat myself to his lordship."

"You'll just have to trust me, John." She kept her voice steady as she led him to the bench she'd recently vacated.

By the man's dour expression, Roanne knew she faced an uphill battle. A good thing she had a secret weapon—he'd never met a stubborn Irishwoman.

The fairies of this land must have agreed with her, for within moments the sun broke through the clouds and the fog thinned.

Roanne sat down. She patted the open space for him to join her.

"I can stand, m'lady."

"We're friends, John. Please, sit."

John crushed his hat to death in his gnarled fingers. "I'm beginning to think his lordship doesn't have a chance against you."

"Let's hope you're right." She smiled. "Now, tell me what you know. From the beginning, if you please."

"'Tain't that easy."

"Aye, it is," she encouraged, keen to hear. "You saw what happened."

He gave her a sharp glance. "I didn't say that."

Roanne swallowed a sigh. Tiny steps, she reminded herself. Take tiny steps. "Then give me the name of the person who witnessed the deed."

"I'll not give you a name."

"Then let's assume you were there. Begin with what you saw."

"'Twas a day much like this. Wet, cool with the

promise of sunshine. I was walking in the woods, no particular reason, when I heard a dog bark. No dogs roam Kirkland Woods, so that meant his lordship was nearby. He always brought one to flush the game." He paused and looked about as though afraid of being overheard.

Roanne gave the man a big smile of reassurance to put him at ease. "Go on, John. You're doing very well."

John swallowed. "I crept through the woods, careful not to make a sound. Sure enough, 'twas the old earl with his favorite hunting dog. The animal had vermin of some kind treed. Squirrel. Marten. I couldn't see what it was even though the branches were bare of foliage. Lord Kirkland commanded the hound to cease his racket, but it refused to obey. His lordship cursed a few times, then set his flintlock against the tree and went to fetch a switch to give the dog a smack."

Roanne thought of the wolfhounds her family raised. No one would dare mistreat those gentle giants. She huffed in disgust. From what she'd witnessed thus far of the previous earl's treatment of the poor souls who were his tenants and his lack of regard, she held him in little esteem. Beating a defenseless animal tipped the scale. Her mind drifted to how different the brothers were. In her opinion, the fourth Earl of Kirkland had been a fiend, and privately she chalked up his demise to fate. Simon cared about the people. He made sure their needs were met.

"That's when it happened," John blurted out.

A quiver of anticipation flickered into existence and Roanne clung tight as if her life depended on it, which very much might be the case. "When what happened?"

John looked around, then started again. "The accident. The hound was yipping and jumping at the tree. Up and down, excited-like. He knocked the gun over, and it went off with a boom. His lordship was less than two meters away, still kneeling when the blast hit him in the back."

Roanne's mouth dropped. "Did you check to see if he was alive?"

John frowned. "'Course, I did. His back was covered in blood, not moving, not making a sound. I was sure he was dead and bolted out of area."

Her heart raced. In spite of the serious situation, a thrill delighted Roanne to finally learn the circumstances surrounding Hugh's death. She'd been vindicated. Her brothers were blameless. Now, it was within her power to put an end to Simon blaming her family. She issued a quick prayer of thanks, and grinned like a banshee.

Next, she grabbed her shoes and stockings in one hand and John Langley's in the other to tug him out of the garden toward the ancestral manor.

"Come, John," she gushed. "We must inform his lordship."

"What happened to discussing it first?"

She held tight to the man's hand and dragged him along. "I truly appreciate you confiding in me. But I be right about needing proof. You have to tell Lord Kirkland, in your own words, what you saw."

"Is that wise, my lady?"

Roanne paused. If John had a change of heart and bolted, she vowed to track him down and drag him into the manor. "'Tis the only solution. Innocent lives are at stake."

With a sigh and a nod, the poacher followed Roanne. *Wait until Simon learned she'd been right.*

****

A commotion at the front door caught Simon's attention. Titus forbade a caller entrance. He couldn't imagine which one of Roanne's relatives the butler debated with when Roanne's voice rose in defiance. He should have known.

"Where is his lordship?" she demanded. "This man has important tidings to share with him."

"M-my lady," Titus stuttered as he tried to explain. "His kind are not permitted entry through the front door. Send him around the back."

"I will do no such thing. He's with me."

"You heard her ladyship." Simon did his best to ignore the sight of Roanne's delicate toes sticking out from under her gown. Besides, curiosity prompted him to wonder why his wife invited a poacher inside his home. "Let the fellow enter, Titus."

The butler's exultant expression plummeted. He hated being overruled.

Roanne whipped off her cloak and shoved it along with a pair of boots and wadded-up stockings into Titus's arms, giving the butler a triumphant I-told-you-so look before turning to face him. "We need to speak with you on a matter of vital importance."

Rory, Sean the Third, and Brian must have heard the ruckus as well for they stuck their heads out of the main dining room. Sean munched on an apple and Brian stuffed a piece of toast in his mouth.

The interest gleaming in their eyes left a lot to be desired. Simon couldn't tell if they smirked at him or were merely curious. It didn't matter. He already vowed to be rid of them before the next full moon.

He sighed. "This way then." He turned on his heels and headed back to the library.

A scuffing of leather followed in his wake. Since Roanne was barefoot, he assumed more than the poacher followed.

Roanne shut the door upon entering with her guest. A second later it reopened, and the three O'Caseys from the dining room stepped inside.

Simon bit back a retort. He swore they had no respect for privacy and doubted any objection would make a difference with these nosy Irishmen.

Roanne eyed her brothers and took a deep breath. "My lord husband, you remember John? He's the one in the woods that day I got lost."

"John and I are well acquainted. You might say we have history together," Simon replied, deliberately sounding droll. "Why don't you get to the point?"

The three O'Caseys spread out in the library as Roanne turned to the poacher. If nothing else, the Irishmen knew how to place themselves strategically. He had to admire them for that.

"John, please tell his lordship what you told me," she said.

John sweep off his battered hat and repeated his tale with his head bowed, eyes downcast.

Simon pursed his lips in concentration. With a man as poor as John, the only thing he owned of any value was his word. In all his years at the estate, Simon had never heard once of John breaking his word.

"You mean to say the flintlock was loaded and primed when my brother set it against the tree," Simon repeated.

"Had to be," John replied. "No other explanation for the accident. Whatever the hound had trapped, he wasn't letting his prize escape. He kept barking and jumping. His lordship hadn't stood up, hadn't even turned around when the dog knocked the weapon over. It struck a rock and fired."

Dead silence filled the library.

Simon's head reeled. The O'Caseys were innocent. A dog killed Hugh.

He rubbed his hands over his face to keep himself on an even keel. He recalled the long scratch like a scar on the flintlock's barrel that had looked new when he examined it. He'd dismissed it at the time, a mistake on his part.

Even so, a sense of exhilaration rushed through him. He stared at the three O'Caseys grinning ear-to-ear as he rose to his feet. "Thank you, John for providing this information. I know your word is your bond."

The man flicked a glance at Roanne. "No real choice. Her ladyship insisted."

That elicited a smile from Simon. "She is persistent, isn't she?"

"Aye, my lord." John fidgeted. "Will that be all?"

Simon knew the man deserved compensation for his trouble and slipped a crown into his hand when they shook hands. A trivial sum to pay for a lifetime of happiness. "I believe so. And John, henceforth the deer park will be open to all my tenants as a means to supplement their tables. Will you spread the word?"

"'Twill be my pleasure."

Simon waited for the man to hurry out.

"I told you my brothers were innocent," Roanne said, her amber-green eyes misty. "I've never lied to you."

Guilt punched him in the gut for the pain and misery he'd put his wife through for blaming her family. It couldn't have been easy for her. Yet, she'd endured with unfailing loyalty. She had believed in their innocence from the very start and never wavered.

"You have my sincere apologies for doubting you and suspecting them." He glanced at the trio of O'Caseys. "If you don't mind, I would like privacy with my wife. There are matters between us we need to settle."

****

Roanne woke up the next morning with a vague memory of tossing and turning as though her sleep had been troubled, which was the farthest thing from the truth. She'd retired happy. She and Simon had talked long into the night, probably much like Dorinda and Murdock had after finding each other.

Climbing out of bed, she went to the window to peer out at the grounds. Wide open spaces always brought her peace of mind. She was going to enjoy living at Hollyhock.

"D'you wish to partake your breakfast up here or will you join the others below?" Millie asked while puttering about the room, tidying up.

"I'm a tad tired. I think I'll eat up here."

"Having so much company does wear a body out," the maid responded. "You have—"

Suddenly Millie stopped and screamed at the top of her lungs.

Roanne whirled around, dizzy from the effort, to see her maid pointing at the bed she'd just left.

Scarlet blood the size of a cart's wheel stained the

sheets.

Roanne became hot and sweaty and chilled to the bone at the same time. Her knees wobbled. She gasped as though out of air. This couldn't be happening. Not now.

She dropped into the chair, weak. Her heart raced as a fast, rapid thumping filled her chest to bursting. Her menses had started, or she'd lost the babe.

Either case spelled disaster for her.

Millie rushed to her side, her round face as gray as her frizzy hair. "Oh my, look at you, you poor child. Your nightshift is soaked in blood." She wrapped her warm arms around Roanne. "Let me get that soiled thing off you and clean you up. We'll need to check and see if you're still bleeding, then into something warm and dry."

Dazed, Roanne let the elderly maid administer as she pleased. Millie made clucking noises like a mother hen, and seemed pleased with whatever results she found. For Roanne, it felt good not to have to think for herself or protest.

With Roanne dressed in a clean nightshift, Millie led her to a chair. "You're going to be just fine, your ladyship. Your menses started."

"I haven't had one for two months."

"Could you be carrying?"

Roanne squeezed her eyes shut. "I—I don't know."

"We'll know soon enough. For now, you sit here while I get a servant to change your bedding, then it's back to bed for you. I'm no expert, but I don't think you'll be riding for quite a while. Not in your condition. Don't you worry, though, you're going to be just fine. I've actually seen this once before. The poor woman couldn't carry a babe to full term unless she took to her bed and remained there while she waited for the babe to be born."

Confused, Roanne worried aloud, "You mean I haven't lost the babe?"

"That's for the good Lord to decide." Deeper wrinkles appeared in rows like ploughed fields across the maid's brow. "Does his lordship know you're carrying?"

"I doubt it very much. I didn't know for sure myself. I mean, I missed my menses, so I hoped, but with our constant bickering, there just hasn't been a chance to discuss the possibility with him."

"He needs to be informed."

Roanne remembered his adamant words about bringing a child into this world without love. Last night's conversation had cleared the air on many things, but not once did either of them touch on affection or love. She had enough love to share and care for his babe all by herself, but couldn't imagine how Simon would react to the news. Delighted. Furious. "Can't I keep it a secret for a little while? I mean, what if I've already lost the babe?"

Millie gave a soft tsk. "I'm no midwife, but have brought five little ones of my own into this world. Lost two between the oldest and second. This happened to me with my third child, a boy, and he's a strapping lad with his own babies now."

Roanne's eyes widened. Her heart beat just a bit faster with hope. "I hope you're right about the babe."

Millie rattled on, "I recognize the signs, and don't think you have to worry. Though I'm sure his lordship will want a doctor's confirmation."

Without waiting to be dismissed, Millie raced away with more speed and agility than Roanne thought possible for a woman of her age and girth.

Alone, her belly tightened in the silence. She laid her hands on it as if feeling for life. Was a babe inside? Roanne's mother had died in childbirth. Did the same fate await her?

When a knock sounded, she called out for the person to enter. A young maid with clean linens stepped inside. She gave Roanne a timid smile, then her gaze widened at the bed, only to flick back in Roanne's direction without a word. Performing a quick curtsey, she hurried over to the bed and began stripping the sheets.

Roanne remained seated. Just yesterday the mystery of Hugh's demise had been resolved. The heavy curtain that wrapped around the manor had lifted. It became a place where people could live in happiness.

Now this. Was she to have no peace?

It didn't seem fair.

The door burst open. Simon stormed inside with a thunderous scowl distorting his handsome face. His long stride carried him across the floor until he stopped in front of her. Entranced by the rise and fall of his broad chest, she waited while his midnight blue eyes bore into her.

"Is it true?" he asked after what seemed like forever.

Roanne sighed and let her arms drop to her sides. Millie told. "I suppose it depends upon what you want."

Simon pointed to the young maid finishing making the bed. "Out," he said, standing beside the chair. As soon as the maid departed with her arms full of the dirty bedding, he knelt beside Roanne and grasped her hands with his. "Are you all right? What happened? Millie wasn't making much sense when she found us in the dining room."

The distress lacing his voice triggered her amber-green eyes to mist. "I think I lost the babe."

"What babe?"

Roanne's pulse raced. Millie had left out the most important detail. Time for explanations. She took a deep breath to muster her strength. "Remember the morning I stopped you in the hall? I tried to tell you then that I'd missed my menses. But, as usual, we argued. Which I admit was my fault. My temper always gets the better of me."

A myriad of emotions flashed over Simon's face, then he surprised her. Instead of criticizing, he released her hands and gathered her into his arms where a wave of warmth—safe and protected—hit her. A feeling of rapture exploded in her being pressed up against his chest. She laid her head on his shoulder where she caught the hint of soap, bay, and his manly scent.

"What about infection? We must do everything possible to keep you safe and healthy. How are you feeling? Are you cold? What can I do for you?"

A new man, like the one she'd wed in Ireland a lifetime ago, stood before her and it warmed her heart. "I am fine."

"What if it happens again?" Simon asked in clear disbelief.

Instinct told Roanne to remain strong. No need to argue. "Faith, and I'll just have to make sure it doesn't. Is that good enough?"

He shrugged his broad shoulders. "I'll feel relieved

after the doctor examines you." He paused and glanced around the bedchamber. "I have a confession to make. I like your temper. You say what you mean and mean what you say. There are worse traits than that. No lies spill out of your mouth when that wonderful Irish temper of yours rises."

"I never considered it a blessing afore."

He brushed her forehead with his fingertips. "You are a blessing, my dear wife. "I need you in my life, standing at my side. From the moment I saw you in Finnigan's doorway, you looked like an angel to me. I'm privileged to have you in my life. Now, you rest until the doctor arrives and examines you."

Whether or not she lost the babe went unspoken.

Chapter Seventeen

It turned out Roanne hadn't lost the baby.

The doctor, a portly man who wheezed throughout the examination, declared her healthy, much to Roanne's relief. A progressive fellow, he did not advocate lying in or taking to her chambers for the duration of the pregnancy. That she wouldn't have tolerated.

Rather, after a week's bedrest, his orders were that she resume whatever activity she chose with the caveat that strenuous exercise be avoided. As if anyone at Hollyhock would let her lift a finger without rushing to do it for her. Every single person in the manor-her husband, her brothers, all of Hollyhock's staff-treated her like she'd changed into the fuzzy ball of a dandelion's seed head and would blow away in a breeze.

They loved her, wanted to protect her. And that included Simon. He'd told her so himself the night before.

When an owl hooted outside her window, the world tipped. Roanne shivered at the thought of the creature being so close. There was no shortage of superstitions about the birds. Owls were long associated with shadows and the Otherworld. It made her fear for her unborn child. She clutched her rosary beads and prayed that it would fly away.

Lying in bed, through the open curtains, she saw no nearby trees for it to perch upon. Roanne sighed with relief. In all likelihood the bird flew past.

Still, it was a bad omen to hear the hooting of the bird of doom in daytime. It prophesized death or bad luck. Was it warning her of the prophecy?

She knew her numbers and to fulfill the prophecy a babe must be born before the first year of matrimony ended. Nearly three months had lapsed. A babe took nine plus months.

A knock sounded on her bedchamber door and it swung open without her bidding the person entrance.

The O'Casey clan leader stepped inside. "How's my favorite sister?" he said, smiling.

Although she recognized teasing, she speculated he had a reason for coming to her quarters. Roanne nodded at him. She wondered what bothered him. He looked tired, as if he carried a heavy load on his shoulders.

"I find myself becoming bored," she answered him.

"After two days of bed rest? Read a book. Or take up needlework or another noblewoman's activity to keep yourself busy."

Roanne wasn't about to heed a lecture, not now. She had enough on her mind to worry about. "Good advice for someone else. Those pursuits didn't interest me afore and for sure, not now. I want to move about, except Simon has threatened to tie me to the bed and Millie backs him if I do. 'Tis unfair, Padraig. I need to be active and I'm trapped-a prisoner-in this bedchamber. Speak with Simon. Use your golden tongue to convince him to change his mind."

"*Ack*, what about the sweet bonny babe? Just be thankful you didn't lose it. The chance still exists.

Better to lay abed so you can walk in sunshine with a newborn in your arms on another day." Padraig brushed his hair back, a habit when he wanted to say more. "'Sides, I'm leaving for Eire in a day or so. Simon has graciously made one of his vessels available to take me and the lads home. We've been absent for too long. Farrell with Finn and Meagan's guidance has been handling most of the duties, but he's young. 'Twas a heavy responsibility I laid upon him. Time to relieve him of the burden."

A moment of alarm rose. "You're leaving me?"

"Not all of us. Murdock, Rory, and Sean the Third will stay. You know Murdock's reasoning and can't fault him. Be happy he found his lost love. Rory likes your husband and wants to strengthen the bond of friendship and family they have formed. Sean the Third...well, what I can say about him. Traveling's in his blood. His desire to see the world will not be quenched. This is as good a time as any, afore he settles down and finds himself a wife."

Before she answered, her door opened again. This time Simon entered, trailed by several of her brothers. She scooted higher in the bed.

She beamed at them. "I've never had so many visitors for a single visit."

"How is my lovely wife feeling?" Simon asked.

He bent over the bed and gave her brow a quick peck. His clean-shaven face and the scent of soap clinging to his skin told Roanne his daily ministrations had been recently performed.

She pouted. "Padraig asked practically the same thing and I'll tell you what I told him—I'm bored. I want to be free of this bed and chamber."

"I have just the solution." Sean the Third stepped forward, a silly grin on his face. "We're going to hold a pissing contest. Want to watch? You won't have to move far. Yonder chair will suit just fine. We'll do so outside your window. Come on, lads, what say ye?"

"'Twill be a hoot." Rory joined his brother's side. "We're going to see who can go the farthest. And the longest."

Sean the Second huffed. "I've heard tell, it's the amount of bubbles as one grows older."

Sean the Third stepped closer to the older man and elbowed him in the side. "That leaves you, Padraig, Brian, and Ian out. You're all too old to play. Think it'll be Timothy, Rory, and me." He seemed pleased with his announcement. "It only takes two to make the contest sporting."

Roanne's eyes widened. "Blessed Mary! What will our servants think of us if we allow deviltry at Hollyhock? They'll gossip to our neighbors."

"They'll tell the busybodies that O'Caseys' enjoy themselves, and be envious, I'm thinking," Sean the Third replied in all sincerity, puffing out his chest.

Roanne glanced at Simon for support. "I pray to the good Lord you haven't blessed this scandalous behavior."

He raised his eyebrows in mock surprise. "This is the first I've heard of it."

"Sure, and he can join us," Rory offered with a grin. "As a matter of fact, a side wager will make it more interesting. What say you, Kirkland?"

Roanne held her breath and waited. All gazes shot to her husband to hear his response. He wouldn't dare participate. *Would he*?

Simon walked around the bed. "What do you have in mind?" he said, sounding thoughtful as he eyed her brothers. A second later, an intense blue gleam in his eyes gave him away.

She slammed clenched fists down on the feather comforter. "No! I forbid it."

"If you're worried about favoritism, you can be the final judge," Simon suggested, a little too eager-sounding for Roanne.

Her family had pulled dozens of ill-advised stunts in her lifetime. Most were done in good fun, but now they dragged her husband into their antics. She wouldn't have it and refused to allow him to join them.

Her brothers pressed around the bed. Looking from one intense face to the other, a thought solidified rock hard. They appeared too serious, too expectant. A gnawing suspicion built within her. She let her gaze stray to the window as she bobbed her head. A pissing contest. No way. She knew her brothers. Tricksters, all of them. They were up to something.

She started to laugh. "Shame on all of you for trying to deceive me. This be a ruse to make me forget my troubles. There be no pissing contest."

"There could be, if you officiate," the younger Sean said, sounding earnest.

She growled at him.

"Fooled you, did we?" Timothy asked from the back of the crowd. "Then we accomplished our mission. Nothing like a good distraction to make a person feel better. Now time for us to depart and let you rest."

"*Ack*, afore I strangle each one of you with my bare hands. None of you should be in here in the first place.

And I'll start with you, my dear lord husband," she said with as much sternness as she could muster.

"And here I planned on kissing you for luck," he replied with a grin. "If memory serves me correctly, we haven't kissed in ages. Do you begrudge me indulging myself?"

She didn't answer immediately. Glaring at her family, they began leaving with loud backslapping and mumbles of congratulations to each other filling the room, Simon among them.

"Not you, my lord," Roanne said.

He put his hand on his chest and mouthed, "Me?"

As if he misunderstood. Blessed Mary! The man could tease and torment with the best of the Irish.

She shoved all thoughts of owls and danger to a dark corner of her mind and waited until they were alone. "Aye, you. We have unfinished business. You mentioned kissing."

He remained standing by the door. "That I did."

"I am free now," she said, raising a brow in a clear dare.

"So you are."

He rushed to her bedside, sat down, and took up her challenge by bringing his mouth down on hers. For several seconds Roanne savored the softness of his lips upon hers. He smelled so good. She loved the feel of his body next to hers. He made her body hum. No question about it. The man knew how to stir her passions.

Suddenly, a powerful urge compelled her to lock her arms around his neck in case he decided to stop before she finished enjoying herself. She promptly opened her mouth to meet his thrusting tongue. Long, deep kisses had her moaning in seconds.

Kissing was definitely a way to erase the effects of boredom.

Simon pulled back, breaking the kiss, his breathing sounded heavier than a moment ago. "Does that satisfy you?"

"Only you satisfy me." She lost herself in his spellbinding blue eyes. "*Ack*, you've stolen my heart and I love you."

His face lit up with a smile that melted her insides. "Did I hear correctly? You said love?"

"Aye, I am sure of it." For one long second, she feared she committed a dangerous mistake, then he pulled her tight against his chest.

"Tell me again," Simon said.

"I love you."

****

Simon savored the change in Roanne. The sweetness. The teasing. If this was what he could expect for the rest of his life, he looked forward to thousands of days of give and take extending through their lives until they were elderly and infirm. Wedded bliss at its very best.

Roanne's fingertips caressed his face. "Show me your back. Please."

He remembered her curiosity the morning of her brothers' arrival. Not once had she made an inquiry, which surprised him. "What am I to receive for disrobing?"

"My undying attention."

Laughter bubbled out of him, surprising him. He could play whatever game his beautiful wife devised. He doubted he could refuse, even if he wanted to, and right now the idea of undressing in his wife's bedchamber offered great appeal. "I suppose that will have to do for now, but I reserve the right to demand a higher form of payment."

A coy smile from Roanne made his heart race. "Well," she teased back, "what did you have in mind, my lord husband?"

"Nothing strenuous. We must consider the health of the babe."

"Mopehead."

"I thought this birth important to you."

"*Ack*, of course, it 'tis. The babe means the continuation of my life."

Simon's gut rolled at the prospect of losing his child or his wife. "I have no intention of letting anything happen to you. Or our babe. You are too intriguing, too beautiful. I daresay entertaining."

She narrowed her gaze. "Not boring?"

"Never that. You make me appreciate the joys of living."

"You flatter me."

"As you deserve."

Roanne huffed. "Pure hogwash, I'm thinking. This is a ploy to not fulfill my request. Remove your shirt or I'll do it myself."

"As you wish." He kept his smile hidden as he pulled the garment over his head. He tossed it on the floor and sat on the bed with his back turned toward her.

Silence stretched for a moment. Voices rising from the grounds below the window distracted him. He shook his head. Surely the O'Caseys weren't holding that pissing contest.

The bed creaked as Roanne shifted closer to him. He dismissed his concern about the O'Caseys. The scent of oranges and cloves tickled his nose. He would forever associate the two scents with his charmingly mulish wife.

At the touch of cool fingers on his skin, a shudder of delight raced up his spine. Neither spoke. Roanne's breathing quickened and little puffs of warm air escaped as her hand traced the outline. He mentally followed her fingers touching the four points of the flesh inspired rood. Tiny scrolls were inside the intersecting lines and she traced each delicate curl.

"The crucifix is beautiful," she said, laying her hand flat on his back.

"Technically, it is a cross. No body."

Her fingers outlined his back again. "I see no scars. You were never under the lash."

He shrugged, dislodging her hand as he turned around. "I was careful not to break the rules. And I chose not to put Christ's image on it in case I erred."

"Irish Catholics call it a crucifix, no matter what. A symbol of Jesus' sacrifice. The four points represent self, nature, wisdom, and higher power."

He picked up his shirt and donned it. "If it would please you, I can add his image."

Her amber-green gaze rose to meet his. "Does the process hurt?"

"Terribly. And it takes a painstakingly long time."

"Faith, then do so immediately."

Simon laughed, delighted with Roanne's wicked sense of humor, even at his expense. He decided on the spot that a little teasing would be worth it. Life with the Irish beauty was going to be interesting and entertaining with her by his side. "You little hooligan! You want me to suffer?"

"Aye. 'Tis only fair, for the way I have the last two months."

"Life isn't fair, my sweet wife. We just have to make the most of what we receive."

"Then I be luckier than most. I found you."

"Lucky me. Technically your brothers found me, but who am I to quibble over the sweet words from your sweet mouth. What shall I do?"

"Kiss me," she said, beaming. "That should keep you occupied and me from being bored."

****

The first day after Padraig and the majority of her brothers departed for Eire, Roanne had a caller-Dorinda.

"Is it true?" the brunette asked, settling in the lady's parlor. "You are with child. I'm so happy for you and Simon."

Already the absence of her family weighed on her, and the Englishwoman's company was a welcome change. "Aye, so it would seem. Faith, I pray the babe arrives in time."

"And why wouldn't it?"

"'Tis all a matter of timing. We were only together once in Ireland."

"Roanne, you're being a worrywart. All will be just fine." Dorinda stopped suddenly, inhaled deeply, then began speaking again. "At least you don't have to worry about living in sin for the rest of your life."

"Whatever do you mean, Dorinda?"

"As soon as my annulment is granted, which should be any day now, Murdock and I plan to wed.

Even though my brother paid a small fortune for the dissolution, the church will not approve our union. Their belief on the sanctimony of marriage remains unchanged. But the price will be worth it to be with my one true love."

Roanne's heart went out to the petite brunette beside her. It wasn't fair that two people as deeply in love as Dorinda and Murdock should be kept apart because of silly rulings of strangers. "Do you plan to have children?"

"Of course, we do." Dorinda twisted her hands in her lap. "Children make family complete. Murdock and I are strong Catholics, but we are willing to consider the Church of England for them. Murdock wants me happy and being with him makes me happy. We don't know what else to do."

"You'll always be welcome in our family. I could not ask for a nicer sister-in-law," Roanne said, meaning it. "You should'na let it put a burden on you. You aren't to blame. I wager you gave no cause for Percy's poor treatment."

Golden-brown eyes warmed. "That's what Murdock keeps telling me, but enough about me and my troubles. How are you and Simon getting along? Or am I being presumptuous to ask?"

Roanne beamed, not ashamed to let her happiness show. "Nay. We're wonderful. He's so caring. He spoils me. My only regret is that we didn't start out this way."

"All you needed was time to get to know one another."

"Solving Hugh's death tipped the bucket. But now time is something we have little to spare. I fear Simon and I might have wasted too much."

Dorinda's expression saddened. "I don't accept that. According to what Murdock has told me of your family history, you certainly have good grounds to stand on. And something I never told Murdock I will tell you. Percy saw your prophecy."

The happiness of the last few days evaporated like fog on a sunny day. She froze, unable to breathe. "W-what? How? When?"

"Percy boasted to me your father was suspicious about the translation and bid him to check the document because he knew Latin, French, and Gaelic. As I understand, it was originally written by a French scribe in Latin, then later transcribed into Gaelic."

Roanne blinked, unable to look away. "Did he tell you the contents?"

"No. I wish he had. If he had, I could provide proper answers to your questions."

The echo of the owl's hooting rolled through Roanne's head and she wondered if it had been a harbinger of disaster. A spurt of determination quickened her pulse. Had Da mentioned his suspicions to Padraig? Was he privy to knowledge no one else had? She cringed ever so little. Of course, her brother was gone now, which meant she was unable to press him for answers.

Roanne sat, transfixed. If a chance existed for Simon and her to find ever-lasting happiness, she had to convince him a journey to Eire was necessary. . . no-imperative.

"I'm going to Eire. I have to see the prophecy for myself."

****

"Simon, we need to talk."

He set his quill down to mark his place on the document and cocked a brow at his wife as she swept into the library without knocking. "Haven't we been communicating with each other already?"

"I've learned something of great importance that I believe you should hear."

"Do tell," he said, trying to lighten the seriousness of her tone.

Roanne scowled at him. "I be serious."

One look at his wife's sincere expression drew all his attention. "Then, by all means, you have my utmost attention."

She seemed to hesitate, her gaze flitting about the room. "This concerns your mother."

His heart lurched. Not exactly the subject he expected. "Continue."

"I know you told me how she died when you were a child. Well, certain sources have come forth to inform me that is a falsehood. She ran away because you were being ignored by your father."

Goosebumps erupted on his arms. He refused to question how his inquisitive wife mustered the knowledge. He swallowed. "I know."

Roanne's amber-green eyes widened. "What do you mean, you know?"

Simon stood and went to the divan. He gestured for Roanne to join him. She did and immediately took hold of his hands. The contact brought a wave of warmth that fortified him.

"A child hears far more than most parents intend," he began tentatively, telling her something no other soul knew. "Between eavesdropping and servants' prattle, I learned quite young what transpired under this roof. And there are always those willing to give details." He blinked, shoving back the memories that came as a deluge. "'Twas easier to perpetuate my father's lie. When I discovered the truth, there was little I could do."

"What if she lives? Are you not curious where she is? How she fares?"

"I know how she fares." Simon refused to enlighten her. He headed for the door. "Come with me, Roanne."

At her hesitation, he took hold of her hand to guide her outside. Roanne didn't resist. He led her to the family cemetery on the far side of the barn. At least a dozen tombstones, some tinged green from moss, others chipped, dating back three centuries were planted in the ground to honor the dead. Two appeared quite new.

He stopped before the closest one. He did not have to read the inscription to know what was engraved upon the marble. Hugh Bradford Lancaster, Fourth Earl of Kirkland. *Born October 30, 1630. Died February 3, 1661.*

A sigh broke the silence as Roanne finished reading. Her colorful eyes looked up at him with genuine sadness. She offered a small smile of condolence.

Tugging on her hand, he led her to another headstone. This one, a large flat stone of granite, untouched by decades of the seasons or moss, contained a cylindrical vial in front of it with a solitary flower. The engraving read: Margaret Jane Wallace Lancaster. Wife and Mother. *Born February 15, 1601. Died April 7, 1659.*

Roannee's gaze shot to him. "Your mother?"

He nodded as words failed him. At her look of sympathy, he swallowed. "Hugh delighted in telling me as a child. Bragged how she couldn't stand the sight of me. I knew it wasn't true, but his words still hurt. There was naught I could do until I returned on my last voyage home. Father had died. I sent men to find her and learned she'd spent the last two decades in the Americas. They reported back that as soon as she learned of father's death, she took a ship to return to England but died at sea. This stone is in memory of her."

"Oh, Simon, I'm so sorry."

A tiny part of Simon's heart melted. His wife was so full of love, and he was grateful she shared a fraction with him.

"I want to go to Eire," Roanne said abruptly.

The declaration didn't surprise Simon. He'd been waiting for it. Expecting it actually. He whistled, low and long. "Absolutely not. Not in your delicate condition."

"Don't worry, I'll be safe."

"You can't guarantee that! There are days of travel, a sea to cross, where fierce storms arise without notice, then another day to reach the O'Casey manor. If you won't consider the safety of the babe and yourself, I will. You will remain here."

A glint in her eyes should have warned him. "There's something important I have to check."

"What?"

"It concerns the prophecy. Dorinda said Da asked Percy to look at it for him. I need to know why."

Interesting. He scowled at her but could tell it did

286

little good. Sailors aboard ship had dreaded his disapproval, yet his darling wife showed no fear.

Roanne grabbed his arm and gave him a little shake. "Oh, my dear husband, cease worrying, will you? In fact, come with me. Please. I insist."

The plea did it. How could he refuse whatever she desired? If returning to Ireland was important to her, he would take her. While the last thing he wanted was to jeopardize her health or that of the baby, their happiness was important, too.

And he feared she'd sneak off alone if he didn't agree.

She stared at him, chin lifted, not blinking, determination written all over the lovely contours of her face. Admiration swelled within him.

The decision was his to make and he did. "You're not traipsing off on your own. I'm coming, too." And perhaps he could keep her out of harm's way.

Roanne gave him a quick kiss. "Thank you."

"When?" he asked, doing his best to sound stern.

Her smile nearly blinded him. "As soon as you're ready."

Chapter Eighteen

A sennight later they boarded the *Black Sheep*, a sleek two-masted brigand. It swept through the foam-tipped, gray water like the friendly dolphins that accompanied them for the first part of their journey and after two days, because of favorable winds, the vessel closed on Dundalk's harbor.

At first Roanne had been torn between seeking more information about the prophecy and fear the voyage would endanger the babe, but within hours of feeling the dip and sway, she acquired a handle on her sea legs and swore the child enjoyed being on the water.

Simon stood beside her at the railing as the first stars appeared in the darkening sky. He caught her hand and brought it to his lips. "Are you sure you should be standing all the time? Mayhap you need to lie down."

"Stop fretting about me and the babe. We are fine. Look at the wondrous sights. The sun as it glistens off the water. The sails snapping as they fill with wind. There is so much to see and hear. Listen to the rigging crack, the waves crash against the ship's prow. I love being on deck, feeling the rocking under my feet while sailors scamper in the rigging."

"Humor me, my love. I cannot help worrying about you."

She leaned into her husband's side, his warmth

chasing away the nip in the air. "This doesn't compare to my first trip. I missed so much being locked away in the captain's cabin. Don't begrudge me this experience."

He released her hand and rubbed his chin. "You don't need to remind me what a cad I was."

"You are forgiven."

The huge grin on Simon's face said it all. It was clear the man thrived in the environment. His face had lit with a smile the instant he stepped aboard, and he hadn't stopped beaming.

It hadn't taken any time for her to decide fresh air was good for the babe, too, as her hands rested on her belly. Too soon for real movement, but she liked touching where he lay.

The only blight on her mind was the thought of the prophecy becoming reality. Even if the babe came in time, it did not assure her safety. She could still die giving birth. So many women did. Would Simon care for the child? Or neglect him like his father had done him? Only time would tell how father and son would fare together.

Tonight, the full moon, a luminous pearl, shone down on the water. Stars glittered all around on a velvet sky of black. Waves splashed against the ship's prow as it sluiced through the water, hurling mists of salt into the air.

She shivered against the ship's railing, damp hair tangled around her head and down her back. It didn't take long for her cape to become sodden, the sprays and waves from crossing the bottomless Irish Sea soaking clear through the plush velvet material to make her gown heavy and cumbersome.

Being cold was part of the voyage, and she didn't mind. Her fondest wish had come true. She was returning home.

Simon had honored her wish to see the prophecy for herself. A step in the right direction.

Strong, familiar arms slipped around her waist. "How do you feel? Are you warm enough? Do you need another cloak?" Simon whispered in her ear. "How's our child behaving? You're not ill from the constant motion. No dizziness or nausea?"

Roanne leaned back and tipped her head against his hard body. "None whatsoever. You need not inquire about my health every second. Our son, for I'm sure he's a boy, is enjoying himself almost as much as his father. He likes being on the water. A true sailor, like you."

"And what if he is a she?"

"A woman knows these things."

Simon lowered his chin to her shoulder and whispered, "Have I told you lately how much I love you?"

So much affection wove through his softly uttered words that she had to keep herself from bursting into tears of joy. "Hm…I can't remember. Tell me again."

"I love, love, love you."

"Words that tickle my heart."

She turned around in the circle of his arms to face his front. The warmth of his body chased away the dampness and cold at the same time. He always brought her comfort. Inhaling, she drew a steadying breath of sweet Irish air as the *Black Sheep* cut through the waves toward the shore.

Everything was clear to her now, very clear and

very frightening. "Whatever happens . . . always remember that I love you so...so much. The prophecy didn't make me love you. You did."

He shook his head. "You are too good for me, my love. I don't deserve you."

Roanne grimaced. Sometimes he reminded her of her brothers, and she wondered if he would ever listen. "Faith, there be no sense to any of this. How the English managed to be leaders all these centuries is beyond me."

The quartermaster shouted orders and able-bodied sailors jumped to obey. The new captain of the *Black Sheep* ran a tight ship.

Simon chuckled. "Always insults, when I'm trying to explain my feelings and actions."

"*Ack*, as if I wish to hear. Best you remember who made my life hell these past weeks. A little suffering will d'you good."

Focusing on the busy quay spreading out before them, for this was a nighttime docking, People ran around the docks under the glare of lanterns. She wondered what lay ahead for her. For the O'Caseys. And most importantly, for Simon.

An instant later, the ship docked, knocking them apart.

"Time to go." Simon led her to where Rory, Sean the Third, Murdock, and Dorinda waited to disembark. "I want to reach the O'Casey manor as quickly as possible."

They hurried down the gangplank. Once on solid land again, the troop of O'Caseys and Simon formed a wedge with Roanne and Dorinda tucked safely in the center through the stevedores gathered to unload the vessel and its cargo.

They hailed a wagon and the entire group climbed aboard.

Hours later, the manor tower rose in the distance. Rain began to fall the last mile. A storm was gathering.

Huddled with his shoulders rounded against the rain, Sean the Third said, "'Tis a sign from above. This is the beginning of the end. We will all perish from simple croup. Tis what weakened Da and let his heart fail. We shall soon join him."

"Sure, and I'll listen to none of your doom and gloom," Rory countered, scowling at his younger brother. "Having to look at your moonstruck face has been enough to depress me. I, for one, plan to toast the devil afore I go to my final resting place."

"Aye," Murdock said, his arm around Dorinda's shoulders. "'tis a fine time to start a new tradition— drink ourselves to death."

****

As the travelers alighted from the wagon, the pack of wolfhounds crowded around them with wagging tails, making forward passage impossible. Braith shot between Simon and Murdock, seemingly unable to decide which one to lavish his attention upon.

Simon kept an arm around Roanne and pulled her close as they swept through the wide double doors of the O'Casey manor. "Thank the Lord that's over and done. I worried about you during the crossing."

She beamed at him and the sight warmed his insides. If he were honest with himself, he would say she hadn't stopped since he agreed to bring her home.

"I loved being aboard the *Black Sheep*. She's a beautiful ship. I swear our babe did, too. Not once was I sick or queasy."

He smiled. "I'm pleased. Mayhap, when this prophecy business is over, perchance our lives can take the shape of normal people."

"Nay, Simon." Anguish touched her voice. "Don't underestimate the prophecy. If the babe isn't born on time, I am doomed."

Simon rejected the idea with a vehement dislike. "Take back your words and don't talk silly. You worry overmuch. I want more than a few months with you. I want us to grow old together. I want to see our children grow old with their children. That is not so much to ask, is it?"

With a sigh, she stopped and faced him. "You mustn't mourn me when my time comes. Have a wake to celebrate our time together. Remember what we shared. It will be enough. I love you, my dear lord husband."

"Roanne," he said, his voice cracking with emotion. He knew the pain of loneliness and had no intention of losing her, of ever being alone again. "Look at me. You aren't going to die. I forbid it."

He hated hearing his sweet wife talk of death when he was determined that they would have a lifetime to look forward to. All the superstitious nonsense drove him insane, but what if he was wrong? He shuddered at the thought, only to be distracted by the light touch of Roanne's hand burning his arm through the superfine of his jacket.

"Have you learned nothing, Simon? You must accept fate. You must."

"Never," he denied. The pain stabbing at him, at the notion of never hearing her voice, never seeing her bright smile or feeling her luscious curves caused his world to crash. "I'll not let you go."

"You are a stubborn, stubborn man."

Her insults lifted his spirits and he'd even grown fond of them. "I cannot help myself. You inspire me, m'lady."

"Deny the prophecy until doomsday, but 'twill not be changing the fact that everything is happening as predicted. Da died during the Moon of Ice, a time of cold and hunger. If that wasn't an omen, I don't know what is."

Simon scoffed as they walked down the hallway. He wasn't ready to believe in superstition. "People die every day. We are born and we die. You can't associate your father's death with an ancient superstition."

She huffed back. "I needed to wed a lord, and you showed up. Oh, aye, you were not a nobleman at the time, but Fate made it happen and you soon became one. No coincidence there. And not through foul means as you first suspected. Even if I am pregnant, the babe must be born before the year is out. That was why my brothers and I were so deeply committed to fulfilling the prophecy."

"You mean bullheaded."

"That, too." Roanne grinned.

Simon gazed down at his wife as they entered the solar where a blazing fire fought off the chill and heated musty wool of damp clothing. Those O'Caseys who traveled with them fanned out in the room, all heading in the same direction to vie for the choicest spot before the scorching heat, alternating between rubbing their backsides and blowing on their hands. He didn't blame them one iota.

An abundance of wildflowers filled the solar. Had word of their arrival reached those who returned earlier? Was the colorful array a welcome for them?

He shook away his thoughts. His priority was Roanne. Never would he give up his Irish beauty. *Never.* He'd searched all his life for the joy she brought into his. No man or prophecy would steal her away from him.

She reminded him of an angel, a seductive angel with blazing red hair spilling over her shoulders in waves of soft curls and honey-beryl eyes full of gold flecks. *His angel.*

Just the sight of her dazzled him with an invigorating bolt of longing. He grabbed her hand and pulled her against his chest, inhaling an orange-clove scent mix with the sweetness of the wildflowers to make a strange and wonderful perfume.

"Tell me about the prophecy," he whispered.

Roanne stared at him, saying nothing, stroking her fingers over the black lapels of his coat. "Why now? What does it matter?"

"Humor me, sweet bird. I want to understand. For you. For me. For all of us. With all my heart, I want to believe the same as you and your family, but I have to make sure no detail has been overlooked."

Roanne raised up on her tiptoes to place a feather-light kiss on his chin. "Lord knows I've repeated myself enough times. But if once more makes a difference, so be it."

His heart beat faster. He kissed her back, his hunger for her rising to the surface. "It will."

Her gaze swept down at his front and she laughed, the bubbly sound a joy to his ears.

Before she recited the prophecy, a loud cackle of laughter invaded the parlor. Their privacy ended with Padraig, Meagan, Brian, Sean the Second, Finn, and Ian walking into the room. Farrell entered last, whistling.

"Good tidings," Padraig greeted when he saw them. "'Tis a pleasant surprise to have my whole family under my roof."

Simon smiled. "Forgive the invasion at this late hour. The fault is all mine."

"He's taking the blame for me," Roanne said. "I am the one who insisted we return to Eire posthaste."

"All are welcome," Meagan answered, sweeping forward to hug Roanne.

"What prompted this visit?" Padraig asked.

"We be sleuthing," Roanne said. "A matter arose during a discussion with Dorinda, and the only way to solve it was to return to Eire."

"Interesting," the clan leader responded. "But there's more to this tale than that, I'm thinking."

Murdock left Dorinda's side to push his way to the forefront and tilted his head at Simon. "Enough chit-chat. Kirkland wants to see the actual prophecy. Dorinda claims Percy saw it."

Dorinda took hold of the big man's hand. With the petite woman at his side, the truculent Irishman settled down.

Simon grinned at him. Clearly the rift between Irish and English had yet to fade, if ever. But Dorinda was putting huge dents in the Irishman's hostility. "The dead don't have tongues that constantly prick at me."

"Speaking of the dead," Padraig joined the conversation. "I have news for Dorinda and Murdock."

Worry flashed into the small brunette's golden-brown eyes as she flicked her gaze at the clan leader, then back to Murdock. He pulled her against his side with the gentlest movement before asking, "good or bad?"

Padraig inhaled a deep breath as if to pace his announcement. "In this case, good news, I'm thinking."

"Out with it, man," Murdock thundered. "Don't be keeping us waiting."

"Percy is dead."

"Good riddance," someone said behind Simon. Mentally he agreed. He'd only met the obnoxious lord once, which had left a sour taste in his mouth, and then there was his treatment of Dorinda, which had been inexcusable.

Dorinda stepped forward to face the clan leader. "What happened to Percy? Did my brother do something?"

Sadness flashed over Padraig's expression. "The financial ruin His Grace orchestrated destroyed him. Left him a pauper, possibly headed for debtors' prison. Percy took the cowardly way out. He hung himself."

Dorinda gasped and crossed herself. Suicide was an unforgiveable sin.

Padraig went on. "I sent a missive to you. It must have crossed on your journey."

Murdock slapped his knee, his gaze peering down at Dorinda. "You know what this means, my love. We can wed immediately. In the church's eyes you are a widow."

Dorinda issued a little squeak of joy and kissed him.

Simon couldn't be happier for his childhood friend. "Congratulations are in order, I think. There'll be a wedding to mark soon. Now if I could hear this accursed prophecy, mayhap Roanne and I can join you in celebration."

Padraig moved closer to Simon. "You mean to say Roanne has never recited it to you?"

"No. Not once. Just hints here and there."

The clan leader frowned ever so little. "For shame on you, sister. Do the honors. He be your husband and should hear the tale from your lips."

A flutter in her throat occurred when she swallowed. Her lips trembled as she mouthed the litany with her eyes closed.

Love and marriage the maid must face
The first eligible nobleman she must wed.
Birthing a child within the year,
Or the maid shall find her eternal bed.

Simon listened carefully, letting a frown form as he concentrated. Gut intuition within him repudiated the ancient words. His insides twisted and set his mind spinning. "That's all to the prophecy?"

"Aye, 'tis the prophecy and it has ruled our lives for all time," Murdock grumbled, as he led Dorinda to the window seat.

"We shall see," Simon said.

A scowl turned the corners down on the giant's mouth. "Nay, you shall see. Roanne be doomed. Unless…"

The reminder that he might lose Roanne enraged Simon. His body stiffened at the thought. "There are always alternatives. I cannot accept Roanne dying."

"Faith," Padraig began, "why the sudden acceptance?"

"I was certain if I knew what you O'Caseys knew, mayhap I could better understand. Have patience with me and repeat the prediction again. Don't leave a single detail out, no matter how insignificant it may seem."

"D'you hear yourself, Simon?" Roanne asked, amber-green eyes bright. "What difference will it make? I've recited the prophecy. Why can't you accept it?"

A knot twisted in his gut. He was missing the obvious. Sighing, he sank into the nearest chair. "Humor me," he said, repeating the prophecy. "'Tis that correct?"

Padraig stepped forward. "Word for word."

A headache developed behind Simon's eyes, one of those throbbing kinds that took days to fade. He hated headaches. "So, once more—when your father died, you pulled out this ancient prophecy to read the instructions written down centuries ago?"

A scowl appeared on Padraig's face. "Read? What's to read? We have memorized the prophecy by heart."

Simon shot to his feet. The pounding in his head increased. "Good Lord! You mean no one saw this...this document?"

"We've lived this long without seeing it. No reason to pull it every generation," Padraig said, although his brow furrowed ever so little.

"Percy saw them," Dorinda said from across the solar. "He claimed there were two documents."

Everyone spun to face her.

"Two?" repeated Padraig. "I know of only one."

"'Twas why the old clan leader requested his assistance," Dorinda answered, taking hold of

Murdock's hand. "He was the only person who read Gaelic, Latin, and French in the area."

"I read Latin and French. Mayhap we should check these documents for…for accuracy," Simon spoke up. One look at the puzzled expressions told him he had stumbled onto an important clue. "Indulge me for a moment. How long has it been since anyone has seen these edicts? Surely you see the wisdom in checking."

The O'Casey scanned the parlor. His worried gaze paused briefly on his wife. "From what Lady Dorinda has just said, not too long ago—Da and Percy. We O'Caseys learned the lyrics while sitting upon our mother's lap, we did."

Simon swallowed, a peculiar feeling developing in his gut. Time to get to the bottom of the conundrum, perhaps past time. "You mean no one *alive* has laid eyes on this prophecy in—how long? Five hundred years. Good Lord, man, how do you know it even exists?"

Heated voices challenged his assertion.

"Trust me, my lord, it does," Padraig said, a calm voice in a sea of turbulence.

Rory laughed. "We be telling the truth and his lordship don't recognize it."

"You understand my skepticism."

"Have a care what you say, Kirkland," Murdock murmured.

"Have a care yourself, O'Casey. You may not like it, but your precious assertion likely might be a figment of one of your illustrious ancestor's imagination. At best, it could be as twisted as those far-fetched tales of dragons being chased out of Ireland by your famous St. George. Dragons…" Simon paused and stood very still, studying his relatives' faces, including his lovely wife, and nearly laughed. A dozen faces stared back at him in shock. "Don't tell me? Oh, Lord…surely, you don't… Dragons are mythical beasts invented to scare children. St. George was a man, not a great warrior. No one has ever seen a dragon."

"Doesn't mean they didn't exist!" Brian claimed from the floor where he sat.

Simon kept calm. "Very well, where is the evidence? Eyewitnesses? Bones? The former has never come forward. Nor has the latter ever been found. Can you not see how things are twisted through time? The same holds true with your prophecy."

"Simon," Roanne said. "You must understand, 'tis what we believe."

The sincerity of her voice came the closest to making Simon believe. "Prove it to me. Show me the document."

"Of course," Murdock snapped. "Think you we're backward? We put our trust in God after we die. While on earth, we believe in the tangible."

"Excellent," Simon said. "Where are they?"

"In a safe place," Padraig said.

Chapter Nineteen

Roanne couldn't believe what she heard. Never in her life had Padraig been evasive. Why start now? "That is no answer. We deserve to see the prophecy with our own eyes."

"If I may be so bold, have someone fetch the documents," Simon said to the O'Casey. "We are all sensible people in this room and need to resolve this matter, here and now."

Padraig shifted his weight as he turned to the youngest O'Casey. "Farrell, fetch the box from under me bed."

The strapping lad raced off with the vigor of the young.

In the wait, Simon turned to Roanne. "If I am wrong in doubting you and your family, you will have my sincere apology," he told her. "I vowed to avenge my brother, except I let grief and guilt keep me from seeing the truth. I had to blame someone…" He let his words trail off, then began again. "I've wasted precious time. We could have addressed the prophecy sooner."

The confession surprised Roanne, but she accepted it as sincere. "'Tis all right, Simon. We didn't have the best start, but that doesn't mean we cannot enjoy our remaining months."

"I want more than months."

The sincerity struck a chord in Roanne's heart. She

laid her hand on his chest. "The time we have will be enjoyed to the fullest. That is all we can expect."

Simon shook his head. "I know that now. Hugh was mean and cruel because he enjoyed being that way. Our father taught him to disregard those around Hollyhock. Neither cared if they hurt another human being. Their lack of concern for our tenants is proof of that. I made my own fortune to prove my worth to them, to my family. If not for Hugh and my father, I wouldn't be the man standing before you today. When our father died, I was willing to try to make inroads into healing the past. That's why I agreed to oversee his estate in Ireland. I had hoped to improve our relationship. Deep down I suspected little chance existed for us to make amends." Simon stared down at her, his hands fisted at his sides. "Seeing the trust and love the O'Caseys shared, I realized what I'd missed. What I would never have. I became like Hugh-jealous-and that jealousy blinded me to the truth."

Roanne's heart raced. She dropped her hand and put it on her belly. Empathy swelled within her. "You could never be like him. Please, heed me, Simon. I—"

Farrell dashed back into the solar huffing and puffing before she finished. He handed a wooden box the size of a loaf of bread to Padraig with a reverence that confirmed the importance of what he held. "Behold the prophecy," announced the young O'Casey.

Roanne pretended not to watch the tension on the clan leader's face, not see him flick a nervous glance at his wife. Over the last few months, worry had marked Padraig most of all. The silver wings on either side of his temples had spread until they touched at the back of his head.

He nodded and held out the box to Simon. "Take it."

Simon accepted the carved strongbox with mitered corners and wooden pegs and alternating *fleur-de-lis* and Celtic triquetra symbols around the sides. The leather hinges were rotting. A loop kept the lid closed with a carved piece of bone.

"You want me to open this?" he asked.

The O'Casey nodded. "You are the doubter. Best prove yourself right or wrong."

Simon held out his hand for Roanne and she took it eagerly. "Stand beside me. I want you near."

In the midst of the solar, she shuddered a little, swallowing down a growing fear that threatened to rip through her and her world. This moment brought them to the beginning of the end.

Fear and tension washed through her, but Simon stood solid and warm next to her. Realization struck her with the clarity of knowing the sun would rise in the east. During the short months of their marriage, he had become her rock.

"Open it, Simon," she said softly. "I am eager to hear what was written on the scroll, no matter what."

"Not afraid?"

Her breath quickened. Anticipation caused her heart to race. She didn't know how much more she could bear. "Terrified, but that'll not change reality. Go on, dear husband, open the box."

Even though her words were meant to encourage, dread filled Roanne. It descended upon her like a great dark curtain, yet at the same time, a calmness settled within her. A sheen of moisture glistened on Simon's strong brow. Her poor stubborn Sassenach was nervous, and she belonged beside him.

He released her hand to slide the carved piece of bone from its loop and lifted the lid. A slighty musty odor rose from the box to tickle her nose. The unfolding of brittle leather filled the quiet room. Two rolled, leather scrolls lay inside.

Simon exhaled a deep breath before reaching inside and lifting out the yellowest scroll tied with a rotting velvet ribbon faded brown. Roanne knew the once-red ribbon signified the blood O'Caseys had shed. Dried flecks of crumbling leather floated to the bottom of the box like tiny motes. The document disintegrated before their eyes.

No one moved. No one made a noise. All gazes fixed on the document in Simon's hands. A symbol of the past, of the future. He stepped over to her desk, unrolling the fragile leather with great care, laying it flat, and skimming the faded surface where words were burnt into the leather.

"This one is in Gaelic," he announced. "A language I cannot read."

"Then read the other," Roanne said, gathering her courage. "It probably came before the Gaelic one."

As though sensing her apprehension, he drew her against his side and kissed her deeply. Was this goodbye? Refusing to dwell on the possibility, she savored the closeness, the sweetness of his kiss, a moment she would cherish forever and always.

"Lord Kirkland, that can come later," Padraig said. "I'd be interested in what you read."

A smile twitched at the corners of Simon's lips. "Would you now?"

"*Ack*, I would. If only I had looked before now."

"But you didn't. You didn't because you believed what you had been told."

Murdock elbowed his way forward with Dorinda at his side. "Sure, and we all did. Get on with it, and read the words aloud, Kirkland."

For a moment, Roanne wondered if anyone else noticed how her contentious brother had for the second time used Simon's title instead of referring to him as a Sassenach. The change heralded acceptance, a belated acknowledgment from her brother for her husband. She smiled to herself at the significance.

Simon took her hand in a gentle grip and smiled at her. "I think we should all be seated."

Roanne shook her head and cleared her throat. She was prepared for the worst. "I'll stay by your side."

Simon's gaze skimmed the closest parchment as if seemingly refreshing his memory on the language. His midnight blue eyes were clear, his voice low as he began reading aloud, "Love and marriage is…"

The beginning was identical, and a collective murmur of agreement sounded very much like an I-told-you-so spilling out of the gathered O'Caseys. The light from the hearth cast long shadows against the walls of the solar. Simon looked up to glare at his audience.

"Silence!" Padraig demanded of his family. "I want to hear without listening to your voices sounding like a flock of hungry hens, squabbling over a kernel of grain."

A twinkle appeared in Simon's eyes—as vibrant as the brightest sky and a bigger smile on his mouth. He turned to Roanne, brushing a kiss across her fingertips even as he adjusted his stance, then began again in his deep voice.

"Love and marriage is the case
When the maid sees a noble face.
Breeding with child within a year
Will cause the blush unseen to vanish
For the maid, the time she must cherish with her
beloved.

The room erupted in shouts. Denials filled the air.

"Which one should we believe?" demanded Brian.

"How do we know Kirkland's telling the truth?" Murdock said, blunt as ever.

Rory grunted. "What happens if she doesn't like her husband?"

Roanne let them vent their frustration. She had her own to deal with. The storm which had started upon their arrival rattled the panes and matched the atmosphere within the solar. Irish weather was always unpredictable and this one seemed no different.

"Faith, read the rest," Padraig demanded, his face pale.

Simon looked at him. "That's all. 'Tis obvious the two renditions don't match. My French tutor told me the problem with translations is more in the pronunciation. French is a Romance language. Latin is a classical language from the Etruscan and Greek language. Sometimes there is no equivalent in Latin to French. Certain words become lost in translation. I'm sure the same case exists for Gaelic, as well."

Roanne had already caught the difference in two words. *Birthing and breeding.* A big difference between the two. It wasn't over yet.

Simon shook his head. "To say someone has played a cruel hoax on you is putting it mildly. Your prophecy is false."

His words proved her suspicion. The sinking feeling in the pit of her belly didn't help.

"You must be wrong," Padraig said. "You misread it. Read it again."

"Nay, I think not. Your prophecy is not, nor has it ever been the forecast of death as you believe," Simon explained. "Rather, it sounds more like a maid's infatuation with her husband and her subsequent honeymoon. That after marriage, if a child comes within the first year, the maid's married life would be forever changed. If I am interpreting this correctly, it advised her to cherish the time with her new husband before their child is born, for from then on, everything would be different."

Sean the Third laughed. "Why would Kirkland lie? He has no reason to build up our hopes for Roanne, only to dash them when the evidence is before our eyes."

Padraig's gaze narrowed. He sank into a chair. Meagan touched his arm as he held out his hand for the scroll. "You mean we've let a foolish ditty to ease a maid's fear rule our lives all these generations?"

****

Roanne and Simon slipped into her childhood bedchamber near midnight. While exhausted, neither were willing to let sleep take them. Word had spread almost immediately of their return and people started arriving shortly after reading the prophecy.

"You were right all along, my lord. Our prophecy did not mean doom and gloom. It was a testament to couples bonding before children came, to make a stronger family unit," she said. "I expect you'll be reminding me for the rest of my life."

"A long life it will be, too. Though being right doesn't make me feel any better. You and your family suffered unjustly for no cause. I'm just pleased everything has been resolved. I love you too much to let you go."

"Sure, and stubborn you be. Methinks you would have tried to stop the sun rising in the morning."

"If it meant saving your life. Aye, I would have tried."

A rumble of laughter rose from the rafters below, dozens of voices raised in joy. Relatives all around Dundalk were filing into the solar, despite the early hour, to celebrate the news. In her mind's eye, Roanne could see Padraig standing before the great fireplace. Rory sprawled on the green pillow seat with long legs stuck out before him. Poor Murdock had lost the spot once his favorite. Thinking of him, Roanne didn't think it mattered anymore. Murdock much preferred to stand close to Dorinda. It had already been announced before Simon and she took their leave that he would return to England with Dorinda. Brian sat on the floor, ready to challenge anyone to pit their strength against him. Finn would stand in a corner and silently suck on his pipe. His wife would be showing off their newborn. The Seans would mingle with the crowd, each grinning ear-to-ear. Ian, in all likelihood, would be outside, checking on the ponies. The crystal-clear scene and the merry noise warmed Roanne's heart.

Let them enjoy themselves. She wanted to be alone with her broad-shouldered husband. The thought made her heart race.

Nothing meant as much to her as the admiring look

Simon aimed at her. "Did you not worry the tiniest bit about what would happen if the prophecy turned out to be true?" she asked.

Simon swept her in his arms and carried her to the large feather bed. "I was a fool not to trust my wife, something I will do with my whole heart from now on."

"Never a fool," Roanne countered. "It was my responsibility to make you understand."

He kissed her neck and shoulders. "You called me one more than I can remember."

"My apologies," she gushed between little titters of pleasure as his warm hand skimmed the length of her leg from knee to thigh. His hands slid up her body, his thumbs gliding over her breasts. She caught her breath, then let it out slowly as warm, melting sensations poured through her. When his fingers found her woman's spot to work a magic only he could create, she nearly screamed. Lord, how she loved his touch.

"Love me, Simon, love me," she whispered. "Admit you like being my husband."

He straightened, grinning. "Immensely."

"Simon…"

"Roanne…"

Ah, it felt good to hold him close, to feel his mouth soft upon hers. Closing her eyes, she buried her face on his chest.

Rolling on his side, Simon caught her against him. His lips met hers. The pounding in her ears came from her heart. She twined her fingers into the thick mane of his dark hair and drew his head down to hers. They rolled on the bed, not Englishman and Irishwoman, not even husband and wife; but two searching souls, desperate for each other.

A word about the author…

Award-winning author Darcy Carson grew up reading everything her mother brought home from the library. Reading romances became her favorite topic. Eventually her love of those novels led her to start writing them. She resides in a Seattle suburb with her husband and a prince of a toy poodle.

Thank you for purchasing
this publication of The Wild Rose Press, Inc.

For questions or more information
contact us at
info@thewildrosepress.com.

The Wild Rose Press, Inc.
www.thewildrosepress.com

www.ingramcontent.com/pod-product-compliance
Lightning Source LLC
Chambersburg PA
CBHW070047030726
47506CB00002B/387